The ~~Grieving~~ Grateful Widow

MARIA MORRISSEY

THE ~~GRIEVING~~ GRATEFUL WIDOW

ISBN: 978-1-5272-9304-5

THE ~~GRIEVING~~ GRATEFUL WIDOW

DEDICATION

Dedicated to my dear friend Marlene.I am so sad that you passed away before you could see my book finished. I hope you are looking down on me and that I have done you proud. xxx

CONTENTS

Acknowledgements

Thank You

Foreword

THE ~~GRIEVING~~ GRATEFUL WIDOW

THE ~~GRIEVING~~ GRATEFUL WIDOW

ACKNOWLEDGMENTS

To my beautiful family and friends who have sat next to me on this rollercoaster ride, holding my hand, screaming and crying with me along the way, and constantly reminding me that there is always something worth getting up for in the morning. xx

To my beautiful Tracey, thank you for all the hugs, kisses, chores, and daily checks to make sure I was alive. I will always love you more than I can say. xx

To my stunning Michelle for dropping everything at the drop of a hat when the going got tough and running to my aid, as always, picking me up and glueing me back together again. I will never stop loving you. xx

To My beautiful ladies Caz and Amy, what can I say? You two will always be in my life like a guiding light, filling my world with love and positivity. Caz, your enthusiasm and excitement for this book is unreal, and you both will always hold a special place in my heart. xx

To my lovely Mother and my Auntie Marie, sorry for all the shocks along the way. You have been amazing despite the crazy situation. I love you dearly forever. xx

To my wonderful Marlene for welcoming me into your home day or night. No matter how late, you would always let me cry on your shoulder. I will be forever grateful to you. xx

To my newest, amazing friend Lee, you were sent to me at exactly the right time. Everything for a reason. Thank you for educating me and coaching me to make changes for the better, and I hope you will continue to do so. I cannot put into words how much you have done for me. The best

THE ~~GRIEVING~~ GRATEFUL WIDOW

way I can explain it is this: You helped me put one foot in front of the other when I did not know how. You have given me so much understanding of how these strange events could have happened to anyone, not just me.xx

Last but not least, to my gorgeous, amazing Archie. You are the perfect dog, sent to me at the perfect time. In our few short months together, we have been through so much trauma, and we are now inseparable. I love you so much, and you were my reason to get out of bed and leave the house every day. So, thank you for making me feel guilty until I took you on walkies. It was the kick up the arse I needed every day. Thank you, my lovely. xx

Thank you to my wonderful Editor, Kathy De Cicco,at Dagger and Kill Ltd,for all her time, effort, and skills.

Thank you to my amazing graphic designer, Declan Cropper. You created my vision of the book cover perfectly.

Huge thank you to Holly Bentley Photography for capturing me in such an amazing light.
@holliebphotography1

THANK YOU

A special thank you to the following people who were generous enough to contribute to making my dream of publishing this book a reality:

Char
Sharon Parkinson
Karen Telford
Michelle O' Pray
Tanya O' Pray
Emily Jane Stevens
Lorraine O' Pray
Stu Leeson
Catherine Southern
Sheena Slattery
Caz Jackson
Amy Burgess
Tracey Harcourt
Ruth Taylor
Charlotte Jones
Kelly Fleming
Susan Nelson
Louise Andrews
Sharan Ingram
Frank Grundy
Charles Ayeni
Moira Slater
Ron Hardman
Sue Hardman
Jason Lloyd
Sylvia Dickinson
Keely Culshaw

FOREWORD

If you ever think that you have met the man of your dreams-at the risk of sounding like a cynic, I would advise you to read these few words of advice before mapping out your whole life with someone. They may just save you from years, maybe a lifetime, of suffering... Or worse.

- Has this man completely swept you off your feet at the speed of light?
- In a short space of time, do you feel like he is THE ONE?
- Does he like all of the same things as you?
- Does he have the same views and opinions as you?
- Is he more romantic than any man you have ever met before?
- Does this whirlwind romance make you feel like you are playing the lead in one of your favourite rom-coms?
- Does he turn up unannounced early in the morning or late at night because he *"just had to see you, even if it's just for five minutes"*?
- You cannot believe that someone out there could be so compatible with you, they are the male version of you.
- This is the kind of love you see in the movies.
- This man is just too good to be true, you have to keep pinching yourself (well, please do, sooner rather than later).

Surely these would be wonderful points, right? Wrong! If this was a once in a lifetime holiday deal, a loan with unreal interest rates,the first thing you would be is suspicious. You would be saying immediately that if it is too good to be true, well then, unfortunately, it usually is.

THE ~~GRIEVING~~ GRATEFUL WIDOW

Please don't misunderstand me, there are such things as whirlwind romances at the beginning, but if you tick most of the other items on that list, I would be more than wary.

The truth is, we do not live in the movies, and it is rare that our lives pan out like one unless we are talking about a dark psychological thriller, which would be quite fitting in my case.

Maybe we should be asking if this person is actually obsessed with us, and that is why they turn up at strange times *"just to see us."*

Ask yourself: is it normal to find a partner who not only likes all the same things: TV programs, films, music, and so on but to have all the same views and morals as you? I suppose it would be nice to come across, but, really, how likely would that be?

When you look at your Mr Right, do you feel like it is looking straight into the mirror? Well, maybe you are, perhaps you are being mirrored and, in actual fact, falling in love with yourself.

Have you ever heard of love bombing? It is a term used for people, such as psychopaths, who go out of their way to show love? Their gestures of love are way over the top, unreal. That is because the emotions are not real. Particularly for a Psychopath, they mimic those emotions, thus sometimes going too far without realising it.

If I had read a book like this five years ago, who knows what I would be doing now. For one, I would not be writing this book for a start.

Warning bells in our mind, our sixth sense, that gut feeling, however you want to describe it,is our self-defence weapon to protect us from the monsters in this world. Unfortunately for me, my alarm system I now know was damaged at a young age, and therefore never did its job correctly. With the amazing support of some absolutely wonderful people, I am learning bit by bit, day by day, how to override this system and sharpen my senses, and to them, I shall forever be in their debt.

For anyone just starting out on a similar road to the one I travelled or for future reference, this is my gift to you. Please use it wisely; not everyone is as fortunate as I am to live to tell this depraved tale.

THE ~~GRIEVING~~ GRATEFUL WIDOW

CHAPTER 1
Bad News

The cars ahead were a blur as tears ran down my face.I used my hand to brush them away as I moved in and out of the rush hour traffic on the M6.

"Come on! For god's sake, get moving!" I yelled at the cars ahead as they started to slow down, silently cursing them for simply being in front of me.

What difference will it make if I get there faster? Will the news be any better? Of course not, but the least I can do is to get home in time to drive the love of my life to the hospital so we can find out his fate together. Bowel cancer. I tell myself that at least they can operate. It will be difficult, but he is young, he is strong. Together we will smash the hell out of cancer.

Stop crying, Julia, I tell myself, *you need to be strong.*All problems canbe solved, and we can beat this. I know we can. We must. There is no alternative possible.

"Oh, for god's sake, NO!"There's a stream of red tail lights ahead of me as, one by one, the cars all come to a stop. Now, what the hell do I do? Trying to fight panic, I see an exit coming up, and I turn off onto the A38. Why did I have to be on the wrong side of Birmingham today of all days? The traffic is heavy, but at least it is moving, but panic still takes over as my body continues to jolt and shudder from the painful hysterical crying that has consumed me for the last twenty minutes.Why did there have to be a serious crash on the motorway today? One so serious that they need to close all three lanes.Is this a complete conspiracy? Why does nothing ever go as it should for me, for us? *We must be cursed,* I think to myself,moving slowly forward, aware that I am losing more and more time.I try my Sat Nav, but it just keeps taking me back to the M6, leaving me feeling like I'm in a film that is being rewound and played over and over.

After several more reroutes back to the M6, I decide to try to follow my nose and find another route. Navigation isn't my strongest talent, and my friends always joke that I can't find my way out of a paper bag. To be fair, that is accurate.I see a name that I recognise, and in some kind of hypnotic state, I find myself heading to Spring Hill, which will take me down the back routes and in via City Hospital.

Rob had called a little earlier to tell me not to panic and to just get to the hospital when I could and that he would get there in a taxi. "Drive safe," he told me, not realising that I was in such a panic. I could barely think straight, but I was doing my best. Bless him. He is worried about me. Even at a time like this, he was still thinking of me. That is one of the reasons I love him so much. You couldn't find a more caring husband than mine. I knew I was luckier than most having such a wonderful, thoughtful, and attentive husband.

He had called me just as I was leaving work, and his first words were to tell me not to panic but that they had his results. He said they wanted to see him next Tuesday, but he insisted they saw him today, Thursday. He knew that, as soon as he got that call, it was bad news, and as soon as he told me, I knew the same. Rob had been quite optimistic during the week, saying it was looking good, and if there was anything bad, he was sure they would be in touch by Friday.

Making my way through Harborne, I was only about ten minutes from the hospital when my cousin, Ruth, called. She was returning the missed call I had made to her earlier during my hysterical breakdown as I left work.

"Hi, Julia," she greeted me. "Sorry I missed your call. Is everything OK?"

"No, it's not," I gulped the words out as I clutched the steering wheel. "It's bad news about Rob."

"What d'you mean?" Concern touched her voice.

"Rob's got his test results back, and they want to see him today." It was taking everything I had not to cry, and I wasn't sure I would be able to stop.

"What have the doctors said?" Ruth asked me.

"I haven't seen them yet." I slowed at a red traffic light concentrating on my breathing. One, two, three, four.

"Then you don't know anything." Ruth was now the calm voice of reason. "Stop thinking the worst and wait until you see the doctors."

"I'm on my way there now, but the bloody traffic is terrible." The tears started as I started moving again.

"Get a grip, Julia." Ruth was stern, knowing that that was precisely what I needed. "You haven't seen the doctors yet, so you don't know anything. Stop crying and pull yourself together."

"I…"I was in severe danger of losing control.

"This is going to be difficult – for you both, but you have got to get your act together. Rob needs you to be strong."

Those few words cut through my fear at what the future was about to bring us, and I took a deep breath. I was never the strong one;Robconstantly has to be strong for me. I am weak. He is strong. He was forever telling me that he's always had a strong mind that comes from his years of being a Mental health nurse.I have never known a calmer man; when I stress over everything, he caneasily sit back and say, what is the point of stressing? Stress is one of the biggest killers. Nothing bothered my husband in that sense. It was a rare quality but a good one to possess. It was also a quality I wasn't sure I actually possessed, but I was willing to give it a go for Rob.

I had no idea what time I finally got to the Queen Elizabeth Hospital.Parking was the usual nightmare it is at any hospital. Somehow, it seemed to be worse here,meaning I had to park what seemed like miles away from the department I wanted.By the time I got to the reception, I could barely talk after running most of the way, although I'm sure the tears weren't helping.The young girl behind the desk waited patiently until I could get enough air into my lungs to give her Rob's name.

"I can take you there," an elderly lady appeared at my side. "I'm Dot, one of the volunteers here." She gently touched my arm, which immediately started the tears again. I honestly don't think I've ever cried so much in all my life, but somehow Dot knew I didn't want to talk. I blindly followed her down the long corridors taking comfort in the fact that every shaky step I took was taking me nearer to my husband.

With shaking hands, I pushed the button to release the door that would give me access to Rob. He was sitting in one of those hospital lounge chairs whilst two nurses, one on each arm, were mercifully doing their best to fill as many vials with blood as possible.My eyes sought his face, and I was reassured to see that his face looked calm. He smiled.

"Hello, lovey," he spoke in his usual sweet way.

Lost in a muddled haze, I found myself sitting in a chair opposite him, nursing a hot drink. A magic cup of tea, as people call it, especially the English. I just sat there clutching my cup, not knowing what to say or do. I just wanted the nurses to finish what they were doing so that I could ask my husband what was happening. After what seemed like an eternity of just sitting, looking at him, I wiped my nose and sipped my tea as they finally left.

I immediately moved to the seat closest to him."When are you seeing the doctor?"

"I already have," he answered.

"Well, what did he say?" I wanted to know, but at the same time, I didn't want to hear the answer.

"It's not good."

"Cancer?"

"Yes."

I took a deep breath. "What kind?"

"Pancreatic."

My heart dropped through the floor. For some reason, I had convinced myself it was bowel cancer, but I had heard the horror stories like most people, and from where I was sitting, this was the worst type of cancer he could have.

"Can they operate?" I asked those three simple words, but they contained all my hopes and dreams.

"No," Rob whispered the word.

The tears took over again, and I had to gather all my strength to stay upright. Rob just smiled sadly, keeping it together as usual whilst I fell to pieces. We didn't hug each other. We just looked at each other with a sense of sadness and hopelessness that I don't think I have ever experienced in my entire life.

It wasn't all that long before we were sitting across from the specialist nurse. As I looked at her, I couldn't help but think she was in the wrong job. Rob was his usual quietly reserved self while I screeched hysterically like a banshee. I just couldn't help it, it was all too much to take in, but then the nurse gave me a look. A look that told me to pull myself together, I wasn't the one who was ill, it was Rob, and he needed my strength and support – not my hysterics. She was that cold; I imagined I could feel a chill around her.

How could my 45-year-old husband be dying? We had only recently celebrated our first wedding anniversary after just four years of being together. I say, celebrated, well we did celebrate the day before, which was lucky as we spent our actual anniversary in the A&E department where another doctor told my husband that he was just suffering from constipation.

I turned my attention back to the nurse, who was very matter of fact in her answers. It felt like there was no emotion behind her words, but maybe that was because she has to deal with such seriously ill patients. Inside, I was screaming and shouting, but I was quiet on the outside, hanging onto the shreds of the tissues I had been handed. What I did manage to take in was that Rob had stage four cancer and that the tumour was very large. We were given a huge folder of information about the type of cancer, types of palliative chemotherapy, but nothing changed the fact that Rob was terminally ill, and they didn't know how long he would live.

CHAPTER 2
The Man of My Dreams

I was on my way home from work, and my brother, Gary, had asked if I would pick him up on the way.I was lucky that the pub was on the edge of town, so I had been able to park easily enough. My thoughts were on getting home and relaxing after a hectic day at work, so when I walked into the dimly lit room, I was intent on finding Gary and leaving. What I hadn't expected was the man with Gary. He was tall, well-built,with dark hair, tanned skin, and gorgeous dark brown eyes.

Immediately he smiled at me before he introduced himself as Roband asked if I wanted a drink.As he went to get me a coke, I remember thinking that I wasn't immediately attracted to him, but the way he looked at me stirred something deep inside me. It was almost like it was love at first sight on his part. Suddenly I wasn't in such a rush to leave.Gary was in more of a hurry to go than I was, so we probably only stayed about an hour as we all kept on chatting and talking. I was fascinated by Rob and the way he kept on looking at me. I had a feeling he was tied up in my future, and when Gary and I left, I knew that I would see Rob again.

Work continued to be busy, but my mind would often stray to how Rob had looked at me that first time we met. I bumped into him a couple of times when he had been out with Gary, and that look was always there. I felt like I was waiting for something to happen between us, something dramatic, something powerful, something that would change my life

Last September, Gary and his fiancé, Louise, had finally decided to get married, in a June wedding just around the corner. It had been a long time coming, but I was excited for them both. It had been a while since I had a good excuse to party, and I was looking forward to catching up with everyone.

The wedding went smoothly, and as the disco was setting up, I could feel someone staring at me. I immediately knew who it was, and my heart was thumping as I scanned the room. There he was, leaning on the bar, glass in hand with his eyes fixed on me. Without even thinking about it, I smiled, and when he smiled back, I knew that there was something between us. Satisfied, I turned away from him and back to my friend, Ruth.

"Let's dance," My new, sister-in law, Louise suggested, so I followed her to the dancefloor. *Pay Phone* by Maroon 5 was playing, but I could see that Rob was still watching me out of the corner of my eye.

"Why do you keep looking at him? She indicated Rob. "You keep looking at him. You don't know Rob do you?"

"Well I've met him with Gary as you know but no not really," I replied vaguely.

"So why do you have that glint in your eye then?" Louise asked as we moved around the floor.

"I don't, he looked over and I'm just politely returning the gesture," I replied. "I've probably only met him the once."

"Just the one time?"

"What do you mean?" I frowned at her before glancing back over at Rob.

"You can't keep your eyes off him."

I moved around the dancefloor so I wasn't looking at him. "He's just Gary's friend isn't he?," I muttered.

"You fancy him!" Louise sounded triumphant, although I couldn't be sure over the loud music.

"Maybe," I was thoughtful. "But he's already in love with me, and one day we'll get together."

For a long moment, Louise looked at me as though I had gone mad and then she laughed as she twirled me around the dancefloor before gasping for breath; we went back to our seats.

"Anyway, you can't date him," Louise told me when we sat down.

"Why not?" I grabbed my drink.

"He's already got a girlfriend."

I put my glass down. "Maybe he's planning on leaving her."

"Doubt it. They've been together years, and there are a couple of kids too." She emptied her glass.

"Doesn't matter," I told her. "We're going to get married one day…"

She looked at me for a long moment. "Drink?" Louise paused. "Although I think you might have had one too many anyway."

What Louise didn't realise was that I meant every word. I just knew that one day he would be my husband. I had a gut feeling about it.

After that, I would often see Rob around town, always in his car, and he would always be playing *Pay Phone* – just like at the wedding. Gary had confided in me that he had a standing joke with Rob and would tease him about only having that one song in his collection. I knew that it was more than that. It was a message to me. I almost felt like he was hypnotising me with delicious subliminal messages.

I stayed in contact with Rob via Facebook, and after many Facebook messages, I was excited to learn that we were both planning on going to The Black Horse to watch England play in the world cup. That meant not only would

I get to see him, but also that we would get to spend a few hours together.

We had arranged to meet up at The Black Horse, and I have to admit that I was excited, so I called a taxi. Rob was there waiting for me,and from the look on his face, I knew that he was pleased to see me. We got ourselves a drink and found a good table to watch the match although I admit that we did more talking than watching. England lost 2-1, but I don't think either of us really noticed. I was having a great time; being with Rob was like being with someone you have known all your life. We had so much in common, and even though I am a chatterbox, he took it all in his stride. He seemed genuinely interested in the many things I found to talk about, and believe me; they were many and varied.

"Are you hungry?" Rob asked when I finally stopped talking for a second.

"Starving," I admitted, although that was partly because I didn't want the night to end.

"How about we pick up a pizza on the way home?" he suggested. "And then I can drop you off home."

"Sounds great to me," I was happy just to spend a bit more time in his company.

"I know a place just down the road."He emptied his glass and stood up.

I grabbed my bag, said my goodbyes and walked out into the night with him. I held his arm as we headed to his car and then to the takeaway, but I wasn't thinking about the pizza.

It probably shouldn't have come as a surprise that we both liked the same pizza, and, like a true gentleman, he even insisted on paying. The night ended all too soon.As promised, he dropped me home, even insisting on walking me to the door. Part of me wanted to invite him in, but I knew he was still with his girlfriend, so that wasn't going to happen. Besides, my almost 17-year-old daughter Lucie was home; she was the only good that came out of my marriage to Simon. It was a nasty breakup. Rob seemed so much the opposite. I'd want to give him all my attention.

"Thanks for a great night," I told him. "I really enjoyed myself."

"Me too," he gently kissed me on the lips sending tingles cascading through my body. No one had ever kissed me like that before.

"Good night," he whispered.

I stood at the door, watching as he walked back to his car.

It wasn't until I got inside with my butterflies still dancing that guilt crept in. What on earth was I doing kissing him? He was with another woman; I had no right to be feeling butterflies. He was not mine. Maybe we could just be friends. He was such a nice guy.

As I headed towards the bedroom, I sternly told myself to behave. We could enjoy ourselves by just being friends. Members of the opposite sex can be friends, can't they? Who was I kidding? I didn't want to be just friends.

It was only a couple of weeks later before I was eagerly waiting for my doorbell to ring. In one of our many conversations, he told me that I was "too bright" to keep on working for other people and to think about setting up my own business. The subject had come up a couple of times in conversation, and I found myself swept along with his enthusiasm that I should do my own thing. There was something nice about someone believing in me to that extent.Rob had told me that he had a new business and that he would help me get started. He also said that he had a pile of work information that he wanted to share, and, of course, I was happy just to see him again.

When the doorbell finally rang, the butterflies danced again, and I had to stop myself from running to open the front door. When I did, Rob was there on the step, clutching not the pile of papers I had expected but four bottles of my favourite drink along with forty cigarettes (even though he didn't smoke). He was so thoughtful and generous that I was having real problems keeping the butterflies in check.

I had to remind myself that he had a girlfriend and I have a daughter, who was conveniently with friends for the evening. But the devil on my shoulder demanded to know what he was doing here with me then? Obviously, there was something wrong with his relationship with her.Besides, it wasn't like we were up to anything. I made sure of that, but we laughed and had fun. Not once did we talk about business. I enjoyed being in his company; he was so charming, so charismatic.

"So," this question had been bothering me all evening, and I was so desperate for an answer that I was willing to risk everything to ask it. "Gary tells me that you've got a girlfriend and that you live together ...?"

"You mean Gemma," he was very calm. "Yeah, we've been together for years now."

My heart sank straight to my boots. "So, you're happy then." My heart was pounding,and I held my breath, determined not to show him I was upset.

Rob shook his head. "We've been stuck in a rut for years now," he told me. "To be honest, we just share a house – we're just like two friends who happen to live together."

I looked into his brown eyes thoughtfully. It was strange, but I believed him, and it gave me hope even as the wheels in my head started to turn.

"Why do you stay together then?" I had to know.

"It just seems easier," He shrugged his shoulders.

"But you're not in love with her?" This was important to me.

He shook his head. "We really are just friends."

Maybe he was going to come on to me. One day, I just knew, he would be my Prince Charming.

He left that night a little subdued, giving me nothing more than a quick peck on the cheek, but I remained hopeful.

Before I knew it, we were Facebook messaging all the time. Then one day, as I left work midday for a lunchtime running errands, he was waiting for me.

"Hi Julia," he greeted me as I walked over to him.

"What are you doing here," I asked. "Is something wrong?"

He kissed me on the cheek this time. "I was in the area, and I thought that I'd like to take a gorgeous woman to lunch."

I frowned at him. "I'm assuming she wasn't available, and you thought of me…"

He laughed gently, and I felt good.

"So, beautiful lady, would you like to come to lunch with me?"

I smiled and nodded, but inside, my butterflies were doing their little happy dance. I wanted to spend every minute with this man, and if that meant paying my bills after work, then I was happy with that.

I only had 40 minutes for lunch, which was just enough time to dash around to the bank and grab a sandwich on the way back to the office.He took me to the Meadow Lark, which was only a few minutes away. It was a lovely warm day, so we sat outside with our sandwiches, chatting away. It was a real effort to force myself back to work. I would have been more than happy to spend the rest of the day just sitting in the beer garden with him.

I was surprised to see him the next day, only this time he had brought lunch for us both. Again, I couldn't get over how thoughtful he was. Within a few days, we took turns bringing lunch and walking the short distance to the park and sharing our sandwiches with the ducks. Every day, I was falling a little bit further in love with this man, this man who was not only involved with another woman but also lived with her. To make things even worse, I was sure that he felt the same way, but maybe that was good. Perhaps he would leave Gemma and come to me…

Things took an amazing turn a few weeks later. Rob had come over to my home. We had it all to ourselves because Lucie was out with her boyfriend, Josh. We had Chinese takeaway and opened a bottle of wine, or maybe it was two. I was sitting on the sofa, cuddled up against the warmth of Rob when he kissed me. Properly kissed me… My world turned upside up as his hands gently caressed my skin. I couldn't have stopped if I wanted to, and I definitely didn't want to. It wasn't long before we moved to the bedroom. We had already passed the point of no return, and as we made love, it was amazing. It felt like so much more than sex, and I could feel true love; that's the only way I can explain it.

"That was…" I paused, trying to think of the right word. "… wonderful." I was lying in Rob's arms, and yes, I felt both satisfied and loved.

"Are you OK?" Rob gently touched my face. "I'm a bit rusty as Gemma, and I haven't had sex for about four years now."

"Well," I suddenly felt shy, "you haven't forgotten much."

As I lay next to him, my mind was whirring. The problem was that I was struggling to believe what he had just told me. It was hard to believe that for four years of a six-year relationship, they hadn't had sex.

"Are you sure you're OK?" Rob sounded uncertain.

"I'm absolutely fine," I reassured him.

"It'll be better next time," he held me tightly. "I promise."

Wow! I thought to myself. I couldn't imagine what would be better, but I was open to experiencing it with Rob.

After three or four weeks, the sneaking around was beginning to weigh heavy on my mind. Who in their right mind wants to be a mistress? I certainly didn't. I also didn't like the thought of Rob going home to someone else, to Gemma and sharing her bed and then coming back to me.

It was consuming me as I tried to work out what I wanted to do. If this really was love, then surely, he would find a way back to me? I knew that something had to change and that I was going to have to do it.

So, it was with a heavy heart that I typed out a Facebook message to tell him that as much as I cared for him, I couldn't carry on this way. I told him if and when the seas were ever calmer, then to hop in his boat and sail across to me. However, not to leave it too long as that ship may have sailed. I was anxious as I waited for his reply. A huge part of me was hoping that he would immediately reply and say he was leaving Gemma and that he would be right around. When he finally replied, I had to take a deep breath before I could read it.Rob said that he was very sad, but he understood my reasons and respected me for it.

So that was it, over as quickly as it began.

CHAPTER 3
Trying to Move On

After that, I didn't contact Rob again, although I often thought about him. I must admit that I was a little sad that I heard nothing from him, but I concentrated on moving on with my life and putting him out of my thoughts. Then after a couple of weeks, I started receiving messages from him again. When I read the first message, my heart leapt, and the butterflies rushed back even if he was just asking how I was.It all seemed harmless enough, the usual type of thing a friend you haven't seen for a while might send. I was tempted not to answer, but I just couldn't do it; there was a part of me that just craved contact with him.

We had only been chatting for a couple of days when he told me that he missed me, and he was worried that I would meet someone else in the time it would take him to leave Gemma.It was the last bit of the message that gave me hope. Maybe he was planning to leave Gemma, and then we could pick up where we had left off.

That was probably the reason I reluctantly agreed to meet him for a drink at The Black Horse. Our meeting couldn't come around fast enough, but I was so nervous that I almost turned around and went home by the time I had parked my car. Taking a deep breath, I walked into the pub and looked anxiously around for him. He stood up and waved at me, and as I walked over to him, all my doubts popped out of existence.

"Hello, lovey." Rob smiled at me, and my stomach did flip flops when he gave me a warm hug. "I've really missed you."

"Have you?" I looked into his eyes that seemed sad.

"Babe, I haven't been able to get you out of my thoughts for a single second."

I shivered as he said the very thing that I had wanted to hear him say. He reached across the table and held my hand. "Have you missed me?"

"Of course, I have, you silly sod." I joked.

"I'm glad."

After a lovely meal, we were waiting for our coffees, chatting about everything and anything, the conversation had been easy. It was as though we had never been apart.

"So, what have you been up to?"

"I've been keeping busy," I didn't tell him that I had been keeping busy so that I wouldn't have to think about him.

"I haven't been able to stop thinking about you; you know that?"

I stirred my coffee. "Me neither," I whispered.

"You are the one for me, the one I should be with."

My heart was thumping in my chest. "I can't be with you while you are still with Gemma, you know that."

"Not a problem. I'm going to end things with her."

I looked up at him, and he was looking at me as though I was the only person in the room. I had all of his attention.

"Do you really mean that?" I was terrified of getting my hopes up and being let down again. I didn't want to have everything and then lose it all again.

"I mean it, lovely," he smiled. "I am going to tell Gemma… but there's a problem."

My world stopped turning, and the butterflies disappeared. "What's that?" If he was going to tell me that Gemma was pregnant, I was going to tip my drink over his head and march out with my head held high.

"Gemma and I are due to go to Florida next month," he was still looking at me. "It's been booked for ages as a treat for her kids."

"So?" I spoke without thinking.

"I can't let them down – the kids, I mean. They have been looking forward to this for months."

"Have they?" As heartless as that was, I really didn't care.

"If we cancelled it now, we'd lose our deposit," Rob held my hand gently. "We can still see each other," he told me. "I don't want to go, but I have to for the sake of the children."

"They could go on their own," I told him.

"Please, Julia," he was now begging me. "As soon as we get back, I'll tell Gemma that it's all over. We can be together; have a fresh start."

I stared into my coffee, trying to find a solution there. I didn't like this; I didn't like the thought of Rob going on holiday with Gemma. Yes, I did feel sorry for the kids, but that wasn't my problem.

"Please, Julia, I can't be without you. There are a few weeks before we go, and we can be together."

If I was honest with myself, I was totally hooked. I felt the same and just had to be with him, whatever the consequences.

Rob stayed with me at least three nights a week throughout the next few weeks, and the nights he didn't stay, he would turn up at 7:30 am. Lucie liked him and was glad to see me so happy. He would tell me that he just wanted to spend a few precious moments with me before going off to work. I felt so loved; I was walking on air. He was just perfect. My daughter got on with him like a house on fire too. He was so kind, generous, always treating us to meals and little gifts here and there.

Rob's Mum, Barbara, lived a short walk away from my house; he always called in and saw me when he visited her. She was nearly 75, and although she was generally in good health, she looked really frail when I saw her. Barbara was only 5 ft tall, only weighed about six stone and relied on

18

Rob to do her weekly shopping. He always told me that they only had each other as the only other family member was Barbara's sister, and she was nearly 86 years old. Rob said to me that his father had died in a car crash when he was just two years of age, leaving Barbara to bring up a small child, and she had been alone ever since. It was evident that Rob thought the world of Barbara as nothing was too much trouble for him. He would do her shopping several times a week, take her to appointments or to visit her sister, and on her off days would do some housework for her.

Of course, this worked in our favour as Rob had the perfect excuse to be away from Gemma and the kids. He would just tell her that his Mum was feeling poorly and that he was going to stay overnight with her when he wasn't "working away." Rob had his own business, and he would just book bogus courses into his diary in case Gemma checked. I didn't really know what was going on between them, but as the few weeks passed, Rob was spending more and more time with me, and that was all I cared about. I was getting to spend time with the man I loved.

I was proud of Rob for what he had achieved with his business in such a short time. He only started in 2013 and had already become a highly successful Physical Intervention Trainer. He would deliver training to agencies who supplied mental health hospitals with staff who trained other staff members to use force appropriately, de-escalate mental health patients' situations, and restrain them safely. Rob had been a mental health nurse on and off for 20 years before starting his business, so this was an easy step for him to make. He even kept his nursing pin-up for a while and was still practising when we first got together.

When he was the Nurse in Charge, I remember him texting me on a break from one of the units he was working at, and I remember being so worried in case he was attacked at work, but this is what he had done for years, and he hadn't had any major issues before. Even when he worked at Ashworth with criminal patients, he had always maintained his safety. I remember being impressed when he told me that he used to work alongside Ian Brady. What an exciting job to do! And something I wish I had been able to do. I have always been interested in how the mind works and why people do what they do.

I wondered about Rob and me, about Lucie and Gemma. Regarding Gemma, of course, I felt guilty. I truly did, but this was now an addiction, and to have someone in my life who wanted to spend every minute with me was a fix I could not do without. I tried to make myself feel better by telling myself that Gemma couldn't be perfect either. I knew this for a fact because not long before meeting Rob, she had been released from prison after serving six months for theft.

The story was that she worked for a loan company for years, when she had an affair with a man from South Africa behind her husband's back, the husband she shared two children with. The man then tried to blackmail her with sex videos, threatening to show them to her family. She agreed to start fraudulently arranging loans for him and his friends and ended up stealing in excess of £70,000 from the company that employed her.

Whenever I thought about the whole cheating scenario, I knew it was nothing to be proud of – and I wasn't and have never cheated on anyone. Also, I reminded myself that Rob wasn't married to her and the kids were hers, so, yes, not good, but not as bad as the cheating she had done on her husband and the father of her children. Also, I always believed the course of true love never runs smooth.

Rob and I were just so perfect together. We had so much to talk about and would stay up until the early hours most nights. I found myself telling him my deepest, darkest secrets, the abusive past I had suffered at the hands of more than one person, including my late ex-husband Simon, who been the absent and very estranged father of Lucie. I talked about how on the surface I appeared to be the most confident, chatty person, but infact it was a mask, a facade. Underneath, I was very insecure. I was always worried about my weight after my teenage years of anorexia that had never entirely left me. It came naturally to open up to him, he was such a good listener, and I knew I could trust him with anything. So, with his understanding and comforting, I felt the weight of the past begin to appear lighter.

We were constantly in some kind of embrace, hugging, kissing, holding hands, and I loved the fact that he would hold me all night whilst I slept. He would call me "my beautiful," and I was in awe that someone could genuinely think that of me. I have never felt beautiful, I'm just average, but he made me believe and feel beautiful. He would wrap me in his arms, and I would feel so protected. He made me feel invincible, something I had never felt before.

We liked all the same films, thrillers and horrors, real crime programs, romance, comedies and dramas. We even shared mostly the same opinions on societal things like politics and had the same morals. We were a match made in heaven. In our own little world, we were in a bubble, if you like, and I didn't want to come out. I must admit, though, the bubble would regularly pop when real life would creep in. I couldn't stand it when Rob would go in another room or out to the garden to call Gemma or answer a call from her. I would always strain to listen, and my stomach would churn when I would hear him saying,"love you, too." Every time he had to go back there, I would hate it, or if he told me he was unable to get away some nights, I would feel deflated. I kept telling myself, as did he, that this was only temporary and we would be together for real soon, and it was going to be worth it.

Towards the end of July, Rob stayed with me practically every night and would leave before 8 am each day to go back and take the kids to school. Obviously, the excuse would be his Mum was "ill." He would even leave his car parked outside of her house so that if Gemma drove past to check on him, she would think he was there. I had asked him, what if Gemma decides to call his Mum or just turn up at the door, but he assured me that would never happen as his Mum wasn't keen on herand for that reason, Gemma never went round. She didn't even have his Mum's number to call her.

I longed for the day when he could have a lie-in, followed by a lazy day with me without having to rush off somewhere. I just had to be patient, and in time, it would all come right. A love like this was definitely worth the wait.

Around this time, I left my job and secured a new one that would start mid-August, so it meant I had some time on my hands whilst Rob was in Florida. He stayed with me the night before he travelled, and it was a very sad occasion as we were both heartbroken to be apart for a whole two weeks.

That night he had sat alone in my bedroom for an hour saying he was organising a surprise for me whilst he was away and that he would have to nip out afterwards. Once he had completed it, we settled in front of a film with my daughter, Lucie, and her boyfriend, Josh. As always, Rob arranged a takeaway and drinks for us. It was a lovely evening, but the later it got, the more panic I felt. What if his plane crashed? What if something happened to him over there. America can be such a dangerous place, especially with all the shootings you hear about. It would be just my luck to have finally found the perfect man for me then for fate to snatch him away cruelly.

We stayed awake most of the night, telling each other how sad we would be without the other and that we would be counting down the days until his return. He would be arriving back on the 20th August (incidentally my daughter's birthday when she would officially turn 17, or more like 17 going on at least 30). He would be coming back early, but I would only see him for a few minutes before I left to go for a birthday meal with family and friends. Rob couldn't come with me as pictures would be shared on Facebook, and we didn't want Gemma to see them.

The morning Rob left for America, I was devastated. I know it sounds dramatic, but I was head over heels in love, and I could feel pain, which was almost physical at the thought of not being able to see him or touch him for two whole weeks. The last thing he said before he left was to remember how much he loved me, and all he would be thinking about was the day he drove back to my house playing Sky Full of Stars full blast so I could hear him arriving. That had become our song. Rob had said it summed up how he felt about me, and from then on, all gifts were star themed. A few weeks earlier, he had bought me a beautiful necklace with a star and a tiny heart attached.

For the next two weeks, I kept myself extra busy.I began painting the house, first the bedroom, then the lounge, and the kitchen. I had them all done within three days as I worked day and night tirelessly until my hands and fingers were sore and blistered from overuse of the paintbrush. To be fair to Rob, I don't know how he managed it, but he was constantly sending me WhatsApp messages and asking how I was, what I was up to, and I was sending him lots of photos of me.

It was in one of those messages that Rob told me he wanted to marry me and that he had never wanted to marry anyone before. This was it, and he really was the one. I had finally found someone who truly loved me and wanted the same as me - marriage! I had waited my whole life for this, and I had always dreamed of being someone's wife. Having my own special day, beautiful dress, the lot. I had given up hope of meeting a wonderful husband with my track record, but now my time was finally arriving at last! Years of bad relationships had happened for a reason, so I would appreciate it and understand what real love was when I did find the right one. Rob was my reward for all the shit I had put up within my life. It all seemed worth it somehow, now knowing this was what was awaiting me.

Another amazing quality about Rob was that he didn't have a jealous bone in his body. He always said he had never met anyone as honest as me, and he knew I meant it when I told him relentlessly how much I loved him. He would sometimes joke that, if anything, I was too honest, but I didn't think there was such a thing. Whilst he was in America, I had told him I was meeting a group of contractors from my old job who were taking me for a goodbye meal. They were mostly very good-looking lads - the kind who work out, all muscles, tan all over, and handsome faces to match. Some men may have been jealous and might have made an issue out of this, but not my Rob. He told me to have a nice time and enjoy myself. Like I say, he trusted me, plus I can't lie to save my life!If there was one thing I hated, it was liars. My Nana always said liars are worse than thieves, and I totally agree with her. As far as I am concerned, if someone lies to you, they are insulting your intelligence by thinking you are stupid enough to believe them. I know he had to lie to Gemma, and I hated it, but I believed it was a necessary evil at the time to protect her feelings until he could end things amicably and as kind as possible.

The surprise Rob had arranged in his absence was absolutely wonderful and made my heart feel fuzzy and warm. He had written me a love letter on beautiful paper for every day that he was gone and had got his best friend to post them each day so I would receive one for each day he was away. It was so romantic! Like a film! Similar to *PS I Love You* but without the distressing element.

Dear Beautiful
Well its Saturday and missing
you already I'll be thinking of
you all the time. You can text me
whenever you feel like. Can't
wait for two weeks' time when I
can see you again, hope you
have a lovely week off, get
plenty of rest, as you know you
need it, love you so much
beautiful
All my love

Rob xxx

Dear Beautiful

Well if this as worked as I planned it, I'll be seeing you tomorrow and I can't wait. Speak soon beautiful.

Miss you.

All my love

Rob

xxx

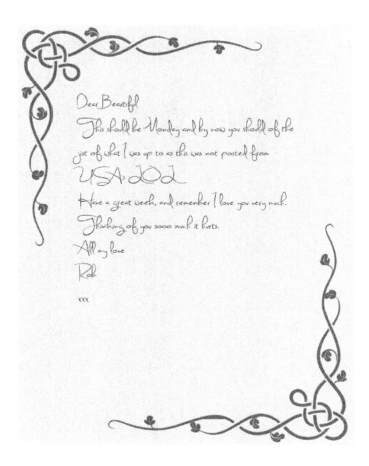

Dear Beautiful

This should be Monday and by now you should of the gist of what I was up to as this was not posted from

USA. JOJ

Have a great week, and remember I love you very much.

Thinking of you sooo much it hurts.

All my love

Rob

xxx

CHAPTER 4
Early Warning Signs

Home from America, Rob and I commenced our beautiful love story once again, spending as much time together as we possibly could, which resulted in him staying pretty much every night now. I couldn't understand why Gemma was putting up with it still, but for some reason, she was. However, I wasn't prepared to continue like this, so I started putting pressure on him about when he was going to tell her so that he could move in with me and Lucie. She needed to know what to expect too. The whole situation was beginning to get silly.

In September, he even came on a night out with me and some friends and family members, and Gemma knew he was going. He put it down to Gary asking him to go, and apparently, she didn't bat an eyelid. It meant we had to tell people not to take any compromising photos of us together in case they ended up on Facebook and she saw them. This is not how it should have been, hiding away in the shadows. It was really starting to frustrate me.

On my birthday night out, I had asked everyone to go in fancy dress as I thought we would look pretty hilarious walking into The Black Horse dressed like that. We didn't half get some laughs from it. I was dressed as Uma Thurman from Kill Bill, in a yellow and black PVC jumpsuit, Ruth was Wonder Woman, Gary was a cowboy Clint Eastwood, my sister-in-law a nun, my sister dressed as Pebbles from the Flintstones, Ginger-Craig was Batman, and then there was Rob who was Jason from the

Halloween movies, in navy overalls and that scary white face with the hair attached.

"Back in a minute," I gave Rob a quick kiss as I grabbed my cigarettes and headed outside with the girls for a quick smoke. The cool night air felt good.

"Hello darling," a male voice made me jump. "Wanna fool around?"

I looked at the man, recognising him from in the pub. Over his shoulder, I could see his poor girlfriend through the window, watching as he had tried to chat us all up.

"Not interested," I told him before turning back to Ruth.

He grabbed my arm and tried to kiss me, and I pushed him away.

"Get lost," I tried to be calm. "I have already told you I'm not interested!"

The man was obviously not listening. "How abou' a quickie... hic," he slurred.

"Get back to your girlfriend," I could sense how quiet everyone had gone. "She's obviously got no taste, so maybe she'll give you what you want."

The man leant in close. "Ya... know you're jus' a whore." I could smell the beer on his breath, but before I knew it, my red mist had appeared

"You're humiliating your girlfriend! Go join her!"

Before I knew it, the drunken letch and I were toe to toe arguing. As his charm hadn't worked, he now decided to go down the spiteful route.

"I wouldn't go near any of you ugly slags anyway!" he spat in disgust.

I was struggling to stay calm. "Apologise!!" I demanded.

"To... ya bunch o' ugly slags? Ain't bloody... hic... likely," he slurred the same distasteful answer right back at me.

My reaction time was second to none. Before I could even think about what to do, I realised I had already done it. I had punched him as hard as I could straight in the face. He lunged towards me to engage, but as I was about to hit him again before he could hit me, Rob appeared out of nowhere. My knight in shining armour! Rob to the rescue! It happened so fast, it is difficult to recall the exact details, but before I knew what had happened, Rob had him pinned to the wall, with one hand round his throat.

"I'm sorry," his poor girlfriend ran out. "Please let him go," she had her hand on Rob's arm as tears streamed down her face. "He's just had too much to drink, and he didn't mean it."

"Let him go," I told Rob. "He's not worth it."

Rob looked at me. "He's just a daft little prick. Let him run along home." The last thing I needed was for us to get arrested and be all over the news in the morning.

Rob showed real control and restraint. "Apologise to your girlfriend," he hissed at him.

"Sorry," the man mumbled the word knowing that he was on the losing side.

"Thank you," his girlfriend was still sobbing as she dragged her idiot boyfriend away. They had only gone a few steps before I could hear her screaming and shouting at him. He deserved it, but as I watched them argue their way into the distance, I felt sorry for her. I could only hope she dumped him that night.

I couldn't help but think if a CCTV operator was watching that whole incident unfold, they would probably be laughing at the sight of all us random characters in fancy dress kicking off. Not my finest hour. It took me a long time to calm down after my angry altercation with the letch and being drunk. I marched down the street ahead of Rob, rambling on with myself, carrying my heels in my hand.

"What the hell did you think you were doing?" he demanded when he caught up with me.

I stopped in my tracks as he was so angry with me. "What do you think I was doing? I was protecting myself."

"You were stupid!" This was the first time he had lost his temper with me. "You put yourself in a dangerous situation. What if that bloke had hit you?" he stared at me, but I could see he was still angry with me. "You could have been seriously hurt – or worse!"

"It all worked out fine," I really didn't think it was a big thing. After four years of being beaten by my ex-husband, Simon, who was also Lucie's father, I had decided that I would never be scared of anyone again and could defend myself against anyone. If I admit it, though, I went too far; I had no fear factor at all, and as I have learned, that is not an advantage in life.

"I don't want to see you get hurt, babe," Rob calmed down slightly. "If anyone is giving you trouble, you come to me, and I'll sort him out."

I watched him walk past me. I wasn't used to having someone to go to as I had always had to fight my own battles.

Things didn't get much better when we got home. Rob shouted at me again; I burst into tears. It wasn't the shouting that made me cry, but it was the fact that Rob was right. I had behaved recklessly. I was crying through embarrassment, shame, and most of all, had I blown it with him? What would he think of me now? Why would he want to be with someone who behaved like that? As an adult and a Mother, I certainly should not be acting like I was back in the playground. I definitely needed to lose that chip. Not everyone who insulted me or was nasty to me was Simon, and I didn't need to prove to the world that I was strong and could look after myself with my fists if need be.

Thankfully, Rob eventually calmed down and apologised for shouting, for which, to be fair, no apology was necessary. He explained that he had been so worried for me and couldn't bear for anyone to treat me badly or hurt me. He would always protect me with his life, and that I needed to realise I don't have to look after myself anymore as that was now his job. It was so endearing; I felt like my heart was going to burst. I could not believe how lucky I was! Most men would have thought I was too much of a handful and run for the hills, but not my Rob. He understood me, knew what I had been through with Simon, and why I had felt the need to toughen up. Throughout our years together, I would often say that there was only a mental health nurse who would stay with me, as no one else would be able to cope with me and my emotional baggage. That was one of Rob's qualities that I found most comforting.

Due to his nursing, Rob understood the dynamics of the abusive relationship I had been in, the type of personality Simon had, and why he did what he did. Rob understood the long-lasting effects it had on me as a person. He always reassured me that it was not my fault. I was only 16 when I met Simon, and he was 27. I didn't know that he was a pathological liar, a woman beater, and a rapist. I endured his cruel torture for four years before gathering the strength to leave when Lucie was just two. I left to protect her, as beating me was one thing, but when he started losing his temper with her, I feared she too could be assaulted. That was more than I could bear.

Interestingly, Rob regarded Simon as a paedophile and said it wasn't natural for grown men to have relationships with young girls who couldn't be considered an adult at that age. It is easier for abusive men to target young, naive girls who can be easily bowled over and manipulated as they do not have the life experience to recognise the signs.

Since Simon, any boyfriends who showed an ounce of aggression towards me were sent on their way immediately. I would never be in that situation again. I was strong enough to walk away at the first sign of trouble.

Rob used to joke that I was so good at getting rid of men; he was always worried in case I suddenly decided to end things with him. I would constantly reassure him that would never happen as I couldn't imagine in my wildest dreams that Rob could ever hurt me physically or otherwise. He was my Prince Charming, the one who had rescued me from all my bad memories. Amazing really, he was the first person who had ticked every box where I was concerned,and he assured me I ticked all of his too. I know that no one is perfect, but he was as near damn it as possible.

CHAPTER 5
Enough is Enough

As the autumn months went on, Rob still seemed no nearer to moving in with me, and I was beginning to think that I had been strung along. At first, the excuses seemed reasonable. He wanted to sort out the bills and make sure he wasn't leaving her in any financial distress. He told me that with the business still being new and people paying late, he had gotten behind with some of the bills at Gemma's house. He was the one in control of the finances and paying all the bills, and he wanted to make sure everything was straight before he left. This seemed reasonable for a short time before I started suggesting that he could still pay back the bills whilst living with me.

So, one night, he told her things weren't working and that he wanted to split up. He didn't mention me and said that he would move in with his Mum for a while.

She didn't take it well; her threats of suicide started. Gemma had then apparently grabbed her car keys and hysterically told him that she would drive her car into a wall. On another occasion, she blocked his car so he couldn't leave and told him she would take tablets. The guilt was clearly weighing heavy on him, and he explained that he felt so cruel running out on her when she had never done anything wrong. And here he was, a mental health nurse; he could see her manipulations. It was just one of those things where he had fallen out of love with her but just stayed out of convenience.

Rob also felt sorry for Gemma because she was now quite overweight and had very little confidence. He didn't want to admit this was another element making him want to leave Gemma, but he knew it was. He worried that his leaving would definitely push her over the edge as she already hated herself. This made me more frustrated as, in the long run, this was crueller to her than just leaving. The wondering where he was all the time, him on his phone when he was there, must have impacted her state of mind. Gemma had even friend requested me, which I had ignored. She was probably also suspicious about that. Plus, her emotional blackmail could go on for years; my waiting around could not.

It was time for an ultimatum. The deadline was set for 1st December, and I made it perfectly clear that it was do or die time. Rob would get no more chances if he didn't leave her. In the weeks leading up to this date, he began to look pale, clammy and stressed more often than not. The stress of all the lying and sneaking around was taking its toll. The sooner this was dealt with, the better for all concerned. I would ask every few days, was he definitely going to do it? Each time I did, he would become agitated and snap at me. Yes, he was leaving, yes, he knew the consequences if he didn't, and no, I didn't need to keep asking him.

So, the 1st December finally arrived, and I was so excited, nervous too, but I had faith that the last thing Rob wanted was to lose me, and that is what would happen, should he not implement the plan. I arrived home from work a little apprehensive and sent him a rushed text.

Well, have you done it?

The reply was not a welcome one. *Julia, please can you come and talk to me. Meet me in Sainsbury's car park in 20 minutes; we don't want Lucie hearing us talk.*

You mean you don't want my daughter hearing us arguing. What the fuck?! – Was my reply.

Within seconds there was another message. *Please, Julia, will you meet me?*

My hands shook, and my eyes began to water as I furiously tapped back. *Fine, see you in 20.*

I knew where he would be parked, his usual place around the back of the store, and as I pulled up two cars away. I could see a pathetic expression lingering on his face. As I got out, I slammed my door, my heart was pounding, and I had to take a deep breath before marching to the car wearing my angriest face. I could feel my cheeks burning as I sat down in the passenger seat of his old but immaculately clean BMW.

"Make this quick," I told him. "Have you done it or not?" I already knew the answer.

"No," he sounded worried. "I haven't, but…"

"Then we're over." I interrupted him. "Unless you go and do it now. This very minute."

I was surprised when he started to tear up. "I was going to Julia, but it's just too cruel to do this to Gemma and the kids right before Christmas."

"And how about me and Lucie?" I fired back. "Isn't it just as cruel to do this to us? Right before Christmas. Lucie was looking forward to spending Christmas with you."

"Please, Julia. Can't we extend the deadline to January?"

"What difference would that make?" I demanded. "There will just be another excuse. Besides which we wanted to spend Christmas with you."

"I promise, Julia. I promise that I will end things with Gemma. Just not before Christmas."

"No," I spoke through gritted teeth. "Your promises now mean shit to me."

He looked at me, shocked.

"You don't even know the meaning of a promise," I spat the words at him, not letting him get a word in. "It's clear you've been leading me on – and I was stupid enough to fall for it. You have no intention of ever leaving

THE ~~GRIEVING~~ GRATEFUL WIDOW

Gemma." Tears began to trickle down my face as my future life disintegrated before my eyes. Hurt was not the word: betrayed, tricked, cheated; there were so many emotions consuming me. Then suddenly, revenge appeared out of nowhere. OK, if he wouldn't tell her, then I could.

"Maybe I should tell her." His face went white for someone so tanned. "I'm going to drive straight there, knock on her door and tell her the whole sordid truth!"

"You can't do that."

"Just you watch me."

"Julia, please don't! Gemma will be devastated."

"Fuck you!" I leapt out of his car, slamming the door behind me, and I didn't look back.

I ran to my car, started the engine, tugging at my seatbelt as I reversed and then sped out of the car park. A quick check-in my rear-view showed me that Rob was right behind me, matching my ever-increasing speed. Funnily enough, by this stage, I had already changed my mind about going to Gemma, but he didn't need to know that. I drove past the turnoff to go home and continued towards Gemma's house. It didn't take me long to realise that he was no longer behind me, and I knew that he had taken a short cut so he could get there before me. My mission, for now, was over. I slowed, found a place to turn and headed back home, my heart rate going like the clappers. As I pulled up deflated, I sat for a moment to wipe my tears before entering the house with my best "I'm fine" face on show. Within a few minutes, the sorry texts began more pathetic excuses and promises. I was too angry to reply, so I ignored them for a good few hours before I felt level headed enough to address them.

After a lot of grovelling on Rob's part, I reluctantly gave in to him and agreed to wait until January for him to leave Gemma. Somehow, he managed to convince me that it would be crazy to throw away a love that we would never find again anywhere else for the sake of a few more weeks. I wasn't happy with the compromise, but then again, I couldn't imagine my life without this man. I knew if I put my mind to it, I could hold on just a few more weeks and that we had a lifetime of Christmases together anyway.

As I came to terms with a longer wait, something happened one night out of the blue. We were cuddled up in bed watching TV when Rob's phone rang. He jumped up, a worried look on his face, got dressed and raced outside. I knew what this meant. He was outside calling Gemma back. After a couple of minutes, he stormed back in.

"Stupid cow," he was rambling. "How did she find out about the money..." He looked up at me. "I've got to go and sort Gemma out, but I'll be back as soon as I can."

I didn't even have a chance to say anything before the front door slammed shut. As I lay in bed, I wondered what had happened. My mind was racing as; clearly, something had happened. Rob had been wittering as he had left, but I definitely heard that he was muttering about money. I pulled the covers up and tried to get back to sleep. Whatever had happened sounded serious, so I wasn't expecting Rob back. To say I was surprised is an understatement as he had been gone less than an hour – and the journey was 30 minutes each way.

Rob didn't say much to me, just that my wish had come true and that it was all over between him and Gemma. He wasn't prepared to go into detail, but the long and short of it was, she knew he had been spending money elsewhere rather than the bills. They had a blazing row, and he had admitted the affair and would go back in a few days to get his stuff. I knew by the look on his face that there was no point pushing for any more information. I had got what I wanted, and I didn't need the details to know that he was mine now and our future together could begin properly.

A few days later, true to his word, Rob came in with a ton of clothes and office equipment. I couldn't stop smiling as I made room in my wardrobe for him. This was an amazing day, one I thought would never come. I was living with someone again.This time though, I was with someone who truly loved me and would protect me at all costs. My daughter and I finally had a good man around the house, and we were all set to become a lovely little family.

During the weeks running up to Christmas, I was so excited, but unfortunately, Rob didn't seem to feel the same. He looked stressed, pale, tired, and on edge all the time. Still, he would be so lovely to me, and I just put it down to him working too hard. A rest over Christmas would sort him out.

One Saturday just before Christmas, we went shopping together in Birmingham. We were in the shopping centre so I could get a present for Lucie when I noticed that Rob was getting more and more irritable.

"How much more have you got to get?" he grumbled. "We've already been in every shop."

I frowned at him, wondering why he was in such a bad mood, "I just want to get something for Lucie," I told him. "What do you think about this?" I held up a beaded necklace that was in Lucie's favourite colour.

"Whatever," he was obviously not interested. "She's your daughter."

I dropped the necklace back on the counter. Rob was getting on my nerves. I had been so looking forward to going Christmas shopping with him, but this was turning out to be one of my worst shopping experiences ever.

"Do you think she'd like this?" I picked up an enamel bracelet, determined to salvage our shopping trip.

"How the hell would I know?" Rob was getting more and more irritable with each passing minute.

I had had enough. "Look," I told him. "If you don't want to be here, with me, then go and wait outside."

He didn't need asking twice, he was out of there like a shot, and I couldn't help thinking that he had orchestrated the whole thing. It had crossed my mind that he was worried about being seen out with me if he bumped into Gemma or anyone she knew. I threw a few things in my basket without even thinking about what I needed. I paid at the till and made my way out of the shop as quickly as possible. I had expected Rob to be outside, but he was nowhere to be seen. Today was turning into the day from hell. Exhaling loudly, I pulled my phone out of my bag and pressed call. No answer, now I was annoyed as I started to walk around looking for him as I went. After five unanswered calls, my blood was boiling, and then the text arrived. *I'm at the car. Meet me there when you're done xxxxx*

Now I was furious, our first Christmas shopping trip together and not only did I have to shop alone, but I also felt rushed and he didn't even have the decency to come and help me with my bags.I marched back to the car, threw my bags onto the backseat, scowling at Rob before getting into the passenger seat beside him.

Sad to say, we argued all the way home about his behaviour. His defence was that he is a man, he doesn't like shopping, and the reason he didn't answer my calls was that he had bumped into a couple with their daughter. He has been friends with this couple for many years and changed this eighteen-year-old girls' nappies when she was a baby. He said that he hadn't seen them for years and had got engrossed in conversation. His phone was on silent, so he only saw my missed calls after he had left them. I must admit that I'm not sure if I believed him, and this showed, resulting in an argument about Gemma yet again.

But we got over it because I kept telling myself, *"Come on! Don't let this ruin our first Christmas."*

CHAPTER 6
Christmas Eve

At least we made it to our first Christmas Eve. After a hectic 24th December afternoon with final preparations and Rob's last-minute present shopping for me, which he said he enjoyed doing. I was looking forward to a more chilled day Christmas day. Rob, my daughter Lucie, her boyfriend Josh, and I were going to have the best day, or should I say we were supposed to have the best day.

"I'm just going to call around Mum's house for half an hour," Rob announced as I was just getting ready to cook breakfast. "I want to wish her a happy Christmas."

I put the eggs carefully down. "I thought we were going to sit down and have a nice cooked breakfast."

"I have to go see Mum," he continued. "And I have to drop her over to her sister about 3 o'clock. She's going there for Christmas dinner."

"Why didn't you bother to tell me this before?" I put the eggs back in the fridge and tried slamming the door, but it didn't work on a fridge.

Rob just sort of shrugged, which just made me even angrier.

"Can you go after breakfast?" I was still trying to salvage our plans.

"I promised Mum I'd be there."

"You could just go round when you take her over to her sister's house."

"It's all been arranged."

"By who? You never mentioned it to me! " I was annoyed that he had not told me any of this in advance

42

about him having to take her somewhere. Our day would now have to work around his Mum's plans. I still thought it odd that he hadn't discussed this before.

"You know what?" Rob snapped at me. "You are turning into a control freak."

I was so shocked that for a few seconds I couldn't answer. "I'm not saying you can't go."

"Too bloody right, you're not!"

"It's all your fault!" I was so angry I could barely think straight. "You only had to think of me and tell me!"

"That's typical of you!" He yelled at me. "Thinking of your bloody self as usual."

"How… dare you!" I screamed back at him.

"You have to control everything," he stopped yelling. "My Mum hasn't got anyone else apart from me and her sister. And you don't want me to see her!"

"That's a load of lies!"

Rob grabbed his coat. "If that's really how you feel, then maybe we should just end things now."

I was still standing speechless when I heard the front door slam.

It took me some time to calm down, but I couldn't let his selfish actions spoil Christmas for the rest of us. I cooked the breakfast through a haze of tears, but as I put the food on the table, I forced myself to stop crying.

Some first Christmas together this was turning out to be. I had spent the morning crying, then we had to have breakfast without him, and on top of that was the stress of knowing he could walk away from the relationship at any time. The thought of losing him terrified me, and maybe I was the one being unreasonable.

Whilst he was gone, I received a message asking me to have a big think about whether things are ever going to work. He accused me of not trusting him and told me that he wasn't prepared to live like that.

I was absolutely heartbroken at how quickly everything had gone wrong. I could barely think straight, and I just wanted this Christmas to end.

Rob eventually came home before dinner; we went into the kitchen to talk. I explained how sorry I was and that, of course, I trusted him. I was just upset that he had not discussed the plans with me and that I had just wanted us to have a perfect first Christmas together.

After we had our Christmas dinner, Rob rushed off to take his Mum to her sister for their dinner. I sat in the kitchen thinking that this was a lie. I felt sure that he would take Barbara over to Gemma's house, and they were going to have a Christmas dinner there.

I couldn't get this thought out of my head. So, I decided to get into my car and driveround past Barbara's house. His car wasn't there, but they could have already set off, or he could have gone straight to Gemma's house. It was pointless me driving around trying to catch him out. As he said, there was no point in a relationship if we didn't have trust. I was just going to have to put my trust in him.

I survived Christmas, Rob survived Christmas, and most importantly, we survived Christmas – with a few hard lessons learned.

CHAPTER 7
Seen in Oadby

Rob was all packed and ready to leave. He had to go away for work, and although my heart ached at the thought of us being apart, it was only for a couple of days. He had told me that when he was earning enough money, I could give up my job and would be able to go with him when he was working away. That was something to look forward to in the future, but I was just going to have to grin and bear it for now.

Rob called me when he was halfway to Crawley and again when he arrived, but not so much when he got into his hotel room as the signal was terrible. He had gone with a colleague called John, so at least he had company.

The next morning, he texted me bright and early, telling me that it was snowing where he was. It was cold and frosty in Leicester, but luckily the snow had not made much of an appearance.

I had been at work about an hour and a half when I received a text from Rob asking me to call him when I got a chance. As soon as it was time for my first cigarette break, I dashed outside to call him.

He told me that he was in Leicester and that he had had to take his Mum to hospital as she had collapsed. I was surprised that he had managed to get back so quickly, especially with the motorway traffic, but when I asked, he explained that he had set off around 1am. He said his Aunt had called him just after midnight to tell him about Barbara. He quickly explained that he didn't have time to talk, but he just wanted to update me. He promised to call later.

As I walked back into work, I realised that nothing made sense.I needed to talk to someone; otherwise, this would just play on my mind and drive me mad.

I quickly called Louise, my sister-in-law.

"Hi, Lou,"

"Hi, Julia. Everything alright?"

"I'm not sure…" I admitted. "Have you got a second? I'm at work, so I can't talk long."

"Sure, what's up?"

"You know that Rob is working away in Crawley?"

There was a pause. "I think you mentioned it."

"Well, his Mum collapsed at home, but I think Rob might be lying to me."

"Oh,"

"He texted me first thing this morning from Crawley to say it was snowing. He said that his aunt called him at midnight, but he always has his phone on silent. And he told me there was no phone signal in his room. So how did she get through? I'm going around in circles trying to work it out." I finally ran out of breath.

Silence.

"Lou? Are you still there?"

"I'm here."

"Did you hear what I just said?"

"I heard," Louise paused again.

"Do you know what's going on?" I demanded. "You've got to tell me."

"Gary was in Leicester this morning," she finally started talking. "It was just before nine, and he mentioned that he saw Rob driving towards Oadby. He tooted his horn and waved but thought it odd that Rob was trying not to be seen and ignored him."

"Maybe it wasn't him…" I had a sinking feeling that it was.

"You know what Gary's like; he caught up with him until Rob looked at him. He said Rob looked guilty about something."

"Maybe he was just picking something up," Now I knew I was clasping at straws.

"Gary texted him and said he thought he was away on business."

"And?"

"He just said that he had had to come back because of his Mum."

"Thanks, Louise," I needed to think about this. "Let's get together soon."

"Sure, Julia. Bye."

This was getting worse by the minute if Gary had seen him before 9 am heading towards Oadby; how could he have just arrived at the hospital now when he called me just after 10 am? My face began to feel hot as my blood began to boil. Why was he lying to me?

I discussed my concerns with a work colleague, and she explained that she had a relative who worked on the medical assessment unit where Barbara supposedly was. She called her and asked her to confirm if Barbara was there. I know she shouldn't have, but I was so grateful to her for doing it. I was shocked when she confirmed that Barbara indeed was there and had been admitted that morning. Well, they do say that most lies are based on some sort of truth. The question was why he was lying about the rest of it? Plus, Louise had sent me a text to say that Gemma had deleted her and Gary off her Facebook page, and she couldn't understand why she would do that all of a sudden.

It was a tough day at work as I found it difficult to concentrate. That evening when I finally got home, I put all of Rob's clothes in a bin bag, and when he texted to say he was on his way round, I managed to act like everything was fine.I wanted to shock him when he arrived and give him what he deserved. I was still so angry with him for lying to me.

Rob walked in, obviously confident that everything was OK even when I asked him to follow me to the bedroom. He sat on the bed and asked me if I was OK. I could see by his expression that he was trying to weigh up what I was thinking.

"Don't bother getting comfortable," I said coldly, "your stuff is in there. Pick it up and get lost!" I spat the last words at him.

"What's wrong, babe?" The colour drained from his face as he tried to work out why I was doing this.

"You are so lucky that I didn't knock on Gemma's door earlier." I could have. I had parked around the corner, waiting for Rob to goin or out of the street. I wanted to catch him red-handed.

"Fortunately for you, I got bored of waiting."

"Why would you do that?" He asked.

"Because I know you lied to me. You never went away, and that you are still seeing Gemma!" I was trying very hard not to shout. "There's no point in denying it."

"I'm not seeing Gemma. It's all over! You know that!" He retorted.

"Well, I don't believe you!"

"I can prove it!" Rob pulled out his wallet. "Look!" He showed me the booking.com confirmation for his hotel.

"That's not proof," I retorted. "It just tells me that you booked a room. It doesn't even show you actually paid for the room – unless you've got a receipt, which you won't have!"

He sighed deeply. "I don't have a receipt – John was going to pay for the room. I left early if you remember."

"Really?" I was still angry with him. "Hotels usually ask you to pay on check-in."

"Not this one. There's an option to pay on checkout at this hotel."

"You're lying," I told him bluntly.

He threw his hands up in despair. "It's clear that you've already made your mind up.

"The only thing I've made my mind up about is that you should leave and not come back."

Rob got to his feet and reluctantly took his bag. He stopped in the doorway, turned to look at me and gave me a sorrowful look before leaving.

I lost count of all of the texts that went back and forth that night as Rob tried to plead his innocence. He finally sent me a screenshot of his booking. I still didn't believe him, so I looked up the hotel's number and called them. The receptionist made it abundantly clear that under no circumstances could a guest make payment on check out. The payment was to be made upon booking or check-in at the very latest, just like I had thought. Did he really think I was that stupid?

We argued over the next few days, and I told him that we were finished and I wanted nothing more to do with him. In the end, he admitted that he had been at Gemma's when I had thought he was away and that he had never left her as he had felt too guilty to leave before Christmas.

I was disgusted with him. As it turns out, the clothes he had brought to my house were just things he didn't wear anymore and that Gemma thought he had spent Christmas with his Mum. I accused him of going to her for Christmas, but he vehemently denied it. It didn't matter now anyway as we were through.

One last thing to do was to make sure that he didn't get away with it though, Gemma deserved to know that he had been cheating us both. I sent her a Facebook message to tell her how long we had been together and that I thought she should know. I told her that I had ended it with him after finding out that he hadn't left her. I texted him, wishing him good luck as I had just messaged her. About an hour later, I got a reply saying that he didn't blame me but that he really did love me.

The following week or so was difficult as I got more and more messages telling me how sorry he was, how much he loved me, and that I was his world. I must admit, when the anger had subsided, I was finding it increasingly difficult to walk away from him. What if this was a stumble in the road? What if he was my only chance of happiness, my soul mate?

Rob even resorted to texting me one day whilst I was at work, instructing me to go out to my car in the car park as he had left an envelope with money on the windscreen for me. He had explained that it was for housekeeping that he should have given me and that he didn't want me to struggle because of what he had done. It was true that I was finding money difficult,but I didn't want to get pulled into speaking to him.

I found myself crying in the office as I was so confused and torn about how I felt. My manager pulled me to one side, and as she already knew what he had done in the past, she was more than suspicious about this new random act. She went as far as to say that he was coming across as a "psycho." Laughing, I assured her that he definitely wasn't a psycho, and before I knew it, I could hear myself defending him and talking about all of his kind and caring qualities. She didn't think it was a good idea to go outside to the car, but I assured her that I would be fine, and she agreed to let me go out but warned me that if I wasn't back in five minutes, she would be coming after me.

I knew Rob wasn't someone to be scared of and that he had done this out of guilt and because of the love he still had for me. I approached the car and must admit that I felt a sense of someone watching me. I looked around the car park and down the side roads, but his car was nowhere to be seen. I told myself to stop being so silly and collected the envelope and looked inside. There was £100 inside the envelope, which would undoubtedly come in useful. I did wonder why he hadn't just pushed it through my front door… Before I could change my mind, I sent him a text and asked him. He quickly replied that he was going to but was worried in case the dog chewed it. He added that he was now back in Leicester, so it was easy to drop it off as he was passing. I decided to accept it in the spirit it was given and then went back to ignoring him.

Not long after that, Louise, my sister-in-law, decided that we should go out for a drink as she had decided that I needed cheering up. We decided to go to the local Wetherspoons for a drink, and we sat at a table by a window upstairs.

I was talking to Louise when I looked out and saw what I thought was Rob's car parked directly across the road. I told Louise to discreetly look and tell me what she thought. She was adamant that it was Rob, but her expression was a mixture of concern and confusion. We joked that he was watching us, but it was a joke for sure. I commented to Louise that there was no way he could know where we were unless...

I wondered if he had followed us, but that would mean he would have had to hide somewhere on my street, follow me to Louise's house and then follow us to the pub without me noticing him in my rear-view mirror.

Louise suggested that maybe he was going to the chip shop, which was on the side where he had parked. The car remained there for around twenty minutes before eventually leaving. The chip shop reason seemed the most likely story, and I didn't give it much more thought.

About a week later, Rob asked me to meet him for a drink and a chat. I made sure that I looked my absolute best, hair, make-up, even a low cut-top. I was determined to show him just what he was missing, what he could have had. Rob was clearly impressed as I walked in but not so impressed at the admiring eyes on me from the lads playing pool, but I was happy. I had created the desired effect.

We talked for some time, and he explained that he and Gemma were now definitely over and that he was glad. He said that the Facebook message I sent had done him a favour. There was no begging for another chance. He spoke more about how he was sorry and that he had ruined everything, and that he didn't deserve another chance. He was right, of course, yet I couldn't help but wish that he would sweep me off my feet and tell me he would do anything to make me forgive him. Strangely we bid each other goodnight so politely, just like a couple of awkward friends who had been estranged for years.

CHAPTER 8
Valentine's Day

Both my family and friends had a lot of opinions over what Rob had done, and none were good. Who could blame them? He had lied to me, and the way he had behaved was nothing short of despicable. Even Gary, who had known him for nine years, said that it looked like Rob had turned out to be "a right weirdo." He was angry that Rob had treated me so badly, but he was also angry that Rob had lied to him too. Garys aid it just shows that yes, he knew him from work and yes, they had a drink together from time to time, but maybe he didn't know Rob. Gary was just like me in that he hated people who told lies.

I had told Rob not to bother me anymore, and for the last two weeks, he had seemed to do that. However, Valentine's night arrived, and I received a text from Rob. It said that he had left me something on my car windscreen and under my back passenger wheel. I rang Garyand told him as I wasn't sure what to make of it. He told me not to go out as Rob could be waiting for me, but I argued that I wasn't scared of Rob and that I didn't think he would be capable of hurting me, but Gary wasn't happy about it. He said that none of us knew what Rob was capable of and that this behaviour was extremely creepy by anyone's book. It was hard to hear that Gary, my brother, could think so poorly of his friend. Still, I believed in my heart that Rob did not intend to freak me out or be creepy; he just wanted another chance.

I waited almost an hour before unlocking the front door and making my way out to the driveway. I looked up and down the road before approaching the car. All clear, so I grabbed the red envelope from my front windscreen before crouching down at the rear passenger wheel. Scooping the ivory colour gift bag up, I took one more look up and down the road before hurrying back through the front door. I breathed a sigh of relief as I locked the door behind me.

Opening the card made my heart flutter as I anticipated his words of heartfelt love. The card said on the front *To the one I love.* As I opened it, a piece of paper dropped out. Unfolding the paper, I revealed two tickets to see Morrissey in March. They had been bought from an online ticket tout, and Rob had paid way over the odds for them. At £180.00 for two tickets, it was a rip-off, but it showed that Rob had gone out of his way to get me the chance to see my musical hero once again. I felt so touched that he had done this for me; I couldn't help but smile.

Inside the card, he had written that he loved me more than he had ever loved anyone and that he would never forgive himself for ruining it all. Tears ran down my cheeks as I read his sincere, heartfelt words.Next, I opened the small, ivory coloured gift box to reveal a white box inside with Seiko etched on the front. Opening the box, I found inside the most beautiful silver watch, with a baby pink face and with little stones embedded around the circular frame of the face. It was gorgeous, my favourite colour, a replacement for my current watch that was bought for me by an ex. Strange to replace one ex's watch with one from your most recent ex.

I called Gary, who was angry that I had gone outside after his warning, and I understood from his reaction that he was not one bit impressed by Rob's gestures. His opinion was that Rob was trying to buy me, but I argued, why would he go to all this trouble if he didn't want to be with me and make up for what he had done? If he didn't care about me, he would have just moved on and forgotten about me.I had always had a gut feeling that I would one day marry Rob, and despite what had happened, I still believed that and just knew that my feelings couldn't be ignored. I knew that I would have to forgive him. He didn't need to know that right now, though. I would keep him waiting. It was the least he deserved. He needed to be taught a lesson about the amount of hurt he had caused with his lies.

As I was mulling everything over in my head, a notification came through on my phone. A Facebook message – from Gemma. Heartbeat racing, I clicked on the message and did a double-take and re-read the message:

Are you and Rob seeing each other?

My heart sank; this could not be happening. Surely, Rob wasn't still with her. Typing back furiously, I quickly told her that we had been seeing each other from June to January but that he had lied and told me he had left her, but when I found out in January that he hadn't, I'd finished with him.

She confirmed that they were still together and he still lived there and asked me when I had last spoken to him.

Anger burned through my body, angry for me and angry for her. We were both victims of his nasty lies. I replied that I had been ignoring him, but he left a card and gifts on my car about an hour earlier.

Immediately she responded, asking could I send her photos of the card and gift?

Of course, I would, snapping pictures of the front and inside of the card, then the tickets, and the watch. I thought this would serve him right. If he thought he could carry on with his secret double life, he had another thing coming.

She messaged back a one-word answer: *Thanks.* Then she was gone.

Feeling rather proud of myself for dishing up some punishment, I picked my phone up and typed a message to Rob: *Drop dead!*

Short and not very sweet at all, but I wanted to get my point across clearly so that he would be in no doubt. I waited for a few minutes to see if I got a reply before blocking him on every type of messaging service and social media site possible. The pathetic reply that I had received before I did this was just this: *Ok, I'm sorry for everything xxx.*

That weekend I went to stay with my sister, who thought that I was so much better off without this liar in my life. She, too, believed that he was trying to buy me back with the extravagant gifts and part of me agreed; although, I couldn't help but think that I had lost my soulmate. I wished things were different.

Around midnight on Saturday, I received a friend request from no other than "Bruce Lee." It wasn't difficult to guess who this was. My sister told me to ignore it, and at first, I did. However, by the next morning, it was obvious that I would accept it and that I had to know what he had to say for himself. Clicking accept, I felt butterflies in my stomach, hoping that he would message soon and not keep me waiting in anticipation for too long.

About twenty minutes later, a message popped up begging me to agree to meet up with him so he could explain himself face-to-face. I replied that I wanted nothing to do with him, but I was lying. Wanting to create a fear that he had lost me forever, I kept up with this facade for days before eventually agreeing to meet him in one of the local beauty spots.

I knew that I still loved him the moment I saw him, with butterflies in my stomach. I tried hard to ignore them as we walked around the lake together. After about two hours of talking, we had come to a stalemate. He had given his apologies, his explanations as to why he lied and that he had been a coward when it came to leaving Gemma and the kids as he could not bear to hurt them. They had all been his family for the past six years, and it wasn't easy to pull the plug on their life together. He confirmed that it had taken losing me to realise that he could not continue to live a lie anymore and that he would do anything to win me back.

Then it was my turn and my time for me to tell him exactly what I wanted. I explained that he would need to work extremely hard to build up my trust as he had drained me of any that I had for him. I started in on him about his phone behaviour and Facebook.

He agreed to stop keeping his phone on silent, that he would go back on Facebook and make it clear that he was in a relationship with me. Childish as that may seem, it was a way that he could prove to me that there was nothing to hide anymore. No more was I going to be the secret girlfriend. This charade had gone on more than long enough.

I also insisted on seeing his new car's logbook to prove that he had got it from his Mum's address, as he told me. He wasn't happy about the phone rule or the Facebook one. He justified this by telling me that he has always had his phone on silent as he gets too many nuisance calls because of his business, and as for Facebook, he didn't even like it, which is why he came off of it in the first place.

Eventually, he agreed to both, but when I asked him when I could see the logbook for his car, he made excuses about showing it to me. Apparently, he wasn't sure where it was and asked if our relationship depended on it. He told me that I needed to start believing some things, or we wouldn't be able to build on our relationship trust.

There was no backing down for me, and I told him to forget it. If he couldn't do these few things for me, then there was no hope for us. This was the position that he had put me in, and he could either like it or lump it. He couldn't just float back into my life on his terms. From now on, it would be my way or the highway.

Finally, he admitted that the car's logbook was in Gemma's address. He was getting it changed now that he was living with his Mum. He said that he had to manage it like this because of credit checks and that he hadn't wanted me to know, so I wouldn't think it was because he was still with her.

Reluctantly he agreed to the phone and Facebook rules, but after hearing this new lie about the car, I told him I didn't think it would work. Not accepting my position, he asked me to go to his car with him, where he presented me with more gifts: a cute teddy and two minion ornaments, as he knew that I loved them. I told him that I couldn't accept them under the circumstances, but he wouldn't take no for an answer.

So, returning to my car with a heavy heart and my gifts, I watched him drive away as my eyes began to fill with tears. I had to stick to this now. I had to accept that I had been wrong and that he just wasn't the man for me as I had first thought.

Over the next couple of weeks, I received the odd text from Rob asking how I was doing. The best thing would have been to ignore them, but I was glad that he still hadn't given up on me. I even agreed to let him pick me up one evening and drive me to a pub for us to chat. The struggle to not throw my arms around him and tell him that I loved him was very real. I was proud of myself, though;I was strong and told him I would never be able to trust him fully and that it would never work.

Tears were leaking down from underneath Rob's sunglasses during our journey back to my house. I just about managed to hold mine in until I was back in the house. It broke my heart to see him like that, as he wasn't the type to cry. It just proved to me that he was in love with me. Was I willing to walk away from the only man that had truly ever loved me?

It wasn't just about me, though, because my daughter, Lucie, was tired of seeing Rob upset me. The last few months had been a rollercoaster of emotions, and it was hard to judge whether the majority had been good or bad. Most of my friends and family were adamant that I was doing the right thing by staying away from him. A few friends pointed out it was OK for them to say that when they didn't have my feelings and they weren't the ones who sat home alone.

Later that evening, I checked that my front door was locked and was astonished to find an envelope with my name on sat on the doormat. It was obvious that it had been hand-delivered and by whom.

I was losing my resolve…

CHAPTER 9
Living Together

It wasn't all that long before Rob moved in, for real this time, bringing all of his prized possessions with him. This was it; we were finally going to build a life together,which felt so right. Things went from good to fantastic in no time at all, and apart from work, we were pretty much inseparable. His mobile was no longer on silent, and although he had promised to go back on Facebook, that had still to happen. It didn't matter that much; finally, I could tell the world he was mine, and I was able to post photos of us together. It was challenging to get a decent photo of him as he was miserable about taking pictures, but that was just part of his personality's grumpier side.

The good times were far outweighing the bad now, and that's what mattered. We were more in love than ever, and Rob never stopped telling me how glad he was that he had not lost the love of his life. It was a fantastic feeling to love and be loved. Finally, I could see my fairy tale ending taking shape. It had been a long time coming, but the wait was well and truly over.

Rob was amazing around the house; he would help out with anything and everything, and it was so lovely to come home and have my tea cooked if he was home first. He was perfect in every way, and I had never been happier. Lucie also had a new friend, Carla, staying at our house. Rob had run across Carla's parents, his friends from 18 years ago when we were trying to Christmas shop for the first time. It turns out they also knew my brother, Gary. Lucie and Carla liked Rob too, which was a massive bonus.

Rob thought it would be great for now-17-year-old Lucie to have someone nearer her age in the house too, and she and Carla acted like sisters. Carla, who was almost 19, had moved in with us - only for a few weeks or a month at most, Rob said, while she got things sorted out financially before moving into her own flat. Both girls used Rob like a taxi service,but he took it all in his stride and seemed to enjoy it. Finally, I was like other people in a stable relationship. However, in my heart, I believed that I was luckier than most as I didn't know anyone who was happy to spend so much time with their other half.

I started to finally meet his friends, something I had been so excited about. Unfortunately, I didn't get to meet his best friend Vinnie due to him having health problems on top of being a parent of children with autism. Vinnie struggled to meet up with anyone because of his lifestyle, so that couldn't be helped. I did meet a couple of his drinking buddies, though, not that he ever drank much. I had never seen Rob drunk as he said that he wanted to make sure when we went out, he could keep an eye on me and keep me safe. I loved this about him because he was so protective, and I always felt so safe around him.

Two friends I did meet, though, left me feeling extremely uncomfortable. He'd been friends with Stacey and Dave for years and was godfather to their eleven-year son, Jack.

I followed Rob into their house, and I was shocked when I met Stacey. She wasn't at all how I imagined her. She was so loud and brash, not someone I would imagine to be friends with Rob. Dave, her husband, sat quietly on his laptop smoking and barely looked up to acknowledge us. The ashtray overflowing on the coffee table looked like the one from the TV show *The Royle Family*. I couldn't help but think that had they been visiting us, we would have at the very least put out a fresh ashtray.

Once the introductions were out of the way, Stacey took the drinks we had brought into the kitchen after passing us one each.

I was shocked when she returned and sprawled herself over the back of the sofa behind Rob and wrapped her arms around his neck, something a partner would do, not a friend. Her husband didn't bat an eyelid. If she could see the look of contempt on my face, she didn't show it.

"I've really missed you, Rob," she stated,still with her arms wrapped around his neck. "I have heard so much about Julia." Stacey glanced in my direction and looked me up and down."Although I do think that she is overdressed."

I raised my eyebrows at her. I wasn't wearing anything special, but she had clearly made no effort and was only wearing a tired t-shirt and her trackies.

However, that wasn't what bothered me. Stacey was easy on the eye, blonde hair, blue eyes, and slim. I wanted to like her but was finding it increasingly difficult

"Do you know," she rubbed Rob's neck, "everyone thinks that Rob is my secret lover."

"Really?" I tried to sound disinterested.

"Really," she replied. "In fact, my Mum made a comment about it only last week."

"And, of course, you told her it wasn't true."

She gave a high-pitched laugh. "You are so funny, Julia."

Now I knew that I didn't like her.

At one point in the conversation, she turned to her husband. "Sorry, you know I love you, Rob, oops I mean Dave."

In my mind, this was the last straw, but how I managed to keep a lid on my temper that night, I will never know.

Rob commented on how quiet I was on the journey home. I put it down to tiredness, and it was weeks later I broached the subject to tell him how I felt. Surprisingly, Rob agreed that Stacey had been behaving as though she was a dog trying to mark its territory. He said that her behaviour had been bizarre that night, and she had never acted that way before. Her behaviour had worried me as Rob would meet her and her son for lunch or go round to her house to see her whilst her husband wasn't there. If she behaved like this when her husband and I were around, what was she like when she had Rob to herself. He assured me that she had never been like that before but that he understood my concerns.If the shoe had been on the other foot, Rob told me he would not be comfortable with the situation either.

Rob decided to cut them all off, even his godson. I was astonished! He told me that I was the most important person in his life and that he wasn't having Stacey causing problems. Regarding his godson, he said that he was a 'brat' who only liked Rob for his money. To be fair, when we were there, Rob was asking if he had been good at school and that if he did well for the next month, he would give him £50. Rob said that he was asked for money directly, or hints were dropped about offering him money every time he saw him.

I did say to Rob that it was his choice about who he wanted to be friends with, but I must admit I was relieved when he confirmed that they would no longer be in his life. There had been enough drama in this relationship for a lifetime. We needed a nice quiet life now, and something told me it would be a lot more peaceful without   them   in   it.

CHAPTER 10
The Perfect Boyfriend

Things had gone from strength to strength for Rob and me. We were so happy and spending all of our time together now. We never got bored of each other, and I was now home full-time thanks to the business doing so well. When Rob worked away, I went with him, and on a typical day, I would spend my time taking care of the house and printing the course paperwork for Rob. We were in love as much as ever, and I didn't mind that Rob had gone back to putting his phone on silent or that he had not gone back on Facebook as promised.

I had no complaints at all; he had more than proved himself to me. He was such a dedicated boyfriend, and he would do anything for me, Lucie, and Carla. He was always surprising me with little treats here and there. He was generous to the girls, giving them lifts, picking them up, and had no problem agreeing to Josh, Lucie's boyfriend, moving in when he had a big argument with his parents. Of course he was only given the sofa as Carla was in with Lucie.

Sure, we all squabbled a bit and got on each other's nerves at times, but for most of the time, we were all happy. Rob had even managed to make it up with Gary, which meant we often spent time with Gary and Louise.

When I gave up work, Carla had not long started her first job, and although most people were happy for me being at home, she was not one of them. We had always got on well, but suddenly her behaviour towards Lucie and me began to change. Overnight, she seemed to become a totally different person, one that was false. If she asked me to do something for her and I agreed, she would have this huge smile on her face and tell me how grateful she was and how much she loved me. But if I said I couldn't do something, her face would turn to thunder, and she would sulk.

Another strange thing was that she seemed to act like she had taken my place in the household since I had stopped working. She acted like she owned the place,which was odd considering that she wasn't technically family and was only staying with us while she got her life and finances straight. Also, she became increasingly bossy with me; although, I wouldn't stand for it and put her back in her place. There was one thing concerning me, and that was how she had begun to behave around Rob.

One night she had been cooking some chicken wings for herself and Lucie. She shouted through to ask Rob if he would like some. He answered her, saying that if there were enough, he would have a couple. A few minutes later, when I went into the kitchen,Carla spun around and, in a condescending way, asked if I could just go out of the kitchen for a few minutes whilst she "cooked Rob's tea." It was an odd thing to say when she clearly wasn't cooking his tea, well, unless he was on some massive diet that I didn't know about. The way she said it was as if to say she was looking after him, not me.

The arguments between myself and Carla got worse and worse over the next few weeks. She was treating me like crap but still expected me to drive her to and from her work each day. I'd had enough!

One evening, on the journey home, she was making digs about me not working. Then she asked whether I had been watching daytime TV all day. I snapped! I told her in no uncertain terms that I did not answer to her and that I had plenty to keep me busy during the day, but even if I did want to sit on my backside all day, then that was my business. To be fair, I felt I deserved a rest after years of working extremely long hours.

Carla was not happy when I told her she had to make her own way to and from work from now on, but it was tough. She had brought this on herself.

When I explained to Rob what happened, he immediately supported me, saying he had noticed the difference in her and that I needed to put her back in her place.

My concerns became more intense as Carla's behaviour began to get even stranger. She started walking into our bedroom with just a bath towel on, or at other times she would have tiny pyjama shorts on with a low-cut top. She would stand talking to us, and out of nowhere, she would bend forward and touch her ankle, revealing the majority of her breasts as she did so. It was all very deliberate and worrying.

I decided to discuss it with Rob one night after she had come in to say goodnight to us, giving me a kiss and cuddle, then doing the same with Rob. The problem was that Rob didn't have a top on, and I thought that it was inappropriate. Rob was oblivious to the behaviours I mentioned and felt that I was overlysensitive about the fact he didn't have a shirt on. He thought I was paranoid because of something that had happened many years ago in my past. He was shocked that I could think this about one of his friend's daughters.

Although not a nice feeling to have, the memory was there, never-the-less. Early on in life, I experienced deceit from a very close family member and, at the time, I had told myself I should not have been thinking what I was. Eventually, though, it was proved that my gut feeling had been right. I needed to learn to trust my own instincts.

So, Carla's behaviour was weighing heavy on my mind. This added to the other things she'd been doing, such as trying to take my role in my house. Did she want to take my boyfriend too? I spoke to her privately about dressing appropriately around others in the house. She was almost 19 and needed to know what was acceptable and what was not. Rob told me her parents said Carla had always struggled with her weight and had very little body confidence, which is one of the reasons why I was so shocked by this new behaviour. No matter what her reasons were, she needed to learn some boundaries could not be crossed.

CHAPTER 11
Unexpected News

Rob and I were in Rugby as he was working, delivering training for his biggest client. I was used to sitting in on his courses now, and I loved to watch him in action. My heart was bursting with pride as I lookedat the class of health care professionals who were hanging on to his every word. The number of people who knew him, respected him, and would speak so highly of him was just immense.

He was constantly being asked questions about his time in nursing, and I would love to hear his stories of when he was the Nurse in Charge. The candidates would ask him many questions about dealing with specific situations, and Rob would happily give them as much advice as they wanted. His knowledge was immense, it was his profession, and he was obviously an expert in his field. Even though he hadn't worked a shift for two years, he was still in his element when advising others.

This is how he had become this particular client's National Trainer. Rob had attended a meeting with the top directors at a well-established, private mental health hospital, and they were so impressed with his experience and the fact that he had the same ideas and morals as they did. The hospital directors told the client they wanted Rob to train all the agency staff that they sent going forward. This was a no-brainer for the client, and so they became Rob's biggest client. His intelligence and knowledge were second to none, and it was easy to see why he gained the respect and interest from everyone he taught.

After the morning session, we took a break for lunch before returning for the afternoon session. I took the opportunity to switch my phone back on and check to see if I had any messages.

"I can't believe this!" I told Rob.

"What's wrong?" All Rob's attention was suddenly on me.

"I've just had a text message from my GP surgery saying that they have made an antenatal appointment for Carla."

"An antenatal appointment?" Rob frowned at me. "Doesn't that mean…"

"… that Carla is pregnant! That is what the message implies!"

"Why did they send you the message?"

"I guess Carla must have forgotten to update her contact details with the practice, and I'm using her old number. Gary arranged it for me when she got a new phone." I was so shocked that I couldn't think straight.

"Did you know?" Rob sounded angry.

I shook my head as I reread the message. My hands were shaking so much that Rob took the phone off me.

"I can't believe this." He told me. "She is living under our roof and hasn't even got the decency to tell us before making a doctor's appointment!" That hardly seemed like the most important detail, given the circumstances.

I agreed but didn't say anything. I just took my phone back off Rob and sent her a text saying that I wanted to speak to her when I got home.

"We need to forget about this for now," Rob told me as we headed back for the afternoon session. "There's nothing you or I can do now."

I had treated Carla like a daughter, particularly as she had stayed living with us longer than initially expected. I knew that Lucie thought of her as a sister. I felt that we were all so close – just like a real family, but I knew Rob was right. I took a deep breath and did my best to put my professional smile on to get through the rest of the day.

After lengthy discussions with Carla, she decided that she would have the baby and had accepted that she and her "mystery boyfriend" would need to start looking for a place of their own. Josh had already moved into his own flat, and Lucie spent most of her time over there. As she got closer to 18, I saw no problem in it becoming "their" flat. I liked Josh because he was respectful of Lucie but not overly protective. All of us met up for dinner most nights, that is, until Carla's baby news. So mostly, Carla was the only one living with us now.

Things continued to be tense over the next couple of weeks as Carla continued to sulk if anyone mentioned the baby. It was like she didn't want a baby, which would have made sense as she had always said she didn't ever want kids, so to have one when she was pretty much a kid herself seemed ludicrous.

Unfortunately, Carla and I had a massive row when I found out that everyone, including her parents, Lucie, Josh, and Gary and Louise, knew about the baby except Rob and me. At this stage, I still didn't know who the baby's father was. Things escalated quickly, and before I knew it, Carla had moved out.

Rob was so supportive and tried to keep my spirits up, but it was not easy. With both Lucie and Josh in their own place and suddenly with Carla gone, the house was very quiet.

After a week or so, Carla agreed to visit and asked if Rob would collect her from Wolverhampton. I was relieved that everything had been sorted, but the relief was extremely short-lived. Initially, I was really upset that Lucie knew about Carla's pregnancy but hadn't told me. After a bit of time, I was just glad that Lucie and I were on better terms now.

Within ten minutes of speaking to me to say she was coming over, Carla called back, her attitude completely different. Her voice was cold as she told me that she was never coming back; she didn't give a reason other than she didn't ever want to come back, especially after she had the baby. Shocked, I tried to get to the truth about what had happened to cause this complete turnaround.

Sadly, we were arguing within minutes, and Carla asked why I had chosen my boyfriend over her, especially as she thought of me as a surrogate Mother. It didn't make any sense – it wasn't like she was my daughter, I had only known her as a teenager. I argued back that Rob had nothing to do with this situation and asked her to explain further. She was adamant about arguing over what seemed to be absolutely nothing until Rob took the phone from my hand and tried to reason with her.

Carla sounded venomous as she told Rob to "Fuck off!" When I heard this, I snatched the phone back and shouted into the phone until eventually one of us hung up. I can't remember whom. Rob then decided to call back and tell her to return the door keys, but, again, this conversation quickly escalated into a shouting match. Rob's anger was way too much, and I was shocked at some of the things he said. He threatened to go there, find her new boyfriend and,i n his words,"chop them up."

I tried to calm Rob down, and once he had put the phone down, I asked him why he had been so vicious. Rob was livid, that she had apparently laughed at him. It was rare to see him this worked up, and it took a lot of talking to convince him that the situation wasn't worth it. I told him that she was just a silly little teenager; it was pointless wasting any more energy on her.

I even spoke to Lucie to see if I could find out what had happened, but she said that things had become strained between them too. She thought that Carla was probably jealous of her and Josh before admitting that they had had a huge argument and hadn't spoken for weeks. I could tell that Lucie was still upset about it, so I decided to try once more to talk with Carla. She had left most of her belongings at our house when she had stormed out, so I knew that it wouldn't be long before she came to collect them. I just hoped that her friendship with Lucie could still be saved.

The next time I saw Carla was just a couple of weeks later, she came to collect some belongings. I had hoped that she would arrive with a better attitude and that I could help resolve things between her and Lucie. No such luck. She marched in behind a friend I didn't know who had been kind enough to drive her over. Carla looked angry and told me in no uncertain terms that she did not want to speak to me. Rob remained unusually calm, and instead of getting involved, he left the room and went to sit in the bedroom out of the way. Carla and I exchanged some angry words, and before I knew it, she was gone.

A week later, her friend returned to collect her bed and other large items and told me that he was taking it to Wolverhampton. However, within a few days, I received a text message from Gary advising us that he had agreed for Carla and her male friend to stay with him temporarily.

Rob was furious about Gary's interference, and this resulted in a short text argument with my brother that ended our relationship too. Rob did not get involved in the argument as the messages were between Gary and me, but he convinced me that losing my brother from my life was a good thing.

Rob and I never spoke to Gary and my sister-in-law again. My half-sister decided to get involved, too, whom Rob had never liked. When we two argued, he encouraged me to end the relationship. Finally, I agreed it was for the best. There had been a lot of bad blood between us over the years, and the final argument was somewhat of a relief as I no longer had to make an effort to keep things on track. I would no longer need to convince Rob to give her a chance, something he had never been interested in doing. Even when we were in touch, Rob would find opportunities to snipe about her. So many of our conversations would be dominated by the opinions of my half-sister.

Within a few months, we had gone from having a full house to Lucie and Josh being gone, along, now, with Carla. I had lost my brother, his family, as well as my half-sister and her family from my life. However all my family hopes and dreams were not gone completely.

CHAPTER 12
Goodbye Teddy

Rob and I finally got engaged months after we had booked our wedding. I know it was a back to front way of doing things, but we knew we wanted to marry the following year, and it was just a case of Rob saving to buy me the perfect engagement ring. Our wedding was booked for the 5th June 2017 at The South Mill in Leicestershire, a beautiful grade 1 listed Tudor Manor house with huge outside grounds. It was a venue fit for a princess, and I couldn't quite believe that I would finally get the special day that I had been waiting for all of my life.

For months, Rob seemed to have an excuse as to why we had to keep waiting to get engaged. He put it down to wanting to get me an amazing engagement ring. He explained to me about all the research he had done on diamonds and how he would get the ring specially made for me rather than just pick one from a jeweller.

It was bittersweet timing as my dog Teddy had been diagnosed with prostate cancer just two months earlier. We were unsure how long he would live, and I was broken-hearted when I learned about Teddy's diagnosis and would sit up with him all night sobbing my heart out. The poor little thing looked fine and would lick my face and try to console me, not knowing that it was him I was crying about.

Rob had arranged for us to spend the weekend in a beautiful hotel in Shrewsbury, and as my birthday was on Sunday, it was the perfect time to get engaged. We spent the Saturday walking around the village, taking in the sights and just relaxing and enjoying each other's time. The following day when I woke, Rob was waiting with a coffee, a birthday card and an engagement ring. Although he did get down on one knee, I must admit it was not the most romantic proposal that ever was. For one, there was no surprise element, but to be honest, all I cared about was the fact that I was now engaged to be married. I had been engaged once before, when I was 16, to Lucie's dad, but that was different. I was in a relationship of fear and had accepted that I was stuck with him for life anyway, so I might as well marry him. Rob, however, was the real deal. I was going to marry the love of my life. The man who treated me like a princess,who was going to give me the fairy tale ending I had always dreamed about.

Two days after our engagement, I was quickly brought back down to earth as my beloved Teddy suddenly went downhill. He had stopped eating and was unable to urinate. I knew the time had come for the dreaded vet's visit. They had warned me I would need to take him in once he got to this point. He had been lying on the sofa with me, extremely lethargic, so I called the vet and then called Rob, who said he would meet me there. Teddy perked up when he saw his lead, and the guilt was overwhelming. When Rob arrived at the vet, we were in the waiting room, and Teddy was so excited to see him. Rob questioned whether it was too soon to bring him in, but I explained how he had been all day and when the vet examined him, he concluded that it was the right decision. Teddy was very swollen and growled in pain when the vet pressed on specific areas. I stroked Teddy's head and kissed him over and over as I said goodbye to him. He gave me one final lick (kiss) before he closed his eyes forever.

Hysterical, I began to hyperventilate, and the nurse took me to a yard out the back, handed me a paper bag to breathe into and got me a glass of water. The pain I felt was unbearable, and to this day, I still cannot think of that day without floods of tears. Rob was also very upset about our loss and was extremely supportive. I went on a mission of scrubbing every inch of the house, anything to keep busy and not think of my poor Teddy.

CHAPTER 13
Storm Barbara

In November 2016, Barbara became seriously unwell. Her breathing was always bad due to her COPD and her refusal to give up her 20 a day habit. Rob was working in Nottingham when he received a call from Barbara, saying that she was frightened as she could barely breathe. He called me as he was flying up the motorway. This was ridiculous. If you can't breathe, you need an ambulance. I was only around the corner from Barbara. Why didn't he send me to her at least? Surely the poor woman could be dead before her son arrived to save the day. It would get on my nerves a little the way Rob and Barbara behaved at times. Only Rob could do her shopping, only Rob could take her shopping or to appointments, and now it seemed only Rob could save her when she couldn't breathe. It was odd. This woman had visited my home a couple of times, yet I was not welcome to go into hers. This did not sit well with me at all.

Rob called me again once Barbara was admitted to a ward and settled. It turns out that she had a touch of pneumonia and fluid on her lungs. The hospital wanted to keep her in for a few days as she was very frail. Her dog had passed away a week earlier, and I suspect that, along with the grief, she had not been taking good care of herself. She still had her greedy 17-year-old cat, so Rob had another job to schedule in, feeding the cat three times a day. It should have been getting two meals a day, but Rob insisted that he would have to go three times a day as that is what the cat was used to. This was just another added stress that he did not need, being as busy as he already was and I had just started a temporary role in a womens refuge, working 3 days a week. The ultimate goal, when we ever had time was for Lee to train me up to deliver training in the business.

A few days later, the doctors discussed discharging Barbara, but they were concerned about her climbing stairs and living independently. This is where we came in. We lived in a bungalow and had a spare room. Excellent. This woman I had spoken to only a couple of times was moving into our modest sized bungalow. Admittedly this was not something I was entirely happy with, yet it was also intriguing to get a handle of what this woman was really like. Rob spoke very little about his early life, and I was hoping that Barbara might fill me in a bit.

The first couple of days of having Barbara with us were uncomfortable, to say the least. We had no bed for her, so we had to give her ours, and we had to sleep on the living room floor.

We were like two bears with sore heads, tired, achy, and bickering at the slightest thing. Barbara, on the other hand, was in her element. Rob was waiting on her hand and foot, and the shopping orders were coming in thick and fast. Some days she would send him out three times as she would keep forgetting things that she wanted.

On top of this, we were feeding her greedy cat three times a day and trying to run a business was just too much. I offered to share the burden. I could feed the greedy cat or go shopping but, no, how silly! Only Rob was allowed to do these things. I wasn't to go into Barbara's house for some unknown reason.

Arguing became a daily occurrence with Rob and me as Barbara was not a good house guest, and if even I tried to bring it up, Rob would hit the roof. He was constantly reminding me of her age, that she was ill and had no one else. Yes. Thank you. I know all that. But did she have to be such an ungrateful bitch about it?

I would watch in amazement as Rob would take his Mother a meal, and she would just take it from him without so much as a smile or a thank you. Even worse, she complained about it, stating that she would not enjoy it because he shouldn't have put the beans next to the mashed potato.

The more I approached the subject of Barbara's bad manners, the more arguments we would have. After a week, we finally got our room back as Barbara had ordered a single bed and mattress for our spare room. However, she was not as pleased about the move into the spare room as we were. Repeatedly, she was commenting that the light was not good enough for her to read her books. She would like the curtains open to look out but needed nets so people could not see in. Did she realise that this arrangement was not permanent? Why did she want to look out of the window with nets on it? She could only see the view of the side of my neighbour's house?

Blood boiling, I came home one evening from work to find that my new net curtains from the kitchen were gone, and of course, Barbara the Bitch had them in the spare room.

"I want a new light bulb," Barbara was telling Rob. "This one is rubbish, and I can't see to read. And I want to read my book."

"But Mum, this is a bigger, brighter bulb," Rob replied. "I've only just taken it out of the box."

"I doubt that," her tone was condescending. "If that were true, I'd be able to see to read, wouldn't I?"

I heard Rob sigh and walk to our bedroom and take the bulb out of our light.

"Better?" He demanded a few minutes later.

"Have you changed it?" She demanded. "Only I can't tell the difference."

"Look, Mum, this is the bulb from our bedroom." Rob was trying very hard to remain calm. "You said you could read fine in there, and this is the exact same bulb."

"The light was right over me when I was reading, so that was probably why it's not good now."

"That can't be right," Rob argued. "The light fitting is in the centre of our bedroom, and our bed is pushed back to the wall."

"I doubt that!"

I didn't hear any more as I was going out to the shops; although, Rob did ask me to pick up a new 100-watt bulb. I was tempted to refuse but only agreed, thinking it would shut her up. I should have known better, as when I returned with it, she still insisted that it wasn't bright enough. Rob even resorted to taking the shade off.

"It's still not bright enough!" Barbara persisted. "I bet Julia bought one of those cheap, no good bulbs."

Outside, I gritted my teeth.

"Now, Mum, you are being ridiculous!"

I wondered, if she didn't have bright bulbs at home, how could this new one still not be bright enough.

A little while later, when Rob went to her house to feed the greedy cat, he returned with a desk lamp that she could bend over her book pages. Guess what? That was no good either.

The door slammed soon after Rob told her it was tough, he had done all he could, and that there was no pleasing her.

Somehow it resulted in another argument for us too.

As time went on, Barbara would try to boss me about and use me as a maid, telling me, not asking me, to make her a cup of tea. She would moan that her porridge was too lumpy, there wasn't enough butter on her toasted teacakes and so on. The one that took the biscuit was when she tried to take the bath that I had run for myself after a day at work. She had no shame whatsoever when it came to being a cheeky nuisance. I can say that I have never met an old woman as nasty in my life, and this was my Mother-in-law to be.   Lucky   me...

CHAPTER 14
Family Problems

The toll of Barbara living with us was unbearable by this point, and I had resigned myself to the fact that we would be stuck with her for some time longer.

I did not believe she was as ill as she said she was a lot of the time. When we were there, she would be running around that house like a little whippet. If we had to work away and leave her for a night or two, she would say that she would be fine. However,upon our return, she would be in bed, telling us how she had hardly eaten whilst we had been away because she felt so ill and had no energy.

Rob and I were planning to go over to Ireland on the Ferry on 29th December, taking my Mum and Auntie with us. One of my relatives there was terminally ill, and it was important to spend some quality time with her whilst we could.

One night I was listening in on Barbara talking to Rob. Although she had kept saying she was much better and that we would be fine to leave her, she was now saying she was too ill to be left alone.

"Can't she just go on her own?" I heard the old bitch ask.

Anger was burning through me, calling me 'she' and having no thought that this was such an important trip for the two of us. It was like she was trying to pull us apart, and so far, she was doing a good job.

Rob walked into the living room with a pitiful look on his face and agreed that maybe I should go on my own. I snapped at him and said that if that had to be the case, I would take his precious car as mine was ready for the knacker's yard and not up to such a journey. This idea clearly concerned him, and he tried to suggest I get a hire car, so I told him that it would not be insured to take out of the country, so he should get a hire car, and I would take his. Eventually, after an hour or so of arguing, I found myself online, changing the ferry dates to January and letting my Mum and auntie Sally know the change of plan.

Barbara had won for now but come January, we were both going, come hell or high water.

The week running up to Christmas was hectic for everyone, trying to get everything ready for the day and finishing off any last work commitments.

That week Barbara had been complaining of being very unwell. By the time Christmas Eve arrived, against her wishes, we had called for the doctor to see her. The doctor was concerned about her becoming dehydrated as she had started with sickness and diarrhoea, now on top of everything else. The doctor suggested, quite firmly, that Barbara needed to go into hospital, but she refused point-blank. That evening, we tried to talk her around to the idea and explained that she would be stuck in A&E for hours if she waited until Christmas Day. Still, she refused.

CHAPTER 15
A Difficult Christmas

Rob and I had wished each other a Merry Christmas and had gone into Barbara's room to do the same. She put on her best "oh don't feel sorry for me" face and asked us if we usually go out on Christmas Day. She already knew the answer to that as she came to us in the afternoons usually.

Trying her best to look sad and pathetic, she told us to carry on as usual and to have a lovely Christmas and that she was just going to stay in her room and have a quiet day. Two minutes after that conversation, I heard her slippers shuffling into the living room where we were sitting. She threw herself back on to the sofa in the most dramatic way she knew how and, in her saddest, whiniest voice, said, "Rob, I need to go to the hospital; I'm really not well. Can you take me in?"

Great job. Instead of going in yesterday like suggested, she waited, wished us a merry Christmas and then bang, hit us with a day at A&E. Seven hours we were in there, waiting for them to put her on a ward. Secretly I hoped they would keep her in as long as possible after putting up with her terrible behaviour and, now, her latest stunt.

That Christmas is the only one in my life that I have not had a Christmas dinner. It was almost 8pm when we got home, so it was too late to start cooking. I just threw a few sausage rolls in the oven (they were part of the Boxing Day buffet) and decided that Christmas dinner would be tomorrow.

During Barbara's stay in the hospital, we went twice a day, brought whatever she asked for, took her clothes home, washed them, and took them back.

I found it extremely odd that during her stay in the hospital, she never once took Piriton to my knowledge. Usually, she took one every day, saying that she was allergic to everything: washing powder, bath soaps, anything that went on her skin. It was like an obsession, something she always had on the shopping list and took everyday.

It occurred to me that, although I had been washing her nightdresses and as far as I was aware had not taken any Piriton whilst in hospital, there were no allergic reactions or skin conditions.

It was a stressful week, to say the least. There was talk of her coming home on New Year's Eve, and I didn't want her ruining that too, so I kept my fingers crossed that they would keep her another night, and thankfully it worked. Not that we did anything special, I think we were both so shattered that we were asleep before the clock struck midnight.

The next day, the inevitable happened, and we brought her home, and the bossing and the ungratefulness picked up from where she had left it. There was no peace from her. She was constantly demanding and at night when we were in bed, those slippers would come shuffling past our room to the bathroom.

Home was not somewhere I wanted to be right now, and it was all because of her presence. In all my years, I hadn't met anyone who would go out of their way to be a burden.

If this was my Mother, she would be polite and grateful and would not want to make our lives difficult, but for this bitch it was like a calling. She would even wait until the last minute, just as I was going out, to ask me to get somethingor try toengage me in conversation.

The day I was meeting with my bridesmaids to shop and make arrangements, she called me in. I told her that I only had a minute as I had to pick up one of my bridesmaids across town and meet the other one to make wedding arrangements.

Instead of saying that whatever she wanted could wait, she started saying that if I was going out, I could pick her up some new pyjamas. Then she began describing to me exactly what she wanted and what she didn't.

I had to be firm with her and say that I did not have time that day and as I had said, I had to go so I could collect my bridesmaids. She gave me the look of a scorned child before saying that it could wait until another day if I did not have time.

Another time, I was meeting a friend for dinner, and she did the same usurping things. First, I ran her a bath, then made a cup of tea, then listened to her wittering on about nothing before I eventually left the house, late yet again.

Most of the time, when I did get a chance to see a friend, I would usually be in tears within a few minutes due to the stress Barbara was putting on me and us as a couple.

I felt like I had nowhere to hide, well, because I didn't.

CHAPTER 16
Happy New Year

We were now in February, and Barbara was still in our spare room. Some days she would talk about how she couldn't wait to go home as she loved her house and all the space she had and that soon she would be well enough. However, if I ever had the conversation with her about her going home, the answer would always be, "Just another week. Then let's see how I am."

"Hello, both," I greeted Rob and Barbara, who were in the kitchen.

"Hi, lovey," Rob answered, but Barbara just turned to me and scowled and turned away and left the kitchen

This was the last straw. "Rob, she's got to go," I told him. "It doesn't matter if she's ill or not. I want this nasty woman out of my house."

"She's not that bad, Julia!"

"I don't care," I was angry and just wanted her to be gone. "I will not be treated like this in my own home."

"She's not well; she can't help it if she's feeling under the weather."

"There's nothing wrong with her!" I yelled, not caring that the woman in question was only next door.

"She's ill!"

"Like hell she is!" I answered. "Besides which, this is our bungalow, and it's too small for all of us."

Rob glared at me and then stomped into our bedroom.

"What are you doing?" I stood in the doorway and demanded an answer.

"Packing." He was grabbing his things out of the wardrobe.

"Where are you going?" I had a bad feeling.

"Well, as you've made it plainly clear that my Mother isn't welcome here, I'm taking her home."

"Good." I paused. "So why are you packing?"

"Because I'm going to stay with her!"

"Why?"

"Mum!" He opened the door and yelled to her. "Get your things. We're leaving!"

I couldn't help but think that this had probably made her day. "You don't have to leave."

"You, Julia, are a horrible bitch!" He shouted in my face. "And I wish that I had never met you."

"Rob…" I was consumed with hate for his Mother.

"Give me my engagement ring back."

I put my hand behind my back. "No."

He grabbed my hand and tried to snatch it off my finger. I flinched as he pulled my finger, but then he looked confused.

He grabbed his bag and ended up marching out of the house without his Mum. He finally came back when he had calmed down, and he apologised. We both agreed that his Mother was a huge strain on our relationship, but hopefully, she would be going back to her own house soon.

One afternoon, Barbara appeared to be in a rather chatty mood, which was not like her at all. Given some of her behaviour, I had actually wondered if she was bordering on dementia. I had never really had a proper conversation with her about anything, especially anything concerning the past. The conversation appeared from nowhere, and I decided to keep quiet,hoping that I would finally learn something about her.

The first thing that struck a chord with me was that she mentioned being on anti-depressants when Rob was a baby. This was strange considering the number of times that Rob had boasted that both he and his Mother had always prided themselves on having such strong minds. So strong that neither of them had ever had to rely on medication to deal with the stresses that life could bring. She went on to tell me how she had married a lovely man called John Carter and that although he was a wonderfully kind husband, she had never actually felt in love with him.

I listened intently, not wanting to mention that I thought Rob's dad was called Michael Carter. Concealing my shock, I remained silent as she proceeded to tell me that she had left John for a man named Michael Dixon and that she had gone on to have Rob with Michael.

By now, I was asking myself, *John Carter? Michael Dixon? Who? Michael Carter...?* And I was wondering if Barbara was in reality or just saying names of people she knew from various times in her life.

Barbara kept telling her story. Michael had been working away a lot, and Barbara had become very low and suspicious of what he might be doing.

Eventually, when Rob was about six months old, she asked a friend to mind him whilst she got the train to Nottingham to find some answers. When she got there, she discovered that Michael was having an affair. She had read some love letters from the other woman, demanded to know where she lived and went as far as turning up on her doorstep to threaten her to stay away from Michael.

My mind was racing as I tried to make sense of what she was telling me. Over time she had called things off with Michael, and other than a few visits to Rob, they had little contact. I concluded that he must have seen Rob at least up until he started school as she had mentioned that Michael had offered to buy him school trousers.

Once she had finished her tale, I decided to confront her with Rob's version of events. Shock evident, her mouth gaped open as I went on to tell her that according to Rob, his dad was called Michael Carter (a combination of John Carter and Michael Dixon, it seemed) and that he died in a car crash when Rob was two years old and that Barbara had been so heartbroken, was widowed young, and had been left to raise a small child on her own. This was why Barbara had lived alone the rest of her life due to being so in love with Michael Carter, the man I now knew never existed.

According to Barbara, when Rob was 18 years of age, there had been talk of him going to visit Michael Dixon, but that Barbara was worried Rob might be violent toward Michael, as he had made comments to her that he would.

When I asked how Rob and her were both named Carter instead of Dixon, she said that after leaving Michael dixon, she decided to use her previous married name of Carter and wanted Rob to share that name.

Twisted, to say the least, to leave your husband for another man, have a baby and then have the gall to change the child's name to the name of the poor husband, I assumed she cheated on was just sick, in my opinion.

More concerning was that Rob had been lying to me the whole time about this, and I wanted to know why. I was marrying him in a matter of months, yet I felt that I didn't know anything about his past. Something so basic as his surname had now come into question, and I was concerned that the information that he had put on our paperwork in order for us to marry might not even be accurate.

By the time Rob arrived home from work that evening, I was ready to pounce. He had barely sat down when I blurted out that I couldn't marryhim. Colour drained from his face. I could see that he was studying me, frantically looking for the reason that could make me say this. He went on to ask me why and when I told him, I have to admit he expressed a mixture of shock and concern.

Silence filled the room as I waited for an explanation, which I was sure that my husband-to-be would have. After a few moments, he began to compose himself before looking me in the eye and saying,"Julia, do you have any idea what you have just done?"

Puzzled and speechless, I urged him with a look to explain himself. Throughout the next five minutes, I said nothing. I just listened whilst Rob told me that if what his Mother had told me was true, then this was the first time he had heard anything about it and that he was in complete disbelief as to why she would tell me such a thing, never having spoken to him about it.

As far as he was concerned, he was born Rob Carter, and his father was a man called Michael Carter. Re-iterating that he was told that his father had passed away when he was two years old, as the result of a fatal car crash, I looked at him suspiciously.

Firing questions at him as if I had him up on the stand, I looked for signs of deceit as he answered how he couldn't know his birth name. He explained that he had never seen his birth certificate, and I wanted to know how he had managed to get a driver's licence and passport. It would have been impossible to do so without declaring his real name and providing his birth certificate.

I have to admit his explanation did not ring true to me. Was he really telling me this? An intelligent person who had heard enough lies in a lifetime to fall for something so ridiculous.

He explained that his Mother had gotten him his first passport when he had gone abroad on a school trip. Ever since then, he had used that passport to renew it and to get a driver's licence. I wanted to tell him that this too did not sit right with me. He had always said to me that Barbara had struggled financially bringing him up, to the point that they could not even afford a camera, hence why there were very few photographs of him as a child. I, for one, had never seen a single picture of him as a child, saying that I had never been into his Mother's house even though at this point the old witch was residing in my home.

I didn't get the chance to interrogate him any further as his confusion turned to anger, then to sadness. With tears in his eyes, he told me that I had no idea what I had just done to him. I had just thrown a bomb onto his childhood memories with no thought of the consequences to him.

Quietly I asked when he was going to have it out with Barbara, and although he said he was going to have to, it was not a path he could take at the moment whilst she was so seriously unwell.

That evening, we were both sitting in bed quietly watching the TV. I was not taking in a single word of what was being said, and Rob looked distracted, too, but sad.

I had never seen him look so beaten down, and I felt a sense of sorrow. I felt that I should be comforting this poor man, but then again, I was also struggling to believe his truth. I half expected him to come out with his usual humorous answer. When on the very rare occasions that I proved him wrong about something, he would laugh and say, "I reject your reality and substitute it with one of my own."

In some twisted way, had he done this with what happened between his Mother and Father? Did he find his version of events easier to live with than the real version? Even if this was the case, I could not justify it in my mind. This version of events had given me empathy towards Barbara (something I now did not believe was warranted). It also instilled empathy with my friends and family when I told them about Rob and Barbara's tragic past.

Rob had turned me into a liar. I had been lying about his father and poor Barbara, the widow when Michael Dixon could still be on this earth for all I know.

However, I was forced to reassess my feelings when Rob suddenly started telling me the truth as he knew it. He said that if it turned out Barbara had lied to him, maybe there was an excellent reason for it, and that possibly was about protecting him.

I could not in my wildest imagination think how lying to him about such a thing could be for his protection, but I kept my mouth shut and just listened. My heart broke as Rob told me one of the most distressing things I had ever heard. He talked of how he did not remember knowing his dad, but maybe his brain had blocked something out, something he had never told anyone about until now.

The guilt that hit me was immense as he tearfully told me of a memory he had as a small boy. What had I stirred up for my poor fiancé? I had opened up trauma from his past without realising that there was even one.

Rob told me that he had a recollection of a man (he did not know who) being in the bathroom in his house. He recalled the man sitting on the toilet with his trousers around his ankles and that he had asked Rob to go to him, and when he did, the man lifted Rob onto his lap.

Rob sobbed as he told me that he really could not remember anything other than that but that maybe he had subconsciously blocked it out. He admitted that there was a strong possibility that this man had sexually abused him but that if he had, it was something that his brain had managed to block out.

This led him to now believe that something terrible had happened and that Barbara had found out, removed the man (most likely his father) from their lives. Then to protect Rob, she had fabricated a new version of events that neither of them would ever have the opportunity to delve into the darkness of such a reality.

As Rob sobbed, I held him and thanked him for being brave enough even to tell me, and I apologised over and over again for thoughtlessly throwing this at him, unaware of the effect it could have on him.

With regards to his name, obviously, his passport and driving licence had that on them, and he assured me there was nothing untoward about his name change. It would not affect anything as it was the only name he had ever known.

Part of me was furious with Barbara for her little outburst and the position she had put me in. It bothered me that she had lied to me about Rob knowing the truth when she had never even told him. It was an awkward situation, but Rob said this sleeping dog would have to lie a little longer until her health had improved and she wasn't as frail.

In mid-March, Barbara finally returned to her own home, and the relief was indescribable. To have our home back to ourselves and the pressure removed was just incredible.

Rob and I were looking forward to our upcoming wedding, and our lives were so busy. I had to keep pinching myself that I was getting married after a lifetime of waiting.

However happy we were, though, there was always room for bickering, and it was always about the same things. Why Rob always appeared so secretive with his phone? It would always be on silent and face down so that I was unable to see the screen. He even got a case that covered most of the phone so that I could not see if anyone did call. Of course, he reasoned that he had just picked a case to protect his phone, and as he was sick of telling me, he kept the phone on silent as people from his courses would randomly call or send messages about work stuff at all hours and he did not want the constant interruption. He would say that a phone was to serve him, not the other way around, and if he wanted to use it, he would, but he was not going to be constantly picking it up and responding to calls and messages.

Then there was his post which was another thing that we would bicker about. He still hadn't had it all redirected to our house, which meant him collecting it from his Mum's house. The few items of post that did come to our house would go in his briefcase with the reasoning that he would read them during his working day as he already knew that most of it was junk.

I would find it so frustrating, but like he said, why was I so bothered? Who do I think is calling or sending him post? He spent 95% of his time with me, and the only time we were apart would be if he was working locally. He wanted to know why I could not trust him even though he had given me a reason not to trust him to start with, but surely, he had proven himself by now. I knew he was right, and I would know if my husband-to-be was not head over heels about me. He was kind, generous, loving, romantic, and wanted to spend all of his time with me. So why couldn't I fully trust him?

Rob asked me why I could not accept his idiosyncrasies and had to question everything? Was it really that strange to hoover his car four or five times a week, polish it whilst sitting in traffic or take it to the car wash three or four times a week? As he said, he had spent a hell of a lot of money on it and wanted to keep it like new. My brother even said to him once as a joke that he must be carting dead bodies around in his boot, and if CSI ever checked the car over, then they would not even find Rob's DNA in there due to his OCD cleaning schedule.

Rob said that just because he did things differently from how I would, it didn't mean that there was anything wrong with how he did things. I knew that I was picking on him at times, but I just couldn't help myself. I would question him on something that I found strange, even though I knew he would prove me wrong. We would have a huge row, and he would probably not speak to me for a night or a day, too, depending on how heated things got. I would then have to make it up to him and apologise repeatedly because I had a suspicious nature and an overactive mind.

Sometimes if I had a bee in my bonnet about something, I would choose to keep it to myself rather than start an argument, but Rob would always know. "Julia, I can see it all over your face. Go on, spit it out. What have you made up in your head this time that you're unhappy about?"

There were times I would feel so guilty because I would convince myself that there was something he was hiding and that sometimes I had checked up on him or caught him in a lie. Only then I was proved to be wrong yet again and felt like a complete fool.

When we were getting on, which was the majority of the time, things were wonderful, and I would scold myself for being so paranoid and creating issues.

I would sometimes make light of my insecurities and tell Rob that I was thankful he had a mental health nursing background and that this was the only a mental health nurse who would put up with me.

However, it was comforting to be given the benefit of the doubt. It meant he understood that I had many emotional scars from my past, left there from a multitude of bad men I had got myself tangled up with. I struggled to accept that those days were behind me, and now I had met a wonderful man. He was the polar opposite of my daughter's father, Simon. I just prayed that my insecurities did not force me to self-sabotage something that was making my life worthwhile.

Rob did nothing but love me and provide for me and keep me safe, but even a nurse or the most patient man in the world was not going to put up with being interrogated regularly for no good reason.

I would often build up a list of things that I thought were "suspicious" and save them up. Sometimes I'd save them for weeks and then wait until he least expected it, throwing them all at him in the hope that I would catch him off guard on something and capturehim in a lie. The result would always be the same, and although I felt relief that he was doing nothing wrong, the guilt of treating him this way would leave me feeling so low.

One particular evening I threw one of my lists at him, and it was one of the times I pushed him too far.

How many times did he have to tell me that he could not live like this, that I was allowing my mind to ruin something so amazing before I learnt my lesson? He believed that I would never know and that the result would be we would split up because he really couldn't take much more. Who could blame him?

My list this time comprised the fact that he was gone almost every time I woke up. Whether it was a workday or a weekend, it would always be the same.

At the beginning of our relationship, he had to do this for obvious reasons, but to me, that shouldn't have continued.

I could wake up at 8am on a Saturday or Sunday and find him already gone. He had been to his Mum's for a cup of tea, gone to do the shopping early, gone to the car wash- all so that his chores would be out of the way so that when I woke up, we could spend the day doing something enjoyable.

On workdays, if I woke up early and he had left a lot earlier than he needs to, I would wonder why but, like he said, he could not predict the traffic, and he could not afford to be late. Then there was the post issue, the phone issue again, and again.

This night, I had gone too far. He had had enough of trying to justify himself when he was doing nothing wrong. As he said, he had always gotten up and out early, and if I thought he was seeing someone else, would another woman put up seeing someone at 7am and nothing else? It made me feel silly. Of course, I knew it wasn't possible for him to cheat, nor did I think he would, but once my mind had those thoughts, they would run away, and I would catastrophise.

Now Rob was talking about calling the wedding off and us splitting up. He said it would be terrible for both of us, but he just couldn't believe that I was capable of changing my behaviour. He said I was just too damaged from my past to be able to trust anyone wholeheartedly. He had even gone as far as to call me Simon (Lucie's dad) and had cried and said that I had become an abuser myself.

He was living on eggshells, and that although he was doing nothing wrong, he was living in fear of the next interrogation and constantly having to defend himself and prove to me that it was all in my head. Rob sobbed and explained how I was continually trying to micromanage him and that I came across as controlling, another thing that Simon had been. He asked me to think back to the times I was afraid to open my mouth and just speak the truth, in fear of whether I'd be believed and what the consequences would be if I weren't.

I cried so hard when I realised what I had become and what I was doing to the man I loved with all my heart. Maybe he was right, and I was too far gone to change. I begged him to give me another chance, but he had heard it all before from me, so I was fighting a losing battle.

"What if I go for some therapy?" I asked hopefully. I explained that I would look into it and promised that I would get help and change. It didn't fill him with confidence.

Reluctantly Rob agreed to stay with me in the hope that I could make a positive change. However, he confirmed that he was very doubtful as he thought maybe I was beyond help regarding this matter.

Thankfully I managed to stop interrogating Rob whilst I waited for some CBT therapy, and I was so grateful that he had given me another chance and was determined to make things work.

I kept my mind busy with wedding plans and work and did not leave myself much time to over-think things that were negative.

About six weeks before our big day, I had my first session with my therapist and threw myself into the plan. I was given homework and useful apps and techniques that helped me treat unwanted thoughts like passing traffic. As a car goes past you in the street, you see it, it goes by, you don't then keep thinking about that car. This was what I had to do with my unhelpful thoughts. They came, and then I had to let them pass, giving them no more thought.

CHAPTER 17
The Wedding

I am told that people had never seen a calmer bride than me. I wasn't one bit nervous about any of it. I later realised this might have been due to the fact that I'd been overdosing on Beta-blockers for the past two months, which I took as a preventative for migraines.

For some reason, I thought that the doctor had told me to take 80mg three times a day when I was told to take it once a day. Stupid me had never checked the box and had continued taking them three times a day. It was only when I took it four times in a day and realised I had taken what I thought was one extra dose that I looked at the box to check what I should do. Only then did I realise what I had been doing. Sometimes I had slept for 17 hours, and I was often so tired. Well, this was why.

Rob had stayed with my cousin's husband Mark the night before the wedding and I had spent it with my bridesmaids Leanne and Ruth. We had got up in the morning in high spirits; Leanne and I doing Bollywood dancing in my bedroom before we got dressed.

We did the usual, went for having our hair and make-up done. I wanted Lucie to join me on these fun bits, but she said it was my day. In the months leading up to my wedding to Rob, Lucie and I had started talking again. The pain of Carla's words and behaviour still seemed to haunt Lucie and me and it had kept us apart for a time. I wanted to know if her life had been caught up with Josh in the same way mine had been caught up with Rob.

The photographer arrived just as I had gotten into my dress with the help of my bridesmaids.

My Stepdad, Brian, arrived, and in no time, we were in a beautiful Rolls Royce making our way to the venue. As everyone says, the day just flies by, and you need to try to savour every moment.

However, there were a few moments I could happily dismiss. Two of her friends accompanied Barbara (the only member of Rob's Family to attend).I couldn't help but think that they were seated together like the three stooges. Barbara didn't smile the entire day, and people I chatted with mentioned as politely as they could that she had been quite rude and dismissive when they had introduced themselves to her.

After the ceremony, as everyone was coming to congratulate us, Barbara gave me a dirty look and attempted to walk past me without a word. Rob saw the obvious expression of shock and anger on my face and stopped her.

"Mum, aren't you even going to speak to Julia?"

Her reply was not remotely kind. "Hello," she muttered and carried on walking.

I decided that she was not going to ruin my day and that I would ignore her behaviour. The only time she smiled the entire day was when she stood next to Rob for a photo.

At the dinner table, they had messed up the seating arrangements at the top table of all places. They had me sitting next to the wicked witch of the west! I tried to disguise my disgust as I said in my most calm and quietest voice that Rob needed to swap seats with me. They were large king and queen style chairs (the queen one being the largest to take into account the huge bridal gown), so they were not the easiest to move. Hence, we ended up sitting in each other's seats. I was a little squashed, but that was more favourable than sitting next to the old witch.

Throughout the meal, Rob was constantly chastising his Mother for complaining as she was sitting and scowling and moaning about how she wouldn't be able to chew the beef with her dentures.

At one point, I heard him talk to her in a rather low but firm voice. "Don't fucking eat it then, just stop moaning!"

She was causing a scene, and after the behaviour I had seen when she stayed with us, it did not surprise me.

At the other end of the table, unbeknownst to me, the best man and his girlfriend were also bickering. What a wonderful top table we had. Hopefully, the speeches would distract people from their rude behaviour.

I had been waiting in anticipation for Rob's speech as I had kept at him to make sure he planned it and he assured me that he would make it as amazing as he possibly could.

A few days earlier, he was sitting in the office after telling me to go shopping on my own. I had been a little disappointed as he had already agreed to come with me to buy clothes for our honeymoon. However, that morning, he had told me that he had things to do and that I should go alone. He went as far as to say to me not to enter the office as he was working on his speech and did not want me to see it. I agreed and left him to it, knowing that he had been working on it with Mark the night before and printing it off. I was expecting something special.

When Rob stood up, I watched and waited for him to pull a piece of paper out of his pocket. This didn't happen; instead, Rob stood nervously, face perspiring, and began to talk. He thanked people for joining us, and he mentioned people who were not able to attend but sent their regards and how happy he was that he and I had met. Then he said he hoped he hadn't missed anything.

"What about you? He's not said anything about you?" I froze as my Mum whispered at the side of me.

"Just one thing," I said to Rob, "you've not said anything about me." I felt so humiliated and had to try so hard not to cry. How embarrassing to have to tell your new husband to say something nice about you. After my prompt, he talked about me for a moment, but it was so pathetic that I didn't even bother to remember any of it. I was too angry to take it in.

The Best Man did a much better job (but also forgot to introduce me). He had a very well prepared and loving speech to give about my wonderful new husband.

Feeling cheated and that he did not deserve my effort, I stood and gave my speech. It was filled with endearing words about Rob, a bit of humour, and it went down very well.

A few of the men at the wedding had joked that they wished their wives had said such lovely things about them on their wedding day. However, I had been at their weddings, and at least they had all made beautiful speeches about their brides on the day, so it was me who was jealous.

As we left the dining room, we were asked to go for a walk around the grounds so that the photographer could get some nice shots of us. Whilst we walked around hand in hand, I spent the whole time with a fixed smile, telling my husband how angry and heartbroken I was and that I could not fathom how he could forget to speak of his new wife during his wedding speech.

Rob apologised repeatedly and blamed it on his nerves and that he had forgotten to take his speech out of his pocket.

There was no point in spoiling the whole day. However, I don't think I ever forgave him for that speech.

The rest of the day and the night went without a hitch. Barbara had gone home in a taxi alone around 6pm as her friends chose to stay and have a good time. I saw Barbara in the corridor just before she left, and I stopped to see if she had anything to say to me other than the snappy "Hello" I had received earlier. She paused to look at me before throwing me a filthy look, then turned and walked away, and she was gone. This was something I later spoke to Rob about in the bridal suite, shortly before he fell asleep at 1am, leaving me thinking about how I had wished my wedding night had been different.

Two days later, we were on our way to sunny Florida, and I have to say that we had the most fantastic time. I loved every minute of it: alligator parks, Universal Studios, Madame Tussauds, and, of course, we had to go to the shooting range.

Rob was so excited to go and shoot a Glock, and I thought I'd enjoy it, but I found the whole situation nerve-racking. The thought of standing in a room with strangers firing deadly weapons scared me. What if someone decided to turn and shoot someone instead of a target?

Wearing ear muffs didn't help as I jumped out of my skin every time a shot was fired. Firing the gun was also difficult as it would jolt back, and I was left with bruises around the top of my thumb.

Rob was in his element, though-boys and their toys. He loved every minute of it, but I was glad to get out of there as soon as I could.

CHAPTER 18
New York

Finally, being someone's wife made me feel overwhelmed with joy. I had a husband and one that treated me like the most important person in the whole universe. The pride I felt wearing my wedding ring and seeing him wearing his was such an unbelievable, heady feeling. I loved just saying "my husband" this and that. I had to keep pinching myself. Marriage to the perfect man had happened to me after all the years of hoping.

I had completed my CBT sessions and believed that I no longer needed help in shutting out any unhelpful or unwanted thoughts. It appeared to be working, and I believe it improved our relationship. We were much happier. Sure, we still bickered at times like all couples, but it wasn't like before. Life was calmer and far more enjoyable, just like life should be for two loved-up newlyweds.

New York:

Rob's dream had always been to go to New York, and although we had just been to Florida three months earlier, he had managed to convince me that we could afford to go. He had been talking about it for years, and his handsome face would light up when he spoke about it being his dream. I was always concerned about money as I had been all my life, but Rob would always tell me that worrying about money was a thing in the past, and I realised now that money was not a problem.

At the airport, we were quizzed by a member of staff about where we were going and why, as we queued for check-in. This was not the first time something like this had happened. When we were flying to Orlando, they had pulled Rob aside with his bag, something to do with checking what his iPad and the wires were. I understood that the security would be rigorous when going to America in light of 9/11.

After a long flight and arriving at Newark airport, we were tired, and I felt horriblefrom the lack of nicotine. All I could focus on was getting through security, collecting our cases and getting outside for a much-awaited cigarette. Unfortunately, my wait for nicotine was about to increase.

Passport control was busy, and I was relieved when it was our turn, and Rob stepped forward to the counter toward the unfriendly guard behind it.

"What's the purpose of your visit?" The guard demanded,

"Holiday," Rob answered.

"And who are you travelling with?"

"My wife."

I expected Rob to be waved forward and for me to show my passport next, but that didn't happen.

"Wait here," the guard growled as he checked my passport.

Within a matter of seconds, what looked like a police officer, gun in his belt, appeared.

"Please follow me, sir." He asked my husband to follow him. "You can wait over there." He pointed to an area where I could stand and wait. Completely shocked, I stood where I was told and continued to worry about why they had taken my husband away. About five minutes later, the officer that had taken my husband away began to walk towards me.

"Excuse me," I stopped him as he walked by. "How long will you be keeping my husband?"

"I expect that it will be some time," he told me. "If you have additional luggage, I suggest that you go downstairs and collect it." He walked off.

Numb and speechless, I decided to do as he said and in no time was dragging two cases behind me, my strength influenced by my anger and need for nicotine. I queued and explained that my husband was upstairs, but could I wait outside in the fresh air? Since my husband had our paperwork, I was told that I was not allowed to leave the secure section of the airport. I had no choice but to wait for him to return before exiting the airport.

Feeling like I was going to explode at this point, I angrily dragged the cases over to a seating area and sat there tapping my foot anxiously awaiting the re-appearance of my husband.

Within 10 minutes, he descended the escalator, and I jumped out of my seat and dragged the cases towards him. He took one of the cases, and we made our way out of the main area. He told me that he had no idea why they took him as he had just sat in a waiting room with other random people who were being interrogated about things on their Facebook pages. When they got to him, he was asked again why he was there and who he had travelled with. He had given the same answers, and then to his surprise, they returned his passport and told him to enjoy his trip.

It was bizarre, but I was just glad we were free to leave. However, we now had to rearrange transport to New York due to missing the originally booked one because of the delay. Rob sorted that out whilst I finally got to dash outside and light that long-awaited cigarette.

Our four days in New York were tiring but amazing as Rob had so many things he wanted to see during our short stay. We walked an average of 10 miles a day. We saw the 911 memorial, the Statue of Liberty, the Empire State Building, Grand Central train station, The New York Times, Central Park, went to the top of the Rockefeller building, and, of course, Madame Tussauds, and much more.

Each night we would just fall into bed and be asleep the moment our heads hit the pillow.

One evening whilst in the Hard Rock cafe, enjoying a huge, mouth-watering burger, Rob began a conversation that came totally out of the blue. For some reason, he mentioned Carla and said that there was something he hadn't told me at the time.

When I had spoken to him years earlier about the strange behaviour that she had been displaying, he had told me he had not noticed anything untoward and that, possibly, I was paranoid.

However, now he was telling me something different. He was now admitting that he, too, had noticed the behaviour and that there was something he hadn't told me.

Dread filled my body as I looked at him intently, waiting to explain what he was talking about. According to Rob, there had been a time when he was lying on our bed oneafternoon watching television when Carla came in to speak to him. He explained that Carla had climbed up onto the bed, lay next to him and wrapped her arms around him in a way that I would often do. He told me that he had been shocked and told her immediately that he did not think her behaviour was appropriate. I stayed silent as he continued to say that she had got up off the bed quickly, giggled and made the excuse that she hugged everybody like that.

Why tell me now whilst we were enjoying New York? I was angry that he had waited more than two years to tell me and was now agreeing that things I had noticed at the time had been there, but he thought it best to ignore them rather than have me over-think everything. This made no sense, and when asked why he was telling me now, he explained that he was concerned that one day Carla might try and split us up by telling malicious lies about him.

I knew what he was trying to get at; however, I played dumb and asked him to elaborate. He went on to say that due to Carla being so jealous of me that she would do anything to ruin my happiness and that he was concerned that she might one day tell people that something had gone on between the two of them.

Yes, it was true that Carla had a history of telling lies, some things quite bad that had been proved to be lies, but I felt uneasy about this due to the signs Rob had told me initially were not there.

Angry but sad, I tried to take in and process the information that he had just sprung on me as he searched my face for clues as to what I was thinking.

Unlike me, I felt calm as I decided just to be honest with what I was thinking. I told him that him saying this now and not at the time could look like there would be truth to these allegations, should Carla decide to throw them out there.

Sitting quietly, he listened carefully as I told him that I was very concerned as this now looked like an attempt on his part to pre-empt a situation. Instead of becoming angry at this, he reassured me of how he would never have cheated on me with anyone, especially Carla, who he thought of as nothing but a child, given he'd known her parents for all of her life.

I can't quite recall how the conversation came to a close, but by the end of it, my concern that something terrible had happened was no more. The subject was never mentioned again, well, until many weeks later.

We continued to enjoy New York and flew home without incident.

CHAPTER19
Too Much to Drink

Rob and I were enjoying a rare and well-deserved day off together, and although he had never been much of a drinker, he had suggested that we leave the car at home and catch a taxi to Rubery for a spot of lunch and a few afternoon drinks.

As we entered the pub, it was clear to see that we had picked a busy time, but luckily, we managed to get a table that had just become empty and made our way to it as quickly as we could.

Rob went to the bar and ordered a burger for him and a bacon, chicken and cheese Panini for me and then returned to the table carrying a pint of bitter and two blue WKDs. It always made me cringe when Rob ordered bitter, as I saw it as an old man's drink. Then again, you could say that blue WKD is a teenager's drink, so who was I to pass judgement?

I had never seen Rob even close to drunk in our four years together as he always prided himself on staying alert whilst out with me as a way of protecting me. A nice sentiment, but it meant that I had never seen him drunk – not even at home either as he always said he did not enjoy a drink in the house.

This particular afternoon, he drank four or five pints but wasn't drunk by any stretch of the imagination. Maybe a little more under the influence than I had seen before, but definitely not drunk.

Out of nowhere, he brought up the conversation about Carla againand said the same as he had in New York. I couldn't understand why he was bringing up the subject again. Well, if he was going to repeat the same thing, then so was I, as I found myself feeling suspicious all over again.

However, when I talked about pre-empting the situation, I was shocked to receive a completely different reaction from my husband. His eyes changed as he leaned across the table.

"Cunt!" He spat the word at me.

As I tried to reply and ask him why he was speaking to me in that way, I was drowned out by the rant of my usually calm husband.

"Don't look at me like that, you fucking cunt! How dare you, how fucking dare you accuse me of something so disgusting!"

I tried to tell him that I was not accusing him of anything, but it was no use. This wasn't my husband I was speaking to. This man before me was completely possessed; his eyes, his demeanour, everything about him had changed. The man in front of me did not resemble my loving, caring, and wonderful husband whatsoever.

"You are fucking sick in the head, you, fucking twisted, evil fucking cunt. How did I marry such a cunt? You can fuck off, Julia! You disgust me!"

I cringed as he abruptly stood from the table.

"I haven't got any way to get home…"

"I don't fucking care!" He replied nastily. "Fucking walk home!"

I watched him with my cheeks burning with shame as he marched out of the pub, leaving me sitting at the table with half a jug of cocktail that I had been enjoying up until now.

I scanned around my environment to find people giving me a pitiful look before turning away and talking in hushed voices. I sat for a few moments trying to compose myself, to look like nothing had happened. I continued to sip my drink, planning how I would walk out of the pub without bursting into tears.

Walking home, crying hysterically, I called my cousin Leanne and tried my best in between sobs to tell her what had just happened. She was angry that Rob had spoken to me that way and struggled to make sense of his behaviour and the whole story about Carla. The fact that he had probably got himself a taxi and left me to walk home too didn't help my husband in her estimations.

I continued to talk with Leanne as I made my way home. The walk from the town centre was just over a mile,but I think I was walking very fast due to the adrenaline.

Once I arrived at the part of Bristol Road where it turned on to West Road (the road that my drive was on), I froze. For a second, I thought I saw Rob on West Road about to turn on to the Bristol Road. What on earth was he playing at, drunk driving? His face appeared to be scouring the street. Was he looking for me? I couldn't explain why but at that moment, I felt fear. Something in my brain was telling me to hide and quick. As he turned onto the main road, I sped up, changing my route to back streets away from any main roads. I continued.

Leanne didn't comment when I told her that I was trying to avoid Rob, which was a good job, because I had no idea myself other than a gut feeling that told me I needed to hide.

I made it home without him seeing me, and after about 15 minutes, I heard his car pull up. I told Leanne I would call her back before I ran to the back door and made my way into the garden. I heard Rob enter the house, stay for a couple of minutes before leaving again. I listened to the car started up, and then he was gone.

I made my way back into the house and called Leanne back and told her that he had now gone again. However, as we talked, I heard the car return. I told her not to call me or text me and that I would be in touch when I could.

Rob looked more like his usual self when he walked into the lounge. He had undoubtedly calmed down, but there was still a sense of anger in the air. He plonked himself down on the sofa.

"Well, where have you been?" he asked.

"I was walking home since you had run off, leaving me penniless. Obviously,you got yourself a taxi home." I replied in a somewhat sarcastic tone.

He looked ashamed. "I'm really sorry for the way I spoke to you," he apologised. "I didn't mean to leave you and let you walk home like that."

"Well, you did."

"It was the drink," he told me. "As soon as I had calmed down, I felt bad."

I wasn't happy with his apology. "Not good enough."

"I tried to find you. I was going to pick you up, so you didn't have to walk home."

His apology wasn't good enough, and I grilled him on why he reacted that way this time when I had only reacted the same way as I had done in New York. I told him that I wasn't prepared to allow him to ever speak to me that way again -and especially not in public. I told him how he had humiliated himself and how he must have looked to strangers speaking to his wife in that way. It made him look like a violent drunk, something we both knew he wasn't.

It was hard to say how long my husband apologised to me or how I managed to forgive him, but eventually, all was well again.

CHAPTER 20
The Little Things

Rob and I were generally getting on well, and I had learnt to try not to interrogate him when I thought things were a bit off.

One thing that had been puzzling me for some weeks was that Barbara's post had started arriving at our house.Some were addressed to her at our address, and some had her own address on but with a redirect sticker.

Rob told me that he had been sick of my moaning about the fact that some of his post still went to his Mum's house,so he had arranged a redirect. Obviously, they had got it mixed up and had now started redirecting Barbara's post to our house instead of his. He told me that he had spoken to them and would refund the redirect charge and sort it out. His post would now be re-directed and not hers.

Rob couldn't understand why it annoyed me so much every time another letter for her arrived at my house. This was my house long before Rob moved in, and to have anything relating to his wicked Mother grated on my nerves. He promised it had been sorted out and told me that I shouldn't let the smallest things annoy me.

He always told me that stress kills, and I needed to chill out, not get stressed over things that didn't warrant it. Besides the post annoyance, the only thing I really worried about was that Rob was working too hard. He looked shattered and needed to look after himself more. He had looked so tired and ill over Christmas after working himself to the bone so that when he did have time off, he was too sick and tired to enjoy it. He always told me I worried too much, of course, and that he was fine. He would continuously talk about all the money we were earning and all the lovely holidays we were going to go on.

My husband was holiday mad, and although, yes, I enjoyed holidays, there were other things I would rather spend money on, like a few small debts I had been paying off since before we were together. They only amounted to about £6,000 and could have easily been paid off in full, but Rob would always promise I could pay them off soon, not now, but soon. This had been going on for years now. Yes, we had paid for the wedding and other things, but in a bad month, we could earn £3,000 and in a good month £9,000. So, my debts, in my eyes, should have been paid off by now.

I was also still annoyed by the fact that since I had gotten rid of my cheap, unreliable car and was still waiting on a better car that I had been promised every month. The better car never came, and I had to rely on using our one car the odd time Rob didn't need it.

I hated it when we were working in different places, and he would drop me off, say in Coventry early, and then drive to Leicester to work. When we both finished working, I would have to wait around whilst he made the trip back to pick me up. It was ridiculous. What was more annoying was that when he was working, and I wasn't, he would take the car, but when I was working, and he wasn't, he would still take the car. He would say it was so he could do his Mum's shopping or in case he needed to go anywhere.

After lots of bickering, I would suggest he do the shopping another day so that he could do what I do and just have a day at home like I had to do. After all, it was only a short walk from our house to Barbara's house,so if he wanted to go and see her, he could. This led to the odd time I had the car, but he would think of a reason why it would be easier for him to drop me off and keep the car. I felt like a child being dropped off at school by a parent. This could easily be resolved by putting a couple of thousand away and buying me a car, but it was a waiting game for now.

I was working in Nottingham, and Rob had a day off, and it had been agreed that I would take the car that day. However, that morning Rob decided he would just come with me to work. Apparently, he wouldn't get under my feet and wouldn't even be in the room with me. Instead, he would go and have a chat with the client I was seeing and that he would sit in the hub area and do some work on his iPad. He said, this way, he could come on breaks and lunch with me, and then at the end of the day, we could travel home together. I was over telling my husband when I thought his ideas were a bit pointless or strange and what would be the reason to cause an argument over nothing, anyway.

When I met him on the first break at around 11am, he told me that he would go home instead of hanging around all day and do any shopping we needed. I asked what we needed and that if we needed anything at all, he may as well just get it from the Tesco next to where I was working. He said we just needed a few bits, that milk was one of the things, and he could not leave the milk in the boot of the car all day. I could see the annoyance in his face when I suggested that he just get it near home time. However, he agreed that I was right and said he would go at the end of the day.

By the time the lunch break arrived, I had checked my phone only to find a text from Rob stating that he had gone back to Birmingham, was going to do some shopping and would be back to collect me later.

Pressing call on my phone, I could feel my blood boiling as I awaited his answer. His voice was happy when he answered. Mine, however, was not. Before I knew it, we were arguing over his 50-mile, each way journey just to get a pint of milk, which was how I saw it.

After trying to reason with me, Rob's patience wore thin and soon, he was shouting at me. I was told how I was trying to micro-manage him. It was none of my business if he did all that driving just to get milk. He was the one who was paying for the petrol.

That wasn't strictly true as all the money that came into the house was "our money", and even though I worked for his company, I never saw a wage as it was just "our money", and every penny went into his bank. Sure, I could have whatever I wanted; all I needed to do was ask when I wanted it. All the bills were paid from my account, but as all the money went into Rob's account, he would have to transfer it to me.

What did bother me was the amount we were getting through each month, and the figures never sat comfortably with me. For instance, one month, he told me we had spent £7,000, and I just knew that couldn't be right. He got annoyed with me and told me to get a pen and pad. He then went online to his bank and read out figure after figure of what we had spent and where and when. It all added up. It turned out we were being stupid with money to the extreme.

I had once mentioned that I would like my own money as it could come across as a bit controlling, me having to ask him all the time. He agreed that we would sort it out soon, but for the time being, it was easier to keep track of "our money" if it was all in the same place.

It didn't bother me usually, but it got right under my skin when he said things like that. I made a mental note to look for the evidence of his supermarket shop when I got home that evening. I don't know what I had expected, but I did think he would have made more of an effort to try to at least make it look like he had been shopping. However, no, other than an extra bottle of milk, I failed to find any other new items of shopping.

When I challenged him on this, he said that he had been to his Mum's house to see if she had needed anymore shopping (even though he had already done her shopping the day before). Since she hadn't and we didn't either, he just picked up milk at the garage.

This had me on the over-thinking train again; where was he dashing off to? Did he even come back to Leicester? Had he been to meet another woman? What the hell was going on that he would argue with me to this extreme just to get away for the day?

We argued for a while until we got back to how much Rob loved me and how could he be having an affair when he spent 95% of his time with me? He was so happy and in love with me, so how could that make sense etc., until we were back to my problem.

Why was I so paranoid? Why did I have to question the smallest of things? Just because someone does things differently from how I do them, why does it have to be wrong?

Rob was back at the point of walking away from me, he had had more than his share of my paranoia, and to be fair to him, I would push and push, only to find out that he could prove me wrong, and then I would be back apologising and wishing I had kept my mouth shut.

Rob said he had not seen me all day and was looking forward to a cosy evening with me, but now I had ruined it, again!

I felt so sad when we argued as Rob would always say that none of us knows how long we are on this planet, and it was a huge waste of our time spending it arguing and being unhappy.

He would tell me how much he loved me and that he was lucky to have me, that we met each other late in life and because we don't know how long we have, we should cherish every moment being happy and not arguing. He was right, of course.

If you had a tick box for how you would like your husband to behave, my husband ticked pretty much all of them. He was caring, romantic, wanted to spend all his free time with me, was not interested in going down to the pub all the time with his mates, didn't come home drunk, was not bothered about porn, did not drool over women on TV or give the glad eye to women in public, listened to what I told him, surprised me with things he knew I loved. The list was endless, and how do I repay him? By interrogating him, that's how.

All this was due to my stupid overthinking and paranoia. I had got to a point where I thought he would probably just leave me because I was making him so unhappy. I didn't deserve him; I knew that which is why I was so paranoid that he would leave me for someone else.

The problem was, it was a vicious circle. The one thing I was afraid of was going to happen due to my paranoia that it was going to happen.

As usual, Rob ignored me for most of the night as I did my best to cosy up with him, give him kisses (that he did not want) and apologise until I had no breath left.

Eventually, he forgave me, as he always would but what was worrying me was how long before he stopped forgiving me, gave up, and moved onto someone else who didn't have half of the issues that I had.

CHAPTER 21
Another Fight

At the beginning of May, things between Rob and I were going very well, and we were approaching our first wedding anniversary. Other than the usual irritating ways Rob had or annoying things that happened, I managed to keep myself in check most of the time.

For example, I had stopped moaning about Barbara's post when it arrived; instead, I would chuck it on one side for Rob.

I tried to keep quiet when he would pick me up and, whilst driving, pick his phone up to disconnect the hands-free. We had already had that argument enough times, and I had never won.

I tried to hold my tongue when he opened a slit in his post, peeked in and then put it away without opening it properly.

I didn't even moan about how many times a week he had to go shopping for Barbara. This annoyed me. The woman was six stone at the very most, and how she could always be needing more and more shopping, I would never know. The last time I mentioned her shopping was when Rob and I were trying to do our shopping, and sure there was no issue with him picking up her shopping too. What I would object to, however, was that I would be asking him if he wanted something only to find he had shot off down another aisle to get something for his Mum. He was making the trip stressful and paying no attention to what we needed or what I needed. I couldn't help myself and make a sarcastic comment about how, as long as Barbara had what she needed, then all was well.

Rob actually snapped in the middle of the supermarket and was shouting at me in the aisle about how twisted I was that I had an issue with him shopping for his 70-odd-year-old Mother, who had no one in the world but him. There were lots of expletives thrown in, and we ended up leaving with only half of our shopping and, of course, all of Barbara's food.

On the way home, he began shouting so much that I was afraid that he might crash the car. When I asked him to stop shouting, he said that he wouldn't stop and that maybe shouting was the only way to get through to me as I clearly didn't listen to anything. He continued that he had had it up to here with me and didn't know if we could stay together as things would never change because I was never going to change.

He dropped me off with the few bits of shopping we had managed to get before tearing off in the car alone. When he returned, I asked if we were still going out for the afternoon, and he told me in no uncertain terms that we were not.

I tried many times that afternoon and evening to get him to speak to me but to no avail. I think that was one of the few times he slept on the sofa.

About a week later, I was excited to be going out with Rob, my cousin Ruth and her husband, Sonny. This was something we had never done together, and it would be nice to see them.

We met at their house, had a drink and then made our way in a taxi to TGI Fridays. It was only a short walk from their home but much easier to get a taxi than to walkany distance in high heels.

We laughed and chatted away. The food was great and the company even better. Ruth and I were drinking Sex on the Beach cocktails, and Rob, who was not usually a cocktail drinker, had decided to follow Sonny's lead and have a Long Island Ice Tea. It turns out that they were really strong, and after the two of them had knocked down £90 worth of them, they were both a little worse for wear.

I had given up smoking and knew that Rob would be annoyed if he caught me having a sly fag that Sonny offered, so I politely declined and stuck to my e-cig.

When we arrived back at Ruth and Sonny's house, Ruth and I were the only half sober ones. Rob and Sonny could barely stand up, and Rob was drinking wine and spilling it all over the dining room floor.

I had never seen Rob drunk in my life, let alone paralytic. He was cracking jokes, dancing, telling Ruth and Sonny how wonderful they were and then went into a big speech (much better than his wedding speech) as to how much he loved me and why and that is why he wanted me to give up smoking. He went on about how life is short and that we met late on in life, and he wanted me around for as long as possible. He even started to lecture Sonny about giving up smoking, which Sonny just laughed off.

After about half an hour, Sonny being as drunk as he was, took himself up to bed, and I decided it was best we made a move too.

We had booked a room at a little hotel, a five-minute drive from their house. As we entered the hotel reception, I was trying to be as quiet as possible so as not to wake up other guests.

Suddenly entering the corridor, out of nowhere, Rob started shouting and knocking on people's doors. Swearing at them and telling them to wake up, and when I told him to stop it, he only got worse. He was shouting about how when he is asleep in a hotel, people always woke him up with their noise, so now it was time for him to get his revenge.

This behaviour was so out of character for him, and I struggled to quiet him down and get him into the room. Once in the room, he seemed to calm down, for which I was thankful. I nipped to the loo, and when I came back out, Rob was half bent over, wearing nothing but his socks, and I couldn't help but think how cute he looked all drunk and naked.

"Aww, are you OK there, babe?" I giggled.

The explosion of anger came from nowhere. I was so surprised that, at first, I thought he was joking.

"How dare you laugh at me! What are you fucking laughing at?"

I told him I wasn't laughing and that he just looked cute in only his socks. This did not pacify him.

"You nasty, cruel bitch! How can you laugh at me? Think it's funny, do you? Do you think me being naked is funny, something to laugh at? You horrible, evil, twisted cunt!"

I tried to speak to him, to calm him down, but it just escalated his anger, so I froze in shock as the abusive words fired at me one after the other.

"OK, so I might not be as in shape as I would like to be. I might have a bit of a belly, but for you to laugh at me, you fucking bitch. You are fucking sick in the head. You, of all people,are laughing at someone's appearance. Imagine if this was me laughing at you naked, you would be crying your fucking eyes out. If this were happening to you, you would starve yourself for a month, you nasty, evil, little fuck!"

I had no idea where any of this was coming from and had learned very quickly that there was no point in trying to defend myself, so I remained quiet, got ready for bed and hoped that his shouting would stop.

Unfortunately, this was not the case as once I was in bed, he began to shout louder, and now he was pointing his finger in my face. I don't have much of a fear factor at the best of times, but I certainly wasn't going to be afraid of my own husband.

Forcefully pushing his hand away from my face, I shouted at him not to do that. No sooner had I pushed it away, it was back, and this time I had actually flinched, so I backed away.

I told him that if he didn't stop shouting, someone was bound to call the police as he sounded that nasty like he would kill me. This made him worse, and he shouted louder and louder.

"Go on then! Someone call the fucking police! Let's see what happens!"

At a loss of what to do, I sat in the chair away from him as he began to tell me that I could walk home from Coventry to Birmingham the next day as he was taking HIS car.

The plan had been that I would keep the car and he would get a taxi into work in the morning as he was only working in a town about eight miles away. I decided not to answer him and instead started packing my bag.

"Go on then, fuck off, you nasty, twisted bitch!" He yelled at me.

Once my bag was packed, I realised I had no cash on me and no money in the bank. I couldn't take the car as I was way over the limit. It crossed my mind to call Ruth and get a taxi to her house, but then that would always be a stain on Rob's character, and I didn't want peopleto know that we had argued.

Instead, I waited until he fell asleep and crawled in quietly beside him. I was too upset to sleep, so I just lay there quietly until the morning when I heard his alarm go off. I pretended to be asleep and lay there with my eyes closed, just listened to him groaning and moving around. I assumed he was getting dressed for work.

Thankfully the next thing I heard was him calling a taxi to collect him from the hotel and take him to work.

Once he had gone, I sat up with a sense of relief. I was just about to get up and look to see if he had left me the car key when suddenly I heard the card click to open the door. Immediately lying down, I pretended once more to be sleeping whilst I heard Rob moving about again.

Within a couple of minutes, he was gone again. I left it a good half-an-hour before I got up and made myself a coffee. With no sleep, I was going to need it to get myself home in one piece.

Rob had left the car key on the dresser, so that was something. I was supposed to go to Ruth's for a few hours whilst Rob worked, but I couldn't face her, and I just wanted to get back to the comfort of my home and see what the results of last night would bring.

Driving on the M6 towards Birmingham, I thought about how this situation might now play out. I knew without a doubt that I had done nothing wrong and that this was all Rob's fault, and that I didn't deserve any of what happened last night. Still, I felt uneasy as I tried to imagine receiving an apology.

Usually, everything was my fault, and although I think at times some of the things weren't all my fault, Rob wouldn't apologise as he didn't see my point of view. Would this be another time where somehow this would be my fault?

I had no idea what he was going on about last night, but what if he was still angry at me? I told myself he had no right, and now it was me with the power as I had the car. If he didn't have a really good apology and explanation lined up for me, he could stay in Coventry as I wouldn't be collecting him this evening.

By the time I arrived home, there was a text from Rob saying that he had been very drunk, couldn't remember what had gone on but that he had a hazy memory of an argument and that he was the one at fault.

Well, that was something, I suppose. However, he could sweat a while whilst I had some time to think and put my feet up with a coffee and answer him if and when I felt like it.

Before I had decided to reply, I received another text asking how I was and where I was. I typed out a quick reply that told him I was home and that I was very upset and that he had been like a monster last night and that I had never seen him that nasty. Within a minute of me pressing send, I received a call from him. Answering quietly, I waited to see if I could judge his mood.

From the start, he was full of remorse. I could hear in his voice how terrible he felt. Mortified about his behaviour, he could not apologise enough. He went on to tell me he was ashamed he had acted in a way that came across frightening. He could not bear to have me afraid of him even for a second. He sounded confused and laughed a little when I told him about what he was saying about his body. Like he always says, he doesn't care about looking gym fit and having a bit of a belly did not matter, and I totally agree; I love him just the way he is. He was the least body-conscious person I knew; that is why it had all been so strange.

He texted me a few more times during the day, additional messages of apology and love. I was still upset with him, but I found it hard to hold a grudge with him. He is the love of my life, after all.

When I collected him, we had another conversation about what he had done, and I could see that it was making him uncomfortable. He apologised again but begged me to stop going over it as he was ashamed enough; plus, after the Long Island Iced Teas, he had the hangover from Hell. I agreed but not before telling him that he had better learn from this and that if we argued over something that I had caused, he had better be quick to forgive and have more patience with me in the future. He agreed but to be honest; I don't know if he really meant it or if it was just a way to shut me up and give his hangover and his ears a rest.

CHAPTER 22
End of the Line?

With three weeks to go until our first wedding anniversary, you would think that our garden would be very rosy indeed.

Unfortunately, my paranoia and nagging were getting the best of me again. I started another argument with Rob about his Mother's post, how he opened his post and the secrecy of his phone.

It had started one evening when I had told him of a letter that looked important and when he would not open it, I asked him what his problem was and why couldn't he open it in front of me. Before long, the argument had become heated, and for once, I told him to give me the keys as I was going out.

He immediately refused, which made me angry that it was OK for him to jump in the car when we argued but that I had to stay in with no choice. Changing my tact, I told him I wanted money instead and to transfer some to me, which he also refused. I then reminded him that as I worked for my money, he had better transfer my salary to me. His response was to tell me that I could have my wages on Friday, which meant nothing to me as I had never physically been paid a salary from his business. We continued to argue, and I brought up the fact that he had given me half of the business, so he shouldn't be controlling all the money.

He laughed at this and told me that I could have half of nothing if we got divorced, as he would move heaven and earth to ensure that he has everything and I would be left without a penny.

In disbelief at what he was saying, I left the room and called Carol. I was in tears and asked her to come and collect me straight away. The poor woman had just gotten home from work but agreed to come right over, being the good friend she was.

I waited about ten minutes in silence, scowling at this man who was supposed to be my husband before leaving the house and waiting on the front for Carol to arrive.

A strange sense of relief and fear hit me as we drove to the end of my street, with me telling Carol to take a left and head to the local Asda. We pulled up in the car park, and I gratefully accepted a cigarette as we got out and talked.

I hadn't smoked for about a month, but that was the least of my worries right now. I explained to Carol about all the bickering, arguments, my paranoia, and how Rob had behaved at the hotel only a few weeks earlier. A look of concern covered her small face.

Admittedly, I expected her to tell me that everything would be OK and that we would work it out. After all, we hadn't even gotten to our first wedding anniversary yet. I felt like a failure in my marriage.

What I expected from Carol and what I heard from her were two worlds apart. Her view was that I was not a paranoid person, and, in fact, I was highly intelligent. She was also in agreement with me about some of the odd behaviour that Rob had been displaying. She believed that he was getting in my head and making me feel paranoid when I wasn't. Her advice was to get out and do it as soon as possible.

When I arrived back at the house two hours later with just over £30 in my pocket and 40 cigarettes, I had pretty much decided that my marriage was over and that I had finally hit a breaking point.

I walked in to find Rob just sat there with a miserable look on his face.

"You're back then," was all he muttered.

I said nothing and just picked up an ashtray from the kitchen and returned with a lit cigarette.

Rob moaned about me smoking again, but I just calmly replied that if I wanted to smoke, I would and that it was my business.

I could see he wanted to ask me how I had bought them with no money, but I wasn't in the mood to enlighten him.

Instead, in a cold voice, I explained that I had finally come round to his way of thinking and that I now agreed that we were never going to work. Even if he was doing nothing wrong, I couldn't cope with the frequent thoughts that told me he was wrong. In fact, I believed that his behaviour was often suspicious.

I told him that although it was sad that we could not make it to our first wedding anniversary, the right thing to do was split up.

I needed peace in my mind and knew I would never get it as long as Rob behaved the way he did. The look of surprise on his face was not unexpected, as usually, I would be trying to hold on to our relationship for dear life. The thought of living without him was still too unbearable to contemplate, but I knew that I was losing my mind and the only hope of keeping it was to be alone.

Rob looked a little unwell, pale even as he clutched his stomach. "Julia, I have been worried sick about where you have been, and I don't feel well as it is. I'm in agony with my stomach, and to be honest, I don't have the energy to argue with you."

Now that I was finally saying we were over, he played the sympathy card, which annoyed me.

As if reading my thoughts, he looked me in the eye and spoke to me in a serious voice. "Julia, I mean it. I could really be dying here!"

I replied that this was a bit dramatic and that I wasn't going to argue with him as I had already said my part. Instead, I walked out, poured a double Baileys, added some ice and took it to the garden along with my ashtray, where I continued to chain smoke and sip my drink.

Rob appeared at the back door, shook his head and walked away. I didn't care what he thought, I was finished with his nonsense. From now on, I was going to do what I wanted, when I wanted.

A couple of hours passed, and I had now relocated to the bedroom, where I continued to chain smoke. I was purposefully trying to annoy Rob and prove that his opinion about what I did no longer mattered to me.

Rob walked into the bedroom and made a couple of comments about my smoking, but when he realised that I didn't care, he completely changed his tact.

For once, I was the one in control of what happened next. He had called my bluff so many times in the last four years about leaving me, but now I was in the drivers' seat, and it would be interesting to see what his next move would be.

Rob was so stubborn, I expected him to agree to split up, hoping that I would change my mind, but if this was the route he was going to go down, he would be disappointed.

I felt like a new woman, hearing my suspicions validated and to think that anyone would feel that way made a huge difference. I had a valid point about the post, the phone, the leaving the house so early even at weekends, being on WhatsApp at 4am when I thought he was asleep. The list was getting longer, and when everything was put together, it didn't look good at all.

I'd been keeping my suspicions to myself all this time and this hadn't been in my best interests, mentally. Even the wedding speech still haunted me as I had started to believe that Rob never wrote one in the first place. If he had, why didn't he pull it out of his pocket? When I asked him for it to see what he had meant to say and keep it in our wedding memory box, he merely said that he hadn't realised I would want to keep it and that he had thrown it away. If he hadn't written one, what was he hiding in the office that day when he would not go shopping with me? Was he lying about working on his finishing touches of the speech with Mark the night before our wedding? He had even said he was printing it out on Mark's printer. It was still something I couldn't forgive.

And what about the postcode on the SatNav the day after my hen night? It was a postcode for a rough area of Birmingham entered just after midnight on the night of my hen night. Rob swore blind he hadn't been anywhere that night and didn't know how the postcode had got there.

My mind was compiling all of my suspicions, and I was worried about what my husband was really hiding. There had to be something. I could feel it in my bones.

Late that night, Rob got into bed, still supposedly in pain, and he did something that shocked me. He apologised for all of the behaviours that led me to be suspicious. He confirmed that although he wasn't doing anything wrong, he could see why certain things would make me feel that way, and he promised that for the good of our relationship, he would make changes to put my mind at ease. Part of me wanted to believe him, but part of me found it so hard to override my gut feeling that there was something very wrong. However, I loved him more than life, and after all the chances he had given me to change, I owed it to him and myself to see if we could make things work.

Over the next two weeks, Rob had gone from eating small meals to barely eating anything. His stomach was constantly swollen, he was constipated all the time, and anything he did eat left him in incredible pain afterwards. He also complained about severe pain in his back. I began to worry when he lost a stone in weight in just a couple of weeks.

The day before our wedding anniversary was a Saturday, and we went to York for a day and night. It was a lovely day, wandering around the shops and treating ourselves to clothes and anything else that took our eye.

We were staying in a beautiful hotel and went back to rest up after our day of shopping before getting showered and changed,ready to go out for an evening meal.

I was relieved to see Rob manage to eat some pizza. The whole night was so romantic, and we talked and laughed all night.

Back at the hotel, Rob started to feel unwell again and apologised to me for not being well enough to make love. I understood, he clearly looked in pain, and his stomach was so swollen again.

Rob was in such agony the following day that he let me drive home, which he rarely let me do. I asked if he felt bad enough to go to A&E, and when he confirmed he did, I was seriously concerned.

Waiting to be seen, we joked about what a memorable wedding anniversary we were having. After a few hours, Rob was taken to a ward, his blood pressure was through the roof, and they needed to stabilise that. He suffered from high blood pressure anyway, but the extreme pain was making it soar. They gave him an enema, and some medication which brought his blood pressure down to a less concerning level and then he was free to go.

A week later, Rob was worse instead of better, and this time we went to the local walk-in centre. The doctor there examined him and said that he wanted us to tell his GP (when he saw him in a week) that he needed an urgent liver scan. Even though liver cancer is rare, it still needed to be ruled out.

Other than that, we were sent home again with no answers. Rob wasn't eating and was still losing weight. About three days before we were due to go to Florida, Rob returned from the GP and told me that the GP had given him some lactulose and was not concerned about him and had given us the green light to go on holiday. Rob said he asked about the liver scan, and the GP told him it wasn't required. He already had about three sets of bloodwork done so far, and there was nothing alarming showing up.

Florida was a complete washout. Out of two weeks, we spent three hours at Universal, made a couple of trips to the pool, and had an hour at the Mall. Apart from that, we were confined to the gloomy hotel room.

Rob was so ill, he was in constant pain and had every over-the-counter medication known to man, but nothing worked. He was not eating and getting weaker by the day. He struggled to get comfortable and slept in his own bed with pillows under his back and stomach for the whole of the two weeks. I was convinced by now that my husband had cancer.

When we arrived home from Florida, we found a letter with a missed appointment for Rob to have a liver scan, something his GP had said was not required. I urged Rob to get an appointment with his GP, and this time I was going with him.

The GP told Rob he was not happy about his current weight because he had lost two and a half stone in just six weeks. His advice was to go home and eat plenty. I was infuriated and made sure the GP knew my feelings. I told him Rob couldn't eat, and that was the problem, and something else quite serious must be going on. The GP didn't say much other than he was concerned, and he'd arrange some scans.

CHAPTER 23
The Car Accident

After cancelling all of the work from the diary, we had the courtesy of almost two weeks to try and take in the fact that Rob was terminally ill. I kept my strong face on in front of him but driving to the chemist or the shop by myself would stem a release of tears. Rob was so weak and had already taken to sleeping a lot and living in bed.

Life was cruel, and I didn't know how to keep going either because I had to take care of Rob and make sure that he was as comfortable and stress-free as possible.

I had to remain focused and I took to writing everything down: work commitments, hospital appointments, shopping lists for Barbara and us, collecting Rob's medication, collecting Barbara's prescriptions. This was not the time for me to collapse and feel sorry for myself.

My first day back at work was incredibly hard as everyone at that place knew my husband and asked about him, the same with the candidates on the course.

I managed to make it to the end of the day and headed toward home. I was going to the local supermarket on the way back to collect our shopping and pick up a few things for Barbara.

All I could think of was getting back to take care of Rob, and it killed me to be away from him, but it was what he wanted. He wanted money coming in, and that meant I had to keep everything going.

After whizzing around throwing everything off my list into the trolley, I dashed to the till. Loaded up and slowly making my way out of the exit, I quickly stopped as two staff members walked out in front of my car. I remember thinking how rude of them to do that as they walked around the side of my car.

Bang! Something hit my car. Before I could work out what was happening, bang, bang, bang! My car went from facing one way to facing another. What the hell had happened? Shocked, I got out of the car to see the vehicle that had just shoved me out of the way was screeching its way up the main road.

People were running, holding their mobile phones up as they filmed the car. When I walked around, I saw half of the car hanging off, touching the floor and fluid everywhere. I became hysterical.

Everything became a bit of a blur, and people were talking to me, asking if I was OK.

"My husband is dying," I told them. "I need to get home to him," was all I could say.

Someone told me that the staff members who walked out in front of me were trying to catch the lads in the car that had hit me.

They had stolen three small, inexpensive televisions. Before smashing me out of the way, they had run into the store manager, pinning him to my car. There was a store manager dent imprinted on the rear passenger door to prove it.

All I could think of was getting back to Rob and then having to tell him about his pride and joy. I had asked my neighbour to knock on my door to let Rob know I was OK as I had tried to call him to let him know that I'd been delayed. He was was not answering his phone. She tried, but he did not answer the door either.

My mechanic Owen came down to see me, and my neighbour Elizabeth came and sat out with me for almost three hours until my mechanic told me to go and that he would wait for the recovery truck on my behalf.

Elizabeth drove me home and I was so relieved to get back to Rob. It turned out he was feeling so unwell that he didn't care what happened to the car but was just glad that I was OK other than the whiplash and shock.

My auntie Sally lent me her car for a month so that I could still get around for work, shopping and appointments, and I stayed on autopilot and kept things going whilst we awaited the first appointment   at   the   QE.

CHAPTER 24
Hospital Appointment

Rob's first appointment at the QE was daunting. The masses of people in the waiting room who all looked terribly ill were so unsettling.

What made it worse was that poor Rob looked worse than most of the people in there. His jeans hung off him as he had lost so much weight at this point. His hair was now a natural grey colour, and his face complexion was almost matching.

To be honest, I don't remember very much about that day other than us waiting hours past our expected waiting time and that Robwas in a tremendous amount of pain.

I spent so much time on autopilot during the whole time of Rob's illness that all appointments, scans, and treatments seemed to roll into one. Eventually, Rob saw the consultants, and they had agreed that he should have some palliative chemotherapy to manage symptoms and hopefully extend his life.

I wish I could describe the feelings back then, but it was as if my brain had shut out and numbed specific memories because to feel them again would be unbearable. The doctors and nurses explained that Rob's treatment would be about getting a balance that suited him. In other words, he could have a lot of treatment and it would make him so sick that he would have no quality of life. On the other hand, he could have less treatment, giving him a better quality of life but for a shorter time.

This decision was something I had to leave up to him. As much as I wanted him with me for as long as possible, I couldn't ask that of him. I didn't want him to be continually so sick and in agonising pain and unable to enjoy any part of life.

Rob, to my relief, agreed to start the chemotherapy and arrangements were made to get him booked in to get it started. Rob was incredibly brave. I was doing my best to be brave, but I just couldn't compare to him.

I tried to keep my tears to a minimum whilst I was around him, but it wasn't easy. Rob was going to be on a powerful cocktail of drugs for his chemotherapy treatment. It consisted of three drugs because his cancer was so aggressive. They did tell us that not everyone was strong enough to undergo it, but they all agreed that Rob was. I was shocked about this because he was about 11 stone and was barely eating anything. He was vomiting quite frequently too, which was a massive concern.

CHAPTER 25
Chemotherapy

Early October, I drove Rob to the QE Hospital for his very first chemotherapy session. He had been a few days earlier to have his bloodwork done, and they had been satisfied that he was well enough for treatment. Again, I had doubted this as Rob had become so weak, he was sleeping most of the time and had been barely eating.

However, we were here, and they began the much-anticipated treatment. Rob already had a port fitted into his chest so that the line could be inserted to administer his chemotherapy. This had been done the week before and would remain in his chest for the rest of his life. When the line was fitted, Rob made a noise like a wounded animal as it was so painful having a needle put into his chest to access the port. He had become so weak recently that even taking blood from his arm was extremely painful. He used to be so strong and have such a high pain threshold. Cancer was destroying him rapidly, and there was nothing anyone could do about it.

The first chemotherapy session was an absolute nightmare. The nurses managed to give Rob the first drug without any problems. Unfortunately, the second one made him projectile vomit within about twenty minutes of it going in. They had to stop treatment at this point, and the doctors were called to see him.

The sickness lasted hours, and they decided that Rob would need to stay overnight to be monitored as he was too ill to travel home.

They said that if they managed to get the sickness under control, he could be sent home the following day with the third drug administered via a pump at home.

It was almost midnight when Rob was settled on a ward for the night, and I had been at the hospital for nearly 12 hours. It broke my heart to leave him behind on that ward. Everyone on that ward, including him, looked close to death.

I told him I would be back in the morning as soon as they said he could leave and asked him where his hat and gloves were as he would need them for coming home since he had to be well wrapped up.

I walked quickly from the hospital to the car park, as it was pitch black, very late, and very cold. Once in the car, I locked the doors and set off to home. I was so exhausted, yet at the same time, so wide awake. After living off two hours of sleep a night for the last couple of months, my body was becoming accustomed to it.

Within about thirty minutes, I pulled onto the drive, ready for a hot drink and a rest. First thing though, I needed to find the hat and gloves.

After checking the hallway, the wardrobe and the office, frustration was beginning to take over. There weren't many things I could do for Rob right now, but finding his hat and gloves to wrap him up after his chemotherapy should be one thing I could do for him. Then it struck me, his briefcase. He had kept them in there before. Rushing back into the office, I found the briefcase, opened it and froze.

Inside was a carrier bag full of what appeared to be letters. My heart sank as I thought back to all the times that Rob would not open his post in front of me or would peak into the envelope without taking the letter out, the post that he always had to collect from his Mum's house, the letter that he would stick in his bag and look at "later." Heart pounding, I opened the bag and tipped the mass of letters onto the floor. Debt after debt after debt, bailiff letters, even court letters for speeding fines, that he told me he had paid.

A total of around £35,000 of debt was lying on the office floor, staring back at me. Making it to the bathroom just in time, I began to vomit. I remember crying, screaming, asking Rob how he could lie to me. Again. How could he have lied to me again?

This was more than debt to me. This was deceit. Rob had promised me over and over that he had nothing to hide, that he would never lie to me again. He told me that I was paranoid and how he had never had a debt in his life. He even said he didn't know how people could live like that being chased by bailiffs.

This was the man who had taken me to America three times in a year, telling me that we could afford it, that we had plenty of money. He even reminded me of what we were earning.

Even when I found debt collection numbers on the phone bill, he still insisted that it was just a mix up over a late car payment.

Rob said if he had been in debt, why wouldn't he tell me? He said he wasn't scared of me and that debt is nothing to be ashamed of, but it is not something he has ever had.

This bag of debt posed the question that if he could lie so convincingly about this, what else was he lying to me about? Dragging boxes out of the bedroom cupboards, I began searching. I was looking for something, anything that proved more lies.

I got all his memory cards out of his camera bags, switched on my laptop, and checked every single card. There were holiday photos of him with Gemma and her kids, even though he told me that he didn't have a single picture of any of them. It wouldn't have been a major issue, but why say that? More lies!

Did he lie about my hen night? The postcode in the SatNav that he said was strange and could not be explained. Why not? It was beginning to look like he had lied to me again and again. After all the lies around the time he was leaving Gemma, I warned him that if he ever lied to me again, I would be finished with him for good.

Oh my God, I had even been for CBT therapy because I was so paranoid as I always accused him of acting strangely with his post and phone calls. When I asked why his Mother's post was being re-directed to our house, he said it was because I had insisted on his post coming to our home. He had paid to have his post redirected, but the Royal Mail had messed it up.

My head was ready to explode. How could I approach my terminally ill husband, who probably only had a matter of months to live, and accuse him of being the biggest liar I had ever met. Deflated, heartbroken, and exhausted, I began to put things back into the cupboards where I got them from. I knew I wouldn't sleep, even though it was already after 4 am. I had to drive to Coventry in the morning to drop paperwork off for one of our staff. From there, I would be going straight to the QE to collect my poor husband, the man who I knew I would struggle to look in the   eye.

CHAPTER 26
Scratching the Surface

After many cups of coffee and no sleep, I drove to Coventry in a daze. When I arrived at the client's office, she took one look at me and told me how terrible I looked. She insisted that I have a cup of coffee with her before I continued on my journey.

Gratefully accepting her kind offer, I took a seat and waited, but my mind was a blur. When she returned, I updated her on how ill Rob was from the effects of the chemotherapy and that I was extremely worried about him. She told me to give him their best and reminded me to look after myself.

As I arrived at the hospital to collect Rob, my stomach was doing somersaults. I had no idea how to behave around him, so I decided to tell him that I was worried about him and hadn't slept much, which would explain why I looked the way I did. Rob had always said he knew me better than I knew myself, so I had a feeling he wouldn't buy my excuse. I didn't have the energy to invent anything more believable, so that is what I went with.

Rob looked so pale and frail when I arrived as he sat at the end of the bed, waiting for the nurse to fit his pump so that we could leave. He told me that they had managed to stop the sickness and that the third drug should be fine. He did ask me a few times if I was sure that I was OK, and I repeated the same answer telling him that I was just tired.

Five minutes into the car journey, Rob was vomiting again. Driving had become a stressful job, trying not to hit bumps in the road as it caused Rob pain, grabbing tissues with my left hand to give him whilst he was vomiting into a bucket. I was glad to get home.

I helped Rob get out of the car and up the front door step. It was frightening how weak and frail he was; it was like he had turned into an old man overnight. It seemed the husband I knew had been replaced with this tiny frame of a man that I barely recognised.

Once he was in bed and settled, I sat next to him and tried my best to act normally. However, just as I thought, Rob was not buying it. So eventually, I bit the bullet and explained what I had found the night before. Surprising myself with my calm tone of voice, I told him that I was deeply hurt and upset about the lies, not the debt and that I wasn't going to start getting angry and shouting as he was in no fit state for an argument.

The shock on his face was evident, but I also sensed remorse. Before he could say anything, he grabbed the bucket and began to violently vomit again. I told him that we should just leave it there as stress was the worst thing for him. He wiped his mouth and said that he was so sorry and ashamed of himself for lying. He said that the debts were old and that he never wanted me to know about them as it was shameful. He said there was nothing any of the debt collectors could do and that once he's dead, how will they get it from him then? He said over and over that there are no more lies.

I told him that this now made me question everything, and I wondered what else could he be lying about. I said that he had made me think that I was going mad and had called me paranoid when I was right in my suspicions. He begged me not to say anymore and that he knew he had behaved terribly and to please not keep talking about it.

When I mentioned the SatNav on my hen night, he began to cry. He said that if I don't believe another word he said, the one thing I had to believe was that he had never cheated on me ever and that he loved me more than anything in the world. He said that he could not bear to die with me thinking that he cheated on me. Any anger I felt was quickly washed away with love, sorrow, and heartbreak.

We held each other so tight as we both sobbed until our shoulders were soaked with tears. Rob said that he would contact the debt collectors and advise them of his situation to ensure that they wouldn't come to the house and that he would get everything in order.

He also assured me that there would be no more skeletons to jump out of the closet. There was nothing to do in this situation but forgive and move on. Without wanting to admit it, we knew time was short and that every second counted.

CHAPTER 27
Difficult Days

Life became increasingly difficult as the weeks and months went on. Rob was going downhill fast. He insisted on me continuing to work, which I did on top of caring for him, food shopping, chemists and hospital appointments.

Rob was shrinking day by day and becoming weaker and weaker. My stress levels were through the roof. Looking back now, I don't know how I managed to cope and do everything that I needed to.

Every minute of the day was like a living nightmare, and I was on autopilot from one chore to the next. Rob had been taking THC oil for a time but refused to take it consistently enough to make a difference.

He was eating less and less now, and he was sick up to eight times a day. The nurses and I begged and pleaded with him to go into hospital for a stay as we were very concerned about him becoming so dehydrated and weak. He would promise me that he would go in the next day, but he would say to give him another day when the next day came.

One thing he hadn't lost throughout all this was his stubbornness and what he said went. At one point, he allowed me to call an ambulance, but after a long wait, he insisted that I cancel it. When I refused, he said that if I didn't, he would refuse to get in it. So again, he got his way.

A few days later, when Rob finally permitted me to call an ambulance, he was in terrible condition. The paramedic told me that in the future, to ignore Rob and call them anyway, and if he was that ill, they would decide whether they took him in.

Rob was so acutely ill that they were unable to take him in straight away. They needed to stabilise his blood pressure before they moved him as it was dangerously low. It took over an hour of him being on a drip in the bedroom (hung on the curtain rail), with his legs being elevated, before they could risk moving him into a wheelchair.

Once Rob was settled into the hospital, I made my way home to my lonely, empty house.

Rob had insisted that I go to work the next day and that he would keep me updated by text. I didn't want to go to work as it was going on 11 now, and I just couldn't face it. My mind was consumed with worry.

Rob had a settled night, and I dragged myself to Nottingham the following day, pretended all was OK, did my job and drove home with my eyes struggling to focus on the road.

As soon as I got home, I had a quick bath, picked Barbara up and headed to the hospital. I told her I needed to stop and get a couple of bits for Rob at the shop, and she decided she would give me a long shopping list of things she wanted. My arms could barely hold the shopping basket as my weary body dragged its way through the aisles. Shopping done, we arrived at the hospital.

Walking along the first set of corridors, Barbara started to feel weak and out of breath. She said I would have to get her a wheelchair, so off I went and was back a moment later with one of those heavy, hard to steer wheelchairs that you have to drag backwards. So now, with barely a hint of energy left, I dragged Barbara along behind me, worried that I would collapse myself at any time.

When we arrived at the ward, Barbara said that she didn't want Rob seeing her in the wheelchair as it would worry him, so she decided to walk the rest of the way, holding on to my arm.

When we arrived at his bed, he smiled but could barely talk due to a lack of energy. We must have been there all of five minutes before he was telling us to go home because he was tired.

We left the ward, went back to the wheelchair, and I dragged her back out of the hospital through the car park and to the car. I dropped Barbara home, put her shopping in the hallway, and went home to collapse into my bed.

Over the next few days, a kind of miracle happened. Rob was fitted with a syringe driver full of anti-sickness drugs, and the change in him was amazing. He had gone from not eating a single thing for two weeks to eating three meals a day, with desserts, in hospital. His sickness had stopped, he was hydrated again, and his energy levels continued to improve. After months of doom and gloom, we were finally turning a corner.

After two weeks, Rob was discharged; he couldn't wait to get home to his 'comfy' bed. He said he had been so uncomfortable in the hospital beds, and he often had disturbed sleep with noisy patients on the ward.

When we arrived home, I supported Rob's weight as I walked him to the front door. As he stepped over the doorstep, his legs gave way, and he fell on the floor. Panicking, I tried to get him back up and asked should I get someone to help, but he refused and said he would be fine in a minute. His leg calf muscles had worn away so badly that he couldn't support his weight from one leg to the other, hence why the step was such a challenge.

Within twenty minutes of being home, Rob asked if I had spoken to his Mum that day, and I told him I had tried a couple of times, but I hadn't heard back from her. He tried calling her a few more times,but after another twenty minutes or so, he said that he was going to have to go round and check on her. I told him he was in no fit state and just to give me his key, and I would have to go round. He was worried that she might have collapsed or had a fall and was insisting on going. I argued with him as he could barely stand up himself, had just fallen, and had his syringe driver hooked up.

Part of me knew that he wouldn't give me his key as he had never let me go in his Mum's house ever. He always said it was because he was ashamed of the house being so run down. Surely, he couldn't care about this right now; he just needed to let me go there and sort this out whilst he got in bed and rested.

Stubborn Rob reared his ugly head, and before I knew it, I was given my orders. He put his syringe driver in his coat pocket, then wearing his pyjamas and slippers, he managed to get back into the car.

Arriving at his Mum's house, I was given strict orders to stay in the car. He wouldn't even let me help him out of the car or to the front door. It was ridiculous, but he just wouldn't listen.

Watching uselessly as he made his way to the front door, I wondered what could be in that house that was so terrible that even under these circumstances, I was forbidden from entering. He staggered over the doorstep and shut the door behind him.

Every second that passed felt like a minute, and every minute, an hour. After about five minutes, I could see the shadow of Rob through the frosted glass. It looked like he was picking up a handful of post. So, his Mum must be OK then, but why was he bothering to look through his post.

Ten minutes had passed, and this time I decided to ignore Rob and approach the house. However, just as I was about to open the gate, the door opened, and Rob appeared. He refused my help to get him back to the car and instead seemed to shuffle along in his slippers like the old man he had become.

When I asked about the post he had collected, he replied that it had all been junk mail and that he had put it in the bin. As usual, I accepted his explanation with a gut feeling that something wasn't quite right. The truth was neither of us had the energy to argue. As he said, the main thing was that his Mum was OK, she had just left the phone in the other room, and apologised for worrying us.

The next few weeks leading up to Christmas were increasingly positive as Rob regained his appetite, and his energy improved significantly. Cheese on toast had become his favourite, and I would find myself in the kitchen at all hours of the day and night, making endless rounds of cheese on toast.

It was the happiest I had been since the diagnosis, and to see Rob eat made me feel on top of the world. It is strange how much joy you can get from something so small when your life is so dark. The tiniest chink of light made all the difference.

Rob was getting out of bed more and had ordered new bedroom furniture, which he said with a bit of help, could be put together before Christmas.

By Christmas, there was a new electric fire in the lounge, a new TV cabinet, a beautiful glass picture of New York above the fireplace and bar one chest of drawers (still to be put together); the bedroom was furnished with beautiful new furniture.

I was so proud of how Rob had achieved so many things when only a few weeks earlier he had been so close to death. The doctor at the hospital had told him that he would have been dead within a week had he not come in when he did. This seemed to have given Rob a new lease of life. It was nice to have this positive and energetic version of Rob, even if it was difficult to reign in his spending.

Argos was delivering parcels two, sometimes three times a day; it was as if he was addicted to online shopping. Whenever I expressed an opinion about the spending, Rob would say that we had plenty of money and that this could be his last Christmas so we should enjoy it. He also said that he wanted a nice home for me, when he was gone, something I could not bear to think about, not for a minute.

Christmas was bittersweet. My Mum and Stepdad, Brian came up for a meal on 23rd December, with which Rob insisted on helping, including baking the biscuits.

As usual, I collected Barbara and brought her to us for an hour on Christmas Day. She had her meal, as usual, then asked to go home. She was always antisocial, wanting to get back to her empty house and watch her TV programmes.

Rob and I did our best to enjoy our time together, but the cancer was always in the back of our minds. Rob still slept a lot, and I found myself lying in bed next to him, feeling so incredibly lonely. He would sleep, as I had the TV on low, but I would see something funny and want to comment to him or wished he was laughing along with me.

Strange thoughts would enter my head, things that were so unimportant. Wondering if Rob would be alive for the next series of a programme we watched together and if he wasn't, would I ever be able to watch any of these shows again? How would I watch anything again without him? We watched everything together, did everything together, told each other everything. Maybe I wouldn't carry on without him, perhaps I would be strong for him for as long as he could hold on, but I would follow him to the grave once the time came. That was the only plan that made any sense.

In November, the hospital had agreed that Rob could have a break from Chemotherapy until at least January. Although he only had two rounds of Chemo, and they were only partial due to an allergic reaction to both one of the drugs and Piriton (which no one had ever heard of before). The hospital said that because his cancer markers had decreased so significantly, it would be OK.

When Rob was first diagnosed, his cancer markers were 600 and something, and they had risen to over 2,600 at one point. However, in November, they miraculously were down to 180. The doctors could not understand it and were amazed. I put it down to the cannabis oil. Even though these results were amazing, Rob refused to take it most of the time, and I was exhausted from arguing with him about it, so eventually, I gave up.

When January came around, we decided that now was the right time to have another dog in our life. We thought it would be company for Rob whilst I was at work, and subconsciously I think we both thought that when he passed away, I would have something to live for.

Alfie was like a little furry angel without wings. A cross between a Jack Russell and a Terrier, he was a cute, scruffy-looking boy. It was clear that he'd been in a bad home before us, but he immediately created a bond with me from the moment I put him in the car.

Alfie immediately settled in with us and was so well behaved, loving nothing more than cuddling up with us. Coming home had become quite sad as Rob was usually asleep, but Alfie changed that as he would spin around in circles to greet me when I walked through the door. His behaviour was second to none, and he was so calm around us and around all the medical staff who were in and out of the house, too. It was like he knew what was happening and wanted to support us, which he did. Alfie is truly a dog in a million. I love him more than life itself.

It was mid-January when Rob started vomiting again, and we were constantly cancelling his appointments with his consultant and for his chemotherapy. Nurses who came out arranged for him to have another syringe driver fitted to combat the sickness and arranged for the GP to visit as well. His health declined more and more over the weeks, and by March, Rob weighed around eight stone, a massive difference to the seventeen stone he was before this dreaded disease began to eat him alive. His appetite was that of a bird, and he was showing signs of giving up.

With little energy, Rob found himself not wanting to talk, even for short periods. He was sleeping more and more, and when he was awake, he would be vomiting. Since diagnosis, it was apparent, Rob's quality of life had declined to near zero.

Besides hospital appointments, Rob had been out of the house three times: twice to his Mum's and once with me to the shop. He had refused to see anyone at all other than his Mum and my parents.

In early March, our GP came to see Rob, and when he went back to bed, the GP asked me how I was. His question opened the flood gates, and tears streamed down my face as I attempted to compose myself enough to answer his question. I explained that I was coping the best way I could by taking care of Rob but that I didn't sleep and struggled to eat from being in a constant state of distress.

We discussed whether Rob should be put through more chemotherapy and the GP explained that Rob was not even well enough to be put through the car journey to get to the QE. He advised me that if Rob went through another session, it would more than likely make his quality of life much worse than it already was. It might only buy him one more day of life, and that we would need to weigh up whether that was worth it.

Reality hit me, that time was coming, and it was coming fast. With the GP's advice, I decided there and then, it would be cruel to ask Rob to go through anymore and that I now needed to make him as comfortable as possible before he passed away.

Excruciating pain shot through every inch of my body, my insides crushing inside me, heart pounding in my head. I have never felt pain like it. Is this what a broken heart felt like? At that moment, it felt like I was dying too. I wanted to scream for help, someone, anyone, anywhere, please do something. People always say that there is always a solution to a problem. What if the only solution is death? The helplessness was overwhelming.

Nothing anyone does can ever make this better; the only change in this situation would be deterioration, then death. I was thirty-eight years old; how could this be my life? Anyone I spoke to would offer support, but nothing they could say or do would help Rob or me. How do you live with knowing that there is no help anywhere? The feeling is indescribable.

I was grateful to the GP; at least someone was being honest and telling me how it was, trying to prepare me for the inevitable. If anyone else had told me what he did that day, I would have probably screamed at them and kicked them out, but fortunately, I have always had a good relationship with him, and I have always had a lot of respect for him. The way he told me was so kind too, and I guess he was just the right person to speak to. He explained so much more in only five minutes than the experts at the QE ever had at any of their consultations. The QE staff still thought Rob was well enough for more treatment when even I, with no medical qualifications, could see that he wasn't.

Over the next couple of weeks, Rob got weaker and weaker.

CHAPTER 28
Back to Hospital

One of the hospice nurses came to the house to check on Rob and give me a new prescription for him as his sickness still hadn't subsided. After checking on him, she sat in the lounge with me, and I asked her opinion on how he was doing. She gave me her honest opinion and told me that she thought he was extremely ill. I discussed with her some of the strange things that he had been saying with regards to the man in the room. Also, he'd been asking about "all" the dogs. It was like he remembered all the dogs that he had had in his life. Humouring him was the best thing to do in this situation. To do anything else would be frightening for Rob. I hadn't realised this but said that I'd do that in the future. Apparently, this can be something spiritual as people often see spirits when they are close to death. Most people just put it down to strong medication.

That afternoon after the nurse had gone, I was in the lounge when I heard a loud thud. Running into the bedroom, I found Rob half in bed and half out. The top half of his body was hanging out of the bed and he had his hands on the floor, supporting the rest of him.

Pulling him back up into the bed, I wondered what the loud thud had been as there was no way he could have made such a noise from half falling out of bed. He weighed so little; it just didn't make any sense.

Sitting on the end of the bed, I just watched him as he lay there looking so sick. His eyes kept rolling to the back of his head, so the whites of his eyes were more visible than his pupils. Terrified, I would shout to him, asking if he was OK, but he said that I was frightening him and to leave him alone. He said he was just resting. This continued on and off for the next hour, and I was petrified of what would happen next.

He had been refused a drip at home to keep him hydrated, and I was concerned that he was becoming severely dehydrated as he hadn't eaten for around four days. I begged and pleaded with him to let me call an ambulance, and he reluctantly agreed.

The two paramedics that came out were so lovely and said it was up to us whether to take him in or not. They agreed that it was unfair not to give him a drip at home, but they felt sorry for Rob, having to be dragged through A&E in his condition. They offered to put him on a drip at home or wait until we got to the hospital. Rob said it was OK to wait until we arrived at the hospital. I didn't know at the time, but I realise now that the paramedics knew that he was in the last stages of his life.

It was hours before Rob was given a drip at the hospital, and I was disgusted that I had to keep asking for them to get it. I couldn't understand why they were letting him suffer like this. It was late at night when we had Rob settled on a ward, and I returned home.

I was confident that Rob just needed perking up in the hospital and that he would come back to me, eating, drinking, and with some renewed energy, as he had done in November.

I was fooling myself. Had I known that this was Rob's last week on Earth, I would not have for a minute considered putting him through the trauma of another hospital visit.

CHAPTER 29
Coming to the End

The next morning when I arrived at the ward, Rob appeared more disorientated than ever. Earlier, he asked me what time had I gotten home and told him it was around 10 pm. Then he said to me that he was asking about the second time I came in. I explained that I hadn't been there a second time and tried to lighten the mood by saying that maybe it was his other wife who visited. Rob looked confused and replied that, no, it was me.

I realised then that this was not my Rob in this hospital bed and that his mind was leaving him. He also said that he had spoken with the staff and that he was coming home later that day.

I waited until the palliative care team arrived and went into a side room with them to discuss Rob's condition. It was as if they didn't have the guts to tell me he was dying. I asked questions about his deterioration and would he improve. Finally, they said that they did not expect him to improve and that I was the best judge as I knew him and how much he had changed in the last few days.

It turned out that he was not offered a drip at home and that dehydration is just another symptom of dying. Apparently, a person stops eating, drinking, and talking within the last few days of their life.

I managed to fight the tears and ask them if he was going to die soon. With sad expressions, they nodded and said yes, it was likely to be a matter of days now.

This terrible scream shot through my ears; I realised it was me. I was beyond hysterical, inconsolable, sat in a room with two strangers, handing me tissues. I couldn't breathe, couldn't cope. Someone, anyone, please help me. I can't do this. My heart cannot take it.

It took some time to compose myself. I sat around Rob's bed with the palliative care team. It had been agreed that he could have his wish and go home that day, and an ambulance had been arranged.

Rob asked me in a confused and childlike manner why I was crying, and I found myself answering in a way that you would speak to a child. I told him that I was just being silly and that I was a bit tired. Strangely, this worked, and he just smiled back at me and then started saying how he would be glad to get back in his nice comfy bed. He then told me to go home and that the hospital would call me later to arrange about getting him home.

I kissed him goodbye, terrified that he could pass away in those few hours when I wasn't there. I was so distraught that I found myself crying and uncontrollably shaking as I made my way down the corridors. Hyperventilating, I struggled to breathe, and before I knew it, I was lying on the floor just before the hospital entrance.

A doctor and nurse stood over me, telling me to breathe, and a woman behind was explaining that she saw me crying and that I just dropped to the floor in front of her and she had been unable to catch me.

I sobbed uncontrollably, repeating over and over that my husband was dying and what was I going to do without him? They got me a wheelchair, took me to Rob's ward without me being in sight of him, and then wheeled me into the nurses' station.

They asked if there was anyone I wanted to call. There was no signal on the mobile, so the nurses offered me their phone. My Mum was only two days into her holiday in Devon and I didn't want to call her in this state, so I called her sister, my Auntie Sally. Just barely able to get the words out between sobs, I explained that Rob would die anytime. Auntie Sally asked if she should call my cousin Ruth and said she would let my Mum know.

As I made my way to my car, a text came through.

On my way now. Am I coming to your house or the QE hospital?

Wow, that was so quick of Ruth to text. I replied that she should come to my house before I got into my car.

I knew there and then that I was in no fit state to drive, but I didn't know when I would be, so I set off, calling Carol along the way. Hysterically sobbing and driving, I told her what was happening and that I was on my way to Barbara to tell her the news.

I was shaking as I walked into Barbara's house (the first time I had ever been in passed the hallway) as I wondered how I could say the words to her. Somehow, I managed to explain and told her that I had to go home and get the house ready for him.

Shockingly Barbara's first reaction was to say that now she had no one and who would bury her now when she dies? I was already in too much shock to even respond. She then said she needed some shopping and didn't feel up to going. I had just told this woman that I had physically collapsed at the hospital and that I had to prepare my home for my husband, her only son, to come home to die, and she wants me to go and do her shopping.

I drove to the shop on autopilot, bought the items, dropped them off, and went home. I called my neighbour Elizabeth and had a cup of tea with her before changing the bed and doing the hoovering.

The next thing I know, Ruth is at the door. Shocked, I opened the door and wondered how she got from work in Derby to home and then to here so quickly. When I asked, she just told me it didn't matter but that she was here now. Ruth had said to me on text a few weeks earlier that she would be there for me when I needed her, and I had assumed she meant that she would support me on the phone. She told me now that this is what she meant, and there was no way she would let me go through this alone. Her boss at work had also been told and agreed that Ruth could just leave and come to me when the time came. Such love and kindness, I was lost for words.

Ruth watched in shock as, like a crazed woman, I ran around the house pushing the hoover. She tried to tell me that it didn't need doing, but I was like a woman possessed, and I just couldn't stop until everything was perfect.

Once done, the two of us headed back to the hospital; Ruth agreed to wait outside the ward while I went to speak to Rob. A time for the ambulance had still not been arranged, and a nurse quietly told me that it might be tomorrow before they could get Rob home. With time not on our side and Rob looking forward to going home, I told them that this wasn't acceptable and that it had to be today.

They then said to me that they were concerned about how I would cope with everything and the lasting implications on me if he died at home. I told him that everything other than Rob's wishes were irrelevant and that I would cope as I had no choice but to cope. They finally agreed that he would be transported home at about 7pm. They would call me when the ambulance had set off.

I spoke to Rob about Ruth arriving to support me and that she would stay in the lounge and that if he didn't want her to see him, she didn't have to. He immediately refused to talk about it, other than to say that he didn't want anyone at the house and that if I drove her home now, I would have plenty of time to get home before he arrived. Realising that there was no point in continuing the conversation, I agreed to send Ruth home and kissed him goodbye.

Ruth also refused point-blank when I told her that Rob wanted me to take her home. She said she understood that he didn't want to see anyone but that I was there for him so she would be there for me. Ruth knew this was too much for me to face alone.

We agreed that she would stay there secretly, making it difficult to pull off with the bungalow being so small. We quickly put a system in place that if she needed the loo, she would text me so that I could say I was going and she could creep in, and when the flush went, Rob would think it was me. The same, if she wanted anything from the kitchen, I'd get a text and say I was going to the kitchen. I don't know how we managed it, but we did.

When the nurses would come, we would tell them not to mention Ruth and explain what we were doing, which they agreed with.

I found out later that Ruth would have conversations with the nurses regarding me. They were all concerned that I would commit suicide once Rob passed away. I was given mental health team contact numbers that I could call anytime, and every nurse that came in was writing notes about me when they visited.

At some point, I had said that when they came to take Rob away, they needed to make sure there was room for me too, as I would be going with him. The thought of life without Rob and the pain I would feel was too much to conceive.

Rob would stay in bed all of the time unless he needed the bathroom and I would have to hold him up to go as he was incredibly weak. Ruth and I managed to keep up the pretence.

One night I had to call the emergency nurse to come out as Rob was in pain. It was a male and female nurse team who attended and when the male nurse was speaking to him, Rob began to look very serious and said to him, "Julia is my wife, you know. Do you know that she is my wife? She's married to me."

The nurse answered that he did know, and after he had left and I went back in, Rob grabbed my arm, and with what looked like an angry expression, he asked, "Hey, does he know that you're my wife? I've told him that you're my wife and that you're married to me."

I replied that he knew and why was he asking? But he just gave me a hard stare and said, "good." The nurse in question found this quite funny, considering he was gay. To me, though, it wasn't funny, it was very strange. Rob had never behaved like that, and he didn't have a jealous bone in his body. It was just so out of character, but then again, he was becoming less like my husband by the hour.

It had been a Monday evening when Rob had come home, and Ruth had said she could stay for a few days, go home and then come back if I needed. My Mum had arranged to get a coach from Devon to Birmingham on Thursday night, so after a lot of persuasion, I agreed that Ruth would go home Wednesday evening. A hospice nurse would stay that night, and then I would be on my own with Rob on Thursday until my Mum arrived in the evening.

Since Rob had come home, my Carol had been calling every evening after work, walking Alfie for me and collecting Rob's Mum so she could visit, and then she would drop her home afterwards. She was an absolute Godsend, and Alfie was undoubtedly grateful for   his   walks   too.

CHAPTER 30
Hidden Visitor

On Wednesday, Ruth's last day, something strange happened. After the nurse had gone home and I went into Rob, he suddenly said that he felt like going for a walk and with energy that I hadn't seen for weeks, he just jumped out of bed.

I panicked as he said he wanted to sit in the lounge, so I ran and told Ruth to hide. She ran and hid in the hallway with the door shut, and I went back and led Rob in. He first sat on one sofa and said he wanted to go and sit on the other one after a few minutes.

Then he asked me to get his iPad so that he could look at the work diary. I wasn't comfortable with this as I was worried he would see an email that would upset him. I had contacted our clients to cancel all future work for the foreseeable future due to Rob having end of life treatment, and I was terrified that he would see that. Managing to distract him, I started a conversation about something else, but after he asked three times and was beginning to get frustrated, I gave it to him.

I had turned his mobile phone off days ago because his watch was connected to it. He had also put his watch on before coming into the lounge, and I was concerned he would realise I had turned it off. Thankfully, he didn't.

In fact, over the next few days, he would press his watch and say that "mitherers" kept calling him but that he was cutting them off. Obviously, this wasn't real, as his phone wasn't even switched on.

Regarding the iPad diary, Rob looked at the dates and asked why I wasn't at work as the diary showed I should be. I explained that I was taking a couple of weeks off to stay with him as he wasn't feeling very well, and I would go back to work soon. He looked a bit confused, but he nodded and put the iPad down, for which I was both relieved and grateful.

After about twenty minutes, I was feeling anxious about poor Ruth hiding in the hallway, so I made an excuse about the front door needed locking and quickly whispered to her to go out and round the back of the house and sneak into the office. She scrambled out into the rain with me, throwing a pair of shoes out after her. Even amongst all this sadness, it was quite a comical situation.

I went back into the lounge where Rob was sitting, looking deep in thought. I managed to pick up Ruth's phone and glasses without him seeing and stuffed them quickly into an old chemist bag. Telling Rob I was just going to put the medicines away, I sneaked into the office and gave a somewhat puzzled looking Ruth the medication bag. She smiled when she looked inside and gave me a thumbs-up as thanks.

Returning to the lounge, I found Rob sat on the edge of the sofa. He asked me to take him back to bed which I did, and he soon settled, so I was able to sneak Ruth back into the lounge. She asked why I didn't just tell him about her being there, and I replied that I didn't want to upset Rob or make him angry. Lying didn't come easy to me and I felt guilty. I had never lied to Rob about anything. This was a white lie for both our sakes and Ruth was going home later, so there was no point unsettling him by admitting it now.

Saying goodbye to Ruth that afternoon was both sad and daunting. I had said all along I'll be fine, I can cope, but now I was going to have to do it. At least the Hospice nurse was coming that night so that I wouldn't be completely alone. Although Rob was in the house with me, it was like he wasn't. Terrible to think it, but my husband had become unrecognisable to me, a stranger I was taking care of.

It was agreed that the hospice nurse would stay overnight and I would have the sofa so I could try to get some sleep. I was told that I wouldn't be in a fit state to care for Rob if I didn't have any energy myself.

The young lady, Kayleigh, they sent was adorable, and I will never forget that night I spent with her. By this stage, Rob wasn't always making sense when he spoke and it was difficult for him to understand why we had someone coming to stay the night. I left Kayleigh in the lounge and went to talk to him. I told him that she had come to help me as I needed to get some sleep and that he could ask her to wake me at any time. He looked so sad, and in his child-like voice (something that had started about two months earlier), he said, "It's OK, tell that lady to go home now, we're OK. I just want you and me to stay in here together. Send her home. Come and lie in here with me" After a bit of persuasion, he agreed to let Kayleigh sit with him for a few minutes whilst I had a bath. Our bungalow was so small that every room was only a couple of steps away from each other, so I could hear Kayleigh chatting away with him. Her voice was so kind and soothing. She was just wonderful to have around.

Once Rob was sleeping, Kayleigh and I sat in the lounge with a coffee, chatting. She was in awe of our wedding photo on the fireplace but at the same time in shock that the frail, now seven stone man in the next room was the strong seventeen stone man in the picture, taken less than two years earlier.

Kayleigh explained that Rob had kept asking where I was and had appeared anxious when I was in the bath. Shockingly though, she told me he had been frightened of a man hiding under her stool. At first, he had told her to "shhhhh," and that there was a man crouched down under her seat. She said he appeared frightened at first but then began to laugh and said that it was OK because it was just a friend of his playing a trick and that he was always doing things like that and hiding.

Hearing this reminded me of a few days earlier when he pointed to the stool, fright in his eyes, asking me what was underneath. When I showed him what was under it, he shook his head and told me to move the stool until it was right up against the bed. I guessed that if it was close to the bed, he wouldn't be able to see anything under it. Things were beginning to get scary for me now. With Rob's body failing, it had been frightening enough, but now it appeared that it was now taking a toll on his mind too.

In the early hours of the morning, I thanked Kayleigh and told her to help herself to anything she wanted and then joined Rob in bed. I must have got a few hours of sleep as when I woke up, Kayleigh had gone, locked up and posted the key back through the letterbox.

CHAPTER 31
Old Friends

Throughout his illness, Rob refused to see anyone other than his Mum and my parents, but now that his mind was clouded, he had started to mention a couple of friends. I tried several times on my phone and on Rob's phone to get through to his best friend Vinnie but to no avail. Eventually, I had to put it into a text to let him know that Rob was very short of time, and if he wanted to see him, it would need to be sooner than later. Managing to get through to his friend Daniel, we arranged for him and another friend Paul to come around 7pm that night.

Throughout the day, we had several visits from nurses and Carol making her usual visit after work and bringing Barbara with her. Barbara spent about ten minutes with Rob, and we were all reduced to tears as they told one another they loved each other. There was a dreaded feeling inside me that Rob wasn't going to make it through the night. My Mum was on her way, but I was so worried that she wouldn't arrive in time.

When Daniel and Paul arrived, I let Rob know they were there and said I would leave them to chat. I returned to the lounge and sat, willing myself to hold in the tears that were so desperate to escape.

Listening to Daniel and Paul, I was in awe at how normal they sounded. They were doing a great job, considering the shock they must have felt at seeing Rob lying there so tiny and fragile. He was not even half of the person they were used to seeing. This was all on top of knowing this was their final goodbye to their friend.

Rob said he was tired, and they walked back through to where I had just knocked a full cup of coffee over. I ran to get a tea towel, talking with them both as I furiously scrubbed the carpet, all the while I was trying not to breakdown.

When they first went into the bedroom, Daniel told me that Rob had asked them who the man was that had just walked out. They said that they hadn't noticed him and that Rob had said that he walked past them and out of the door.

Daniel and Paul ~~e~~hugged me and told me to call if I needed anything, and then they were gone. Rob and I were alone in the house, and he was tired again. I cuddled him for a while, he told me he loved me and I told him I loved him too. Soon he was asleep again.

My Mum arrived by taxi at around 10:30 pm. The poor woman was exhausted, travelling all day to get from Devon to be with us, and the stress of the whole situation was clearly etched on her face. Like everyone else, she knew that this could be the end of my life, not just Rob's, as I had been vocal this past week at not being able to live without him.

I checked if Rob was awake, and finding that he was, I asked if my Mum could pop in and say hello. He smiled and agreed, so she went in for a couple of minutes. Convinced that Rob would die that night, I was glad that they got to see each other one last time.

Rob only ever spoke a couple more words that night and then never   spoke   again.

CHAPTER 32
At the End

Startled, I woke around 5 am to a noise that I can only describe as a wounded animal.

Many years ago, whilst on holiday in Ireland, a deer had jumped out in front of my car, and when I went to check on it, it was making this awful mournful sound and its eyes were so wide with fear. Over the years, I had tried to forget it as it haunted me, but now I heard that same noise again.

Heart pounding in my head, I sat up fast and looked at Rob. His eyes were just like the deer's eyes, open as wide as they would go, staring helplessly, fearful, and God, that sound, it was unbearable. His breathing sounded laboured, and I was convinced that he was going to leave me at any moment. I stroked his head and tried to reassure him, telling him that everything would be OK.

Holding back tears, I called a taxi for Barbara and arranged to have her brought round to the house as soon as possible. It was horrendous. I lay beside Rob as his Mum held his hand. My Mum was making hot drinks and once Rob seemed calmer and the noises had stopped, I stepped out of the room for a quick cigarette.

Although Rob had lost his ability to talk, he still knew we were there, as, within a couple of minutes of me leaving the room, he started to make that horrendous noise again, this time louder than before. I ran back in, comforted him again, and he seemed to calm a little.

Over the next couple of hours, his Mum said we should get a nurse to come out as she thought Rob was in pain. I told her that he was dosed up on medication and that nothing else could be done. I really thought that this was just the sound of someone dying. I feel guilty now, as it turns out he was highly distressed and agitated.

The nurse arrived around 10am, as she was calling in routinely. When she saw him, she asked why I hadn't called them. This made me hysterical as I felt so guilty that I had been letting him suffer. She assured me that I wasn't to know. She gave him more medication and said if he got like that again, to call her straight away and that she would come back.

Barbara started going on about how she knew we should have got a nurse.

"Thanks for making me feel fucking worse, Barbara. Now can you shut up about it? Rob needs peace." I told her.

She deserved me to speak to her like that. Barbara had hardly seen him throughout his illness and she had been no support and just a hindrance – especially to me. She was a burden on top of everything else I had to contend with, and now she thought she could come in at the last minute and throw her two pence in. Well, she was wrong.

At one point, Barbara went into the lounge and sat with my Mum and said to her she was thinking of getting me to drop her off home and that she would come back later. What part of your son is dying did this selfish old bitch not get? As if I could leave Rob and be fit to drive her home? The selfishness of the woman riled me up so much.

Rob had started to stare up at the ceiling; his eyes looked like they were following something around the room. About a week earlier, we had been in bed when the dog suddenly stood up; his ears perked as he started staring at the ceiling, following something around the room. It had freaked me out, but Rob had said he had probably just seen a spider. I agreed with Rob so as not to disturb him, knowing that there was no spider and that the dog had been acting very strangely. Now Rob was doing the same as the dog. He looked terrified as his eyes followed something (that I couldn't see) around the ceiling. The wounded deer noise was back too, and I've never been so frightened in all my life. I had the nurse come out again and she gave Rob more medication and again, he calmed.

His Mum came in and out. I know it was hard for her to deal with and sitting on a stool when she was so frail was painful for her. At some point, Barbara said something about when Rob worked as a carer at the old folks' home up the road. She said he would help them with meals, bathing, toileting etc. My heart sunk. How could he have lied about this too? This revelation meant that Rob had never been a mental health nurse. I knew for a fact that he would have never done that job just a few years ago if that had been the case.

It was difficult to gauge whether or not Rob knew that his Mum had just revealed his biggest lie. This was not the time for asking questions or being angry. It would have to wait. Regardless of the lies, Rob had told me, he was my husband. He loved me, and I loved him, and he was dying. Lies could wait until after he was gone.

I started talking to Rob about all the things we had done together, such as our trip to New York, which had been his life-long dream. He seemed to be reacting, so I did my best to continue.

I put on our wedding songs, our first dance: Sky Full of Stars by Cold Play. I sobbed and sobbed as I held him and tried to continue talking about how happy he made me and that our wedding day was the happiest of my entire life. I told him that I would always love him and that it was OK for him to go and that he doesn't need to keep hanging on.

I began to pray for death as the situation had become so severe that I couldn't bear for him to suffer for another minute. Rob's breathing became more and more laboured, and he started making a gurgling noise. I had read about this and thought he was about to take his last breath. However, instead of stopping breathing, he began to choke. I leaned him forward slightly and was horrified to see black liquid spurting out of his mouth and running down his chin. I grabbed a wipe quickly and wiped it away.

Around 1.30 pm, two nurses arrived again to check on Rob. I told them about the black liquid, and they said not to worry as that sometimes happened. I can't remember what she said to me, but I think I remember her saying it was to do with his stomach lining. I asked the male nurse how we could clean his mouth as the black stuff was all over his teeth. He got something out of his bag, dipped it in water and wiped it around the inside of Rob's mouth.

The nurses gave Rob yet more medication. I asked if they thought it would be long now, and they sadly shook their heads, checking that I had the number to call when needed. They left me holding Rob and sobbing hysterically to our wedding song.

At 2 pm, Rob took a long gasp, and I thought, *oh my God, this is it*. I froze in shock, and Barbara just stared vacantly at him. We waited a moment, and then he took one more breath.

He was gone.

At the precise moment that he took his last breath, the doorbell rang. Luckily for me, it was the hospice nurse who had called in on Saturday to see Rob. She had been trying to call me, but I had my phone switched off. She had become concerned and decided to call in and check how we were.

My Mum had let her in, and she had called out, asking was it OK to come in. I whimpered back to her to come in. I told her that I thought he had just passed away. She checked him over and confirmed that he was gone.

There were no words to describe what I felt in those moments. I suppose there was relief as the last few hours had been so horrific, but there was terror now that I was alone, followed by the realisation that death had arrived after all those months of fearing it. Of course, I was heartbroken.

I lay holding Rob's lifeless body and sobbed and sobbed. I kept asking out loud what was I going to do without him.

Rob's Samsung watch flashed, and a message appeared that said: *Time to get moving*. His watch may have been clever with heart monitors, and God knows what else on it, but it wasn't that fucking clever. It didn't recognise that he was dead.

The next hour or so was a bit of a blur. The hospice nurse had phoned for the on-call GP who came out and officially pronounced Rob dead. The nurse came back to detach the syringe driver, and between her and the hospice nurse, they got Rob cleaned and dressed in fresh clothes, ready for the undertaker.

Within minutes of Rob passing away, it struck me hard that he no longer looked like himself. He didn't even look human, more like a waxwork doll. It was terrifying to look at him.

The nurses had to catch me as I almost collapsed at one point. They took me into the lounge, where I sat with my Mum and Barbara. Barbara wanted to go home, and to be honest, I didn't have the strength or patience to ask her to stay. The truth is, I could have done without her sitting there talking about how she had nothing to live for. I was a 38-year-old widow in severe shock.

We arranged to have her taken home, and then my Mum and I sat there in shock. Every few minutes, I would go in to check on

Rob, just as I had when he was alive, but every time I went in, he looked less and less human. Eventually, I realised that there was no point in keeping going back there. Rob had gone.

All I could focus on right then was the blaring radio blasting out tunes from across the road. I told my Mum that I would ask them to turn it down as the noise of power tools and music was getting on my last nerve.

My Mum knows my temper and thought it would be best if she went, but I jumped up and ran out before she could stop me. Wild hair, haunted face, pyjamas and slippers, I must have looked like a mad banshee. I marched over and shouted to them, but they couldn't hear me over the radio, so I shouted louder. I yelled at them, asking if they could please turn the music down as my husband has just died, and all I could hear was that noise, driving me mad. The shock on their faces was evident as one apologised and told the other to turn it down. I snapped a thank you at them before I made my way back into the house.

Rob's body remained in my bed until around 6 pm when the undertakers arrived. I spoke with them briefly, and they took Rob out through the back of the house. I decided not to look out of the window as I did not want another haunting image - this time of Rob in a body bag being put in the back of a van.

After they had gone, my Mum and I started throwing away the bedding and clothes Rob had been in, and I began scrubbing the bed. There is no dignity dying at home, something I have had the misfortune of learning, and the aftermath is far from pleasant.

It was strange, but after a few hours of Rob being gone, I not only felt numb, but also as if Rob had never been in the house, in my life, or even that he existed at all. Maybe it was grief, but as the days went on, that feeling began to intensify.

I focused on the funeral and all the other things I had to deal with, such as death certificates, bills, and debts. I would stay awake all night writing in my notebook a list for each day of tasks that I needed to complete next. It was the only way that I could function. At the top of each list were the instructions of "Call Lucie about what has happened" and "Make sure Lucie knows when the funeral is." I said out loud, startling my Mum, "I would like Lucie to be there for me."

My Mum was concerned as I still would not eat, and she knew that I wasn't sleeping either. She would see me wandering to bed with my notebook and then would hear me walking in and out of the office and the kitchen all night. I would keep the coffee flowing all night long until the early hours, and this would give me the energy I required to complete all of my tasks.

After the funeral was arranged, I had to put together a fitting eulogy for Rob to be read in his honour. I needed to speak to Barbara and get details from her about Rob's early life as I knew very little about his younger days.

Barbara wasn't remotely interested in the eulogy, and as soon as I mentioned it, she asked if I needed to do one at all. She said that at her brother's funeral, they didn't have anything like that. I bit my tongue as I explained that I had heard them read out at every funeral I had ever attended.

I sat with my notebook and started to ask her a few basic questions about her beloved son. Firstly, I asked where he was born and was shocked when she repeated the question back to me, wearing a confused expression on her face. Surely, this was the most straightforward question for her to answer. Finally, she answered me.

"Well, it was the maternity hospital in Birmingham, wasn't it?"

"Rob said that he was born at Woodlands Hospital in Coventry." I was trying very hard to keep my temper under control. "Is that right?"

"Yes," she told me. "It would have been Coventry, wouldn't it?" This was ridiculous. She only had one child. How could it be so difficult to remember?

So it continued. Every question I asked would be repeated back to me with the same confused expression. It was like pulling teeth. I decided to get this over and done with as quickly as possible. I needed to get away from her as I couldn't bear to be around this woman right now. Her behaviour wasn't normal, and my fragile mind couldn't cope.

In the end, I established that Barbara thought that Rob was born at Woodlands Hospital, Coventry, the name of the primary school and high school that she thought he attended.

When I asked her which University Rob had studied at (he had told me that he did his nursing degree at Birmingham University), one of my suspicions was confirmed.Barbara told me that Rob had never been to University.

In my heart of hearts, I had known on the day Rob died that he had not been a mental health nurse. Barbara told me he had worked as a carer, but now I had to ask the question outright. I explained to Barbara that Rob had said to me that he had done his nursing degree at University and that he had been a mental health nurse off and on for the past 20 years. This created a genuinely puzzled expression. She proceeded to tell me that Rob had never been a nurse, had never been to University and other than working in a care home for a short time, his working life had never been in the care sector. She recalled that he went to college for a short time when he was about seventeen but couldn't even remember what he studied.

She did say that she knew he had been an assistant manager in a food shop when he was younger, that he'd worked in night clubs and she also recalled the kitchen fitter place where he'd worked and met my brother.

Shockingly, Barbara was not too concerned about her son's massive lie and excused it by saying that he probably just said that to get his business started.

I was utterly disgusted with them both: Rob for lying to me all these years and Barbara for not caring one bit. This was more than just a white lie to get his business up and running.

This was a sustained lie that he had perfected over time. The number of times he had given me medical advice as he was a nurse was frightening. There were even times in my life when I had been depressed, and he would tell me how he had never suffered from depression, putting it down to his strong mind and his mental health nursing background.

On his courses, he would confidently tell people about his nursing experiences. He could also easily reel off different types of medications and treatments.

Rob had even assessed my cousin, who was diagnosed with Paranoid Schizophrenia at the age of 21. My cousin's parents were feeling desperate at the lack of support from the mental health services, and Rob offered to see him and see if he could help. They had brought my cousin to the house and Rob had given them a detailed account of what he thought was going on and listed off medications that he may be put on or was already taking. Rob even explained the side effects of different medications and discussed behaviours that they may start to see, advising them how to deal with them. Rob also explained that he thought my cousin had Paranoid Schizophrenia before he was diagnosed. Rob was correct, and the masses of prescribed medications matched what Rob had discussed with them.

Rob's knowledge on the subject of mental health was vast. I recalled all the conversations he had with the nurses who came to the house to tend him. He would discuss things that had changed since he did his general nurse training.

When Rob had taught courses, other mental health nurses would agree with everything he said regarding different conditions, behaviours, treatments, and medications.

It was clear that my husband had a remarkable memory. It was frightening how convincing he had been, not just to me but to the people he met every day.

Thinking back to the testimony that a director of a top private mental health hospital had given him made a cold shiver shoot up my spine. He had gained his biggest training contract thanks to that testimonial. They were so impressed that, as a mental health nurse, Rob had the same insight and values. They even went as far as to say that they only wanted the agency to send staff to them that Rob had trained.

Rob would often analyse my behaviour, and if I was feeling down, he would use his "expertise" to guide me. I couldn't help but think back to a time when we watched a police documentary, and there was a man who was obviously mentally ill. The man claimed to have been a doctor and walked around his house wearing a stethoscope. When the Police arrived at his property, he asked which force they were from and proceeded to tell them that he used to be a sergeant in the police. Rob was in hysterics, laughing loudly at this man's behaviour.

"Can you believe people like him actually exist?"He managed to say in between laughing.

I laughed too and then joked that what if he was like this man and that he hadn't really been a mental health nurse.

"What if you were actually a patient instead," I even went as far as to say.

Rob laughed even louder at this and asked that if he hadn't been a nurse, how would he know everything he did.

I continued to laugh and poke fun at him by mentioning the fact that I had never seen his Nursing Degree.

Rob continued to laugh loudly for a few more seconds before his expression changed from happy to serious. "Do you really think I'm not a nurse?" he asked me.

"Of course not," I replied whilst trying to contain my giggles.

Rob wasn't laughing anymore though and looked concerned that maybe I doubted his qualification. "Julia, seriously, do you really think that I could lie about something like that? Imagine going around telling everyone I've been a mental health nurse for twenty years on and off." He still looked worried. "God, if I did that, it would make me a psychopath."

The laughing returned.

"Of course, I don't think that," I reassured him. "And I agree that someone who lies like that to everyone would indeed be a psychopath."

Sitting there in Barbara's tobacco-stained house, the reality hit me. In the words of my own husband, he was, in fact, a psychopath. My blood turned cold as I knew deep down that this was just the beginning. The lid was off this particular can of worms and what would come next was terrifying to imagine.

Only I could be in this situation, a widow at 38, heartbroken at losing my beloved husband in such a cruel way, finding out that my husband, as I knew him, never existed.

For now, though, I had a funeral to arrange. The investigation of my late husband was on hold for now.

CHAPTER33
The Funeral

Pouring myself a large Disaronno and Coke, I tried to ignore the aggravating wittering of Barbara's best friend as we waited for the arrival of the funeral car.

My Mum and Stepdad, Brian sat quietly, seemingly trying to ignore the pointless rubbish coming out of Ann's mouth. I had allowed her to come to support Barbara, but I just wish she would shut the hell up right now.

Zombie-like, I drifted in and out of the lounge, anxiously checking my watch. It was like an out of body experience: I wasn't really there. I was just floating around, watching the small gathering in my house.

Family members began to arrive outside, and the reality of the situation suddenly became very real. I was looking for Lucie, but as soon as I saw Ruth, the tears started flowing, and I wondered how I would get through the day.

Samuel, the undertaker, arrived, and we made our way outside. Samuel was one of the kindest men I had ever met. He was the one who had come to collect Rob the day he passed away and had kept in touch with me regularly since. I had called him in floods of tears and hysteria when I had found out about Rob's huge lie and about the fact he had spent all our money without me knowing.

In a panic about what to put in his eulogy, my mind was racing as I tried to make any sense of what I had learnt. The Celebrant, Eleanor, was coming to the house to discuss the service and eulogy, but I was in such a state. Samuel had felt so sorry for me that he dropped everything and drove straight to my house to check that I was OK. He sat with me and the Celebrant whilst we tried to think of a solution to a rather unusual situation. We agreed not to mention anything about his earlier years of life or career. It was the only way because if we mentioned his career and that he had been a nurse, then half of the congregation would have known that he was not a nurse. If we didn't mention his nursing claims when talking about his career, the other half of the congregation would have thought it odd.

Although I didn't know how I felt about anything anymore, we had agreed that Eleanor could read out what I had written the day after he passed away. After all, it was the kind of thing people would expect. Knowing in my heart that there would be worse to come, I couldn't feel anything at all. I recall asking Samuel if he had ever come across anything like this in all his years in the business, and I had expected him to tell me that he had. However, he was totally shocked and explained that he had never seen anything like this in all his years. I had initially said that I did not want the coffin to be lowered at the end of the service, but I changed my mind during that appointment with Eleanor and Samuel.

"Drop the lying bastard!" I told them.

My Mum, Barbara, and gobby Ann sat in the back of the hearse with me, eyes glazed, struggling to recognise any of the roads leading to the crematorium. I could feel my legs shaking as I stepped out of the hearse to a relatively small gathering of people waiting outside of the crematorium.

Sad to say, but the majority of the people were there to support me and barely knew Rob. Just like at our wedding, his Mother was the only family member who attended. Other than my friends and family, the majority of the gathering was made up of work acquaintances and the few friends of Rob's that I knew about. I had asked Rob's friends if any were in contact with Carla's parents and if anyone knew about Carla's whereabouts because I thought they could be faces for him.

Everything was a blur as people hugged me and tried to keep me standing as my legs were like jelly. I managed to pull myself together for long enough to ask people to carry the coffin. Two of Rob's friends and two of my cousins agreed to carry him in. I followed behind whilst Rob's favourite song, *Seven Years*, played. It was a song I hated, yet a song he loved, so it was only fair that I had it played. The screen above the Celebrant showed pictures of Rob, pictures of us together, wedding, honeymoon, and holidays that we had shared. The pictures continued on a loop. They say a picture tells a thousand words. Those pictures told of a wonderful husband, a couple madly in love, a marriage made in heaven. Those pictures told a thousand lies.

Eleanor introduced herself, said a little about Rob, when and where he was born and that he had been only 46 when he passed away. She then read out what I had written:

"To think less than two years ago, I read out a similar speech on our wedding day about how amazing Rob was. I could have never imagined that we would be here now, saying goodbye to him. Since Rob and I got together, I always lived with a fear that I would lose him because what we had found seemed too good to be true. Rob was the most amazing, generous, and loving person I have ever met. He really was my fairy tale ending and it breaks my heart that our fairy tale was so short-lived. My fear came true, and on 10th April, my world ended. Rob was my prince who swept me off my feet and carried me away to my happy ending.

Rob's dream was to go to New York and when we got there, he was like a kid in a sweet shop. We walked over ten miles every day; he had to see everything. When we were having a drink in a bar, he turned to me and said, *'I've ticked everything off my bucket list. I only had two things on it; the first was to marry you, and the second was to see New York.'* He said, *'If I died tomorrow, I would die happy.'* I am so glad that he fulfilled his dreams in his short 46 years on this Earth. Rob was incredible and showed his strength and bravery throughout his short illness, refusing to give up. Even at the very end, he kept holding on as he did not want to leave me or his Mum, Barbara, behind. Rob loved his Mum dearly, and nothing was ever too much trouble. He would do anything for her. They had a small family and depended on each other throughout life, just the two of them. We will never come to terms with Rob being taken from us far too early. My heart will never mend, and I will always love you Rob, and be so appreciative of our wonderful time together. You were always telling me life is too short; we just never realised how much so. Goodnight, my beautiful angel, until we meet again, which I know we will."

Sky Full of Stars played as we all took time to remember Rob in our own way. Tears flooded down my cheeks uncontrollably as I listened to the wedding song of our first dance.

Rob's all-time favourite song by Fleetwood Mac, *Everywhere,* played as we said our final goodbyes and made our way slowly out of the crematorium.

Barbara had refused to go to the wake and had been quite nasty about it, so I'd told her to make her own arrangements from the crematorium and to leave me to my own.

I sat at the wake, drinking drink after drink. In my developing haze, I thought I saw Lucie's hair; *good that she's here*, I thought. Drink some more. I didn't even bother approaching the buffet as I knew I wouldn't be able to stomach anything. I concentrated on getting as drunk as I could before the bar closed and on going out every few minutes for a smoke.

I learnt something new about my husband from a lady who attended the funeral. She was someone he had been training for years, and she appeared to have so much admiration for him as did almost all of the people he had trained. According to her, Rob was the best trainer that they had. He would make the courses fun and ensure that they did everything they needed to as quickly as possible so that they could get an early finish. This meant that he would then take them all to a pub and buy everyone a few drinks.

I was shocked, as Rob didn't drink much, and he was constantly texting, telling me that he would get finished as early as he could, but that 3pm was the absolute earliest he could get out. If he left any earlier than that, the company contracting him would question the course's quality. His priority, he told me, was to get finished and get home to me. Never once had he texted me and said he was going for a few drinks with the course candidates. The fact that he had a twenty-mile drive home meant that he shouldn't have been drinking either.

According to this lady, they would often finish around 1pm on the weekends and go to the pub where Rob was so generous and treat them all to drinks. Clearly, this was just another part of my husband's life I was unaware of. As dark secrets went, this was hardly major.

Two of my good friends Ava and Georgia, came to speak to me before they left, and I found myself whispering to them that I had begun to find out things about Rob and that my life with him had most probably been a lie. I told them about the nurse lie, the money he stole, the money he had spent and that he had never done karate in his life, let alone become a black belt.

This was something Barbara had revealed to me, she had bought him plenty of Bruce Lee films during his youth, but that was as far as the whole martial arts story went. The shock on my friends' faces was evident; however, Ava being as blunt as a spoon, said, "Fuckin' hell Jules, that's awful, but this will make a hell of a book. It will be a best-seller. How exciting!".

I laughed as Georgia shot Ava a knowing look and told her that I was actually living through this; this was my real life. I could not yet contemplate my unknown future. However, I laughed and told Ava that she was right; this would have to become a book someday as it was just too bizarre not to be. I hugged them both and said my goodbyes before returning to my Drink Yourself Stupid Mission.

It was fair to say that by 4pm, my mission was complete.

CHAPTER 34
The Investigation of My Husband

Knowing that I had a big job ahead, the first thing I did was to start looking through Rob's emails for any clues about what my husband had been doing, safe to say, behind my back. I spent hours upon hours searching through his iPad, checking email after email.

One email that was alarming was sent to Royal Mail, supposedly from Barbara. It was an arrangement for a re-direction of all her post to come to our house. He had also emailed her catalogue company again, posing as her to notify them that she had moved to our address.

"For fuck's sake, Rob!" I shouted out loud. "What the fuck have you been doing?"

As I finished my little outburst, I got a fright. Out of nowhere, the song *Don't Go Breaking my Heart* flashed up on the iPad and began to play. There was no sound as the device was on silent, but it frightened me nevertheless. I quickly pressed stop and put the device down. Was he still here? Was he asking me not to tell Barbara about him? Not everyone believes in ghosts, but I believe in them; although, I have never been afraid of them. Whatever people want to believe, it was certainly a strange thing to have happened.

The next day, after filling in Barbara on my findings, she revealed to me that Rob had stolen £7,500 from her. He had done this whilst he was dying. Somehow, he had managed to empty her entire bank account, even using up her £500 overdraft that she had never used herself. She had said it was around October 2018 that she had called him crying because she had just found out all of her money had been stolen. He had told her not to panic and that he would come over and speak to her.

Unbeknownst to me, this was the time he had asked me to take him to visit his Mum for half an hour. It was to go and admit that he had stolen every penny she had. Barbara cried as she explained that Rob had told her how sorry he was. Sobbing, he had told her that he panicked after I had my car crash, the car had been written off and he took the money to buy me another car to get to work. She said that he promised to pay her back and had since paid just £750 back to her. He had told her that when my compensation came through, he would give it to her. She said that she couldn't be angry with him as he was so thin and so ill. Then when he begged her not to tell me, she agreed and told him not to worry about anything.

Disgusted and shocked, I put Barbara in the picture about how my car only cost £2,000 and that I had taken out a loan to buy it. Any compensation money due would come to me as I was the one who had been injured. Now that Rob had left me without a penny to my name, I would need it just to keep a roof over my head.

I was so baffled as to what he could have spent the money on. It just did not make any sense. We had plenty of money coming in with what I was earning and the fact that Rob was also being given a generous allowance from the government because of his terminal prognosis.

Throughout Rob's illness, his spending was extreme, but he had kept telling me not to worry as we had plenty of money.

It turns out that when Rob passed away, I was left with just £550 from the last course I had delivered. Other than that, there was nothing left. With the business earnings, what Rob received in benefits, and the £7,500 he had stolen meant that he had spent almost £30,000 in eight months, literally from his death bed.

I had never seen a single bank statement in all the time we had been together but knew it was something I would have to look into. Re-directing Barbara's post now made sense; Rob was hiding her bank statements from her for as long as possible.

I asked Barbara to request bank statements to see if he had been paying for things with her card. I couldn't imagine, with him being so ill, that he had been able to draw that amount from the cash machines. He didn't even have access to a car and was so unwell that he never left the house.

In the past, she had asked him to keep hold of her card as he did all her shopping, but since he had been ill, he had given it back to her.

Barbara refused to request bank statements in order to get dates and details of how Rob had stolen the money. Her attitude was the money was gone, and there was no point raking over the details.

My theory was that he must have stolen the money before his diagnosis as he was pretty much housebound after that. Rob telling Barbara that the money was for a car became even more ludicrous as I recalled the car crash had happened two weeks after his diagnosis when he had already been very sick.

Leaving Barbara's house reeling, I was determined to find out more about my husband's secret life. Even though I was so angry with him for what I had already found out, I felt guilty for speaking badly of him to his Mother or to anyone.

I walked through the house, and as I got into my bedroom, I experienced another shock. Rob's wedding ring had been around my neck on a chain since theday he had passed away and was secure. However, as soon as I entered the bedroom, it dropped from my neck and landed on the floor. It was as if someone had opened the clasp. I believe that he did this because I was betraying him by the way I had been talking about him. To be honest, my first thought was that he had done it, and my second was that I was glad he did. Rob did not deserve to have me crying over him, protecting his good name, and missing him. He had been appropriately named because we all had been "Robbed." I just didn't yet know to what full extent.

This man was not my husband but a complete stranger, and there was going to be no more sentiment as far as he was concerned. I dreaded what I would find out next, but I had to know as much as I could about this stranger who had been living in my home for the past four years, the man I had loved for the past five.

I must admit that I had no idea when I started to investigate my husband that there would be so much to find. It became more than a full-time job for me as I found myself at all hours of the day and night pulling everything out of cupboards, drawers, checking his phone over and over, along with his iPad.

Whilst going through one of his boxes from the bedroom cupboard, I couldn't believe my eyes as I pulled out two police warrant cards. They were in genuine police wallets, with metal badge numbers and emblems. One was for Derbyshire Police, and the other was for Merseyside. Inside each were laminated warrant cards with my husband's name and photograph on them. My heart was pounding as I tried to think of a reason why Rob would have these.

A memory flashed through my mind of Rob, thinking he was funny because he had an app on his phone with a police siren and blue and red flashing lights. He had linked his phone to his Bluetooth one time and played the siren. As it boomed out, I angrily told him to turn it off quickly as he could be arrested and jailed for impersonating a police officer. He just laughed it off and said it was a joke. At the time, of course, I believed that it was a joke, but now, holding these warrant cards in my hand, it appeared that the siren and lights were part of something much darker.

Rob had collected different kinds of knives and also had a Samurai sword which hadn't seemed sinister at the time; however, I was looking at my husband and everything he owned with fresh eyes now. I decided that I would have to give these items to the police, but first, I needed to check if anything else needed to be added to the list.

Luckily Rob had left me with some passwords for some things, and one of those things was his bank account. Unfortunately, I soon discovered Rob had closed an account I had not been aware of, and he had also closed his savings account in November before he died. Fortunately for me, I realised that there was only a few months' worth of statements when I finally got access online to his accounts.

As far as I was aware, Rob had always kept the majority of his money in his savings account. I had the idea that he probably had made payments and transfers from that account which was why he had closed it. The conniving bastard had closed the account from his death bed to ensure that even when he was gone, I couldn't find out where all of our money had gone.

Unfortunately for him, I soon found out the details and contacted the bank to request statements from all of his accounts, including the savings account. The lady at the bank was amazing and offered to send me all statements since the account had been opened, and I gratefully accepted. When they arrived, they would certainly be an eye-opener for me.

One place I still had to check was the spare room at his Mum's house. He had always told me that he had "a few bits" stored there because our house was so small.

I called Barbara and explained that I needed to collect Rob's belongings because there was stuff I needed regarding the business, and I needed to get the business closed down asap. She tried to make excuses and asked me to come another day, but I was worried that she might hide things from me, so I insisted on coming this day .Luckily, after a bit of persuasion about business details, I knew she wouldn't understand, she agreed reluctantly.

I felt strange walking up the stairs at Barbara's house because this was the first time I had ever been up there. I walked into the spare room, as indicated by Barbara. I scanned the room of boxes and bags, and one thing caught my eye immediately. The left side of the room was piled high with boxes and on top of them was a stack of RBS bank statements. *"Yes!"* I heard the voice in my head shout.

Finally, I would get to look at a bloody bank statement after all these years. Picking them up, I felt my smile disappear. My mouth gaped open. I could not believe what I was seeing.The bank statements were all addressed to me. I flicked through them as quickly as I could to confirm that they were all in my name. Going back to the top, I checked the date on top of the statement.

These were dated back as far as February 2014. Rob and I got together in June 2014. My own partner had hacked me; he had printed a stack of my bank statements off. He had been looking at my statements before we had ever gotten together. Why was he looking into my finances anyway? How did he hack me? Why did he want to know about my finance before he was with me? I felt a cold chill down my spine. My "wonderful husband" was giving me the creeps. The quicker I got this lot back to the safety of my home, the better. I sprang into action and found myself running up and down the stairs until the hallway was full.

I filled the passenger seat, the back seats and the boot of my car with all the boxes. Once the car was packed and the spare room was clear, I felt a sense of relief that the stuff was safe and that nothing else could be hidden from me now. I hadn't slept at all for two days, but I just knew as I unloaded the boxes that this would be another all-nighter for me.

My living room looked like a bomb had exploded, and I could barely see an inch of carpet for all the boxes and bags covering it. Time to open Pandora's box and see what kind of Bastard I was dealing with. Part of me felt excited to get some answers, some payback for all the times I had been called paranoid when I questioned something that didn't feel right. What a player he was to project all that negativity onto me!

CHAPTER 35
Pick a Box

Opening the first box, I found masses of paperwork—debts, debts, and more debts, dated from years before we got together. There were lots of discs and memory cards which I put to one side to check out later.

I found a DBS document that stated two driving convictions from 2007 and 2008. He had received a community service order of 120 hours.

There were four counts of making a false statement or representation in order to obtain benefit or payment. He received a conditional discharge for 12 months on all counts and ordered to pay £85 in costs. It turns out he also had to retake his driving test in 2009. I found a provisional licence and a driving test paper for that year.

I found a judgement addressed to Mr G Carter for a debt that he owed a man who lived in the area. How could a court judgement have the wrong initial for his name?

More concerning were the letters I found next. The name on the letters was Gemma's ex-husband, but the address belonged to Barbara. From what I could gather, Rob had committed fraud by pretending to be Gemma's ex-husband and had taken personal loans out against her house. The house was still in joint names with her ex-husband.

It dawned on me that to get money from a re-mortgage, Rob would have had to set up an account in Gemma's ex-husband's name to get the funds. This was serious fraud.

From the letters, I concluded there were two loans with approximately £12,000 still to be repaid. The last letter was dated 2016 and had been written on with pen which said 'Income and Expenditure forms' followed by some figures that looked like workings out of how to pay it. As I placed it to one side as evidence for the police, I wondered if Gemma was aware of this and if she had been involved. After all, she had experience in bank fraud. Either way, the police were going to be notified.

Among the masses of paperwork that I had gone through, I discovered a workbook from a training course, not one that Rob had delivered but one he had attended. It was a Mental Health awareness course, so this must be where he got the basics from originally. As I scanned through it, I came across a section of psychiatric conditions with depression listed at the top and anxiety underneath. Rob had drawn an arrow between the two words and wrote evil twins next to it. It didn't make sense to me, but why would it when I am of sound mind?

Inside a blue ring binder was where I discovered the method to my husband's amazing memory. It was clear from everything that I had revealed about him that he had an impressive memory. His mind was like a sponge in retaining information, particularly regarding his "nursing profession."

The first page was titled *Memory,*and there was a list of numbers 1-40,and then each number had a word or words next to it:

1. Pen
2. Swan
3. Breasts
4. Sailboat
5. Hook
6. Trunk
7. Cliff
8. Snowman
9. Balloon + stick
10. Laurel & Hardy
11. Penis
12. Duck
13. Double chin
14. Channel 4
15. Pregnant Women
16. Pipe
17. Fishing Line
18. Shapely Women
19. Flag
20. Swan + Football
21. Pole

22. Goose
23. Bum
24. Chair
25. Cymbal + drum
26. Cherry
27. Boomerang
28. Egg timer
29. Sperm
30. Breast on Ball (s)

There were no words following each of the numbers 31-40, but underneath the list, the word *Recall* was underlined

Recall
Primary -You recall the beginning of events
Recency- You recall events which are recent
Linking- You recall things which are connected better.
Outstandingness- You recall anything which is strange and outstanding.
Review- You recall more things if you review them more.

Underneath these were notes about study times and a diagram to show how much studying was required to be able to recall a certain amount of information.

The next couple of pages were numeracy related with a lot of workings out that did not make much sense to me, but to be honest,maths has never been my strong point.

The following page was truly over my head. It was called *The Major System* and consisted of the numbers 0-9 with letters circled next to the numbers.

Underneath were more sets of numbers and lots of words to each group of numbers.

The next page was filled with drawn-out tables with groups of numbers going vertical and horizontal with words in each box. There was no real reason for it, but there were many changes from blue ink to red throughout the writing.

Another cryptic page was just called *The Code,* and again my mind was unable to process the meaning behind any of it. What did stand out, though, was the bizarre sentences that were alongside the numbers.

4000s – Touch) Shannon Doherty has more roles over Jason, Gemma's vagina bulges.

8000s – Rainbow) ROY Gave Bob Instructions, Vera Bryony gobbles willies

Another page was titled *Chinese Solar System*. Again, there were numbers, this time starting at 9001 and, again, these had strange sentences next to each one.

9008– John's son charged a fee, and her indoors paid.

There were pages of what looked to be historical facts, and after these, there was a page titled *Swedish* with numbers on it. Then this page also included a selection of words written in English, followed by what I would assume to be the Swedish version. However, after googling the so-called Swedish equivalents, I did not find any of them to be real words, so I was at a loss with that one.

There were even what appeared to be tests where words were written in blue, and then what I think is supposed to be a foreign word in red. They had all been marked with ticks next to them and even scores added at the end that said "95/102 V.Good Rob."

Hand on heart, I cannot tell you for sure if this was the writing of two different people or whether this was all Rob. If asked for an opinion, mine would be that it was all him, just using two different pens. Maybe there had been two personalities at work here. Nothing would surprise me anymore.

At first, I was tempted to think that maybe this file was something Rob had kept since childhood, but then I came across a page full of figures as though he had been working out finances involving thousands of pounds. The last three pages in the file contained pencil drawings of skulls with all the different areas labelled in pen. Again, it had been marked with ticks by each word.

It turns out that *The Major System* is a legitimate way to train the brain; unfortunately, my brain wasn't feeling sharp enough to understand the workings of it, given all I had been through. What I think I do understand is that the ramblings in this file were that of a mad man, someone very intelligent yet unhinged at the same time. Was this a way of remembering all his lies, people's bank account details, digital passwords?

It   was   definitely   possible.

CHAPTER 36
Discs and Memory Cards

There were so many disc and memory card to check, but I had to make a start.I loaded up my laptop and started with the discs first. There were discs full of holiday photos of Rob, Gemma and the kids, so nothing sinister there.

However, the more I checked, the sicker I felt. One memory card had over 1,000 photos on it. There was nothing bad about the photos apart from the fact that they were all mine. The photos had all been downloaded off my iPhone without my knowledge. For some reason, Rob was keeping them on a memory card. Absolutely astounded, I began to rack my brains and try to think how he had been able to do this without my knowledge. Had Rob done this when I had been asleep? Why did he even want them? It just didn't make any sense.

This, along with the bank statements, proved that any privacy I thought I possessed had been totally violated by the man I loved.

I found another memory card full of email addresses and what looked to be bank account numbers, along with Gemma's ex-husband's name and what I assume was his date of birth. Had Gemma given him this information, or had he found it himself? He was undoubtedly capable of doing it himself. After all, he had been hacking everything of mine from what I could determine since the day we got together.

The next disc had a booking form on it. It stated that a wedding in Clear Water, Florida had been arranged, and the contact email address he had put on it was in the name of a John Taylor.

Rob had always told me that he had never thought about getting married before he met me, and yet he had arranged a wedding at a place he had suggested to me. I had told him that even though it sounded nice, I wanted my big day in the UK so that all of my family and friends could attend.

I also found a disk with Rob and apparently his first serious girlfriend Charlotte's engagement party photographs on it. So, I now knew for definite that he had been engaged before.

One of the discs was particularly disturbing as it had documents with the following information:

- How to scam people
- How to hack computers
- How to make mail bombs
- How to make your own lab, sabotage and subvert information pack
- How to be invisible, including using ghost addresses and learning Arabic.

However, the next memory card in my stack to review was the sickest of all. There were screenshots of text messages between Rob and Gemma's daughter (who would have been around 12 years of age at the time).

Text from Rob at 23:43:

Crank love more than anything in this world i really do you cant comprehend how much I love you is that much it hurts xxxxxxxxxxxx

Reply from Gemma's daughter:

Good haha love you too xxxxxxxxxxxx

Reply from Rob:

Love you gorgeous, no matter how much we argue you'll always be my special little girl and il protect you with my last breath xxxxxxxxxxxx

Reply from Gemma's daughter:

Haha thanks, going to sleep now right love you too xxxxxxxxxxxx

My opinion on the messages is that Rob is texting as if he is talking to his partner and that Gemma's daughter is replying just like the little child she was. These messages alone look inappropriate, to say the least, but adding them to the next picture on that memory card and it made me want to throw up.

The following two images on the card were of Gemma's daughter. She is just about identifiable because the camera is aimed down from her face and has been zoomed in to take a shot of her cleavage. Yes, of a twelve-year-old girl. It does not look like she was aware of the camera, so the bastard obviously has taken it sneakily.

Tears stung my eyes, and my stomach was churning; saliva began building up in my mouth. I felt sick to the core. All the times that he had told me how close they were and that he was like a second father to her had come back to haunt me.

I recalled a time when we had argued not long after he had left Gemma. He had told me that he didn't have contact with her kids as he believed they all needed a clean break. This particular night, I thought I saw him looking at a new text that came through after midnight and that her name was on the text. We argued because Rob was adamant that he didn't even receive a message, let alone one from Gemma's daughter.

We argued and argued because he refused to let me look at his phone. He said that if I didn't trust him, then we shouldn't be together. I argued that he needed to prove himself to build trust. We argued for about two hours until I eventually got dressed and walked out of the house in a temper.

I drove to the all-night garage to buy some cigarettes. When I returned, we argued until he told me he would sleep and not speak to me again that night.

Seeing what I had on this memory card concerned me and led me to believe that the message that night was exactly what I thought I saw.

My worst nightmare was becoming a reality. The stranger I knew as my wonderful husband was, in fact, a predator, a paedophile, a monster.

Shivers ran through my body as I began to recall stories that Rob had told me about paedophiles who he had worked with. He would go into details that would turn my stomach as he explained how many of them would tell him about their crimes as a way of sexual gratification. The paedophiles would tell him that they believed it was the young child's fault; the child was abused because of wearing short skirts, sitting on their knee, and had been "flirting with them."

Rob had said that this was the worst part of his job as a mental health nurse because the things he would hear regularly would sicken him. This was one of the reasons that he took regular breaks from the profession -to protect his mental health. Only I knew now that this had all been untrue, and I feared that the stories he had told me could be his recollections of his own crimes.

Out of all the things I found out about Rob, nothing was worse than this.

How could I have shared my life, my bed, with someone so twisted and so sick? I couldn't bear to think about it but took comfort from the fact that my mind had already blocked out any emotion and feelings that I had for him. Numbness was saving my life right now. Thank God I had this strange sensation. I was never married, never lived with him, never knew him. My mind put on an act that told me this whole thing was just a terrible story someone had told me, even though it was shocking and disgusting. I had no connection whatsoever with this evil monster.

Everyone Rob met was fooled by his illusion, and that was a hard pill to swallow. He had managed to keep his reputation intact, hide his dark side and secrets, and leave this Earth as a person who people would mourn. His desire to be respected and be the good guy was something that he could do during his life.

It was my duty now to make sure that he would not be afforded the same courtesy in death. Knowing that I was not going to appear as the grieving widow would be difficult to digest. Still, there was no way that I was going to look like a cold, heartless bitch for getting on with my life, whilst people felt sad at how my poor, wonderful husband suffered at the hands of a terrible disease, then lost his life at a young age. As far as I was concerned, that Bastard had many more years on Earth than he was entitled to. And as hard as it was to come to terms with the fact that the past five years of my life were a lie, I knew that I was glad he was dead.

Dying a slow, painful, undignified death was a fitting end for the monster. There had been no justice in most of his life, but at least there was a degree of justice in the final months of his life.

The only regret for me was that I had done everything in my power to make him comfortable. He was shown so much love, dedication, and care. I had been put through the horror of watching him die, and ultimately I had been played right until the very end. The monster had gone to great lengths to ensure he would be remembered with love and respect, making provisions to hide things even in his last months of life, and he died believing that he had protected the image he had worked so hard to create and maintain.

The best revenge is a dish served cold, and oh, was I going to serve it. His good name and reputation would be destroyed forever once I revealed the ugly and disgusting truth.

My friend Ava, at the funeral, had suggested everything I was finding out would make a great book. I took that to heart, so, Rob, this book is my gift to you, and I hope you get to read and enjoy it in   Hell!

CHAPTER 37
Pornography

Surprise should not have been something I felt after what I had already seen on previous discs. However, each disc I looked at met me with a new and sickening horror.

One of the many things that I had loved about my husband was that he wasn't what I would call "pervy." He wasn't one of these guys who would comment on other women's anatomy, and that was something I really valued. Respect for one another in a relationship was something that I had always valued. I didn't believe that it was respectful to sit and watch a film with your other half and lust after or comment on the people on screen.

Pornography was a big no-no for me, and if a partner of mine were found watching it, I would feel betrayed and hurt. Thankfully this wasn't an issue I had with Rob as it was clear it didn't interest him at all, or so I thought back then. We had discussed it several times, and he would tell me he did not understand the attraction with it as he would rather see things first hand. Putting it down to his nursing background, he had explained that maybe he saw anatomy in a different way to others and believed it was nothing to get excited about.

I was comforted by this and the fact that he didn't seem to ogle other women whilst we were out,giving our relationship what I believed to be a unique strength. The odd time that I would accuse him of checking out another woman, he would calmly dispel the idea and explain what he had been "looking at" rather than ogling the woman in question.

Seeing what was in front of me now on my laptop, I felt like an absolute idiot. Not that I have any real experience of looking at pornography, I felt confident enough in my judgement that what I was looking at was hard porn. Sitting shaking, I forced myself to focus on the screen whilst fast-forwarding video after video. I checked each video to ensure they were all adults and no children were involved, but it still sickened me to my core, but the review of the discs needed to be done.

There were videos of oral sex, resulting in a disgusting display of ejaculation. Other videos were of hard sex, but one video was extremely troubling. It was of a young woman who looked like a teenager about age 15. She was dressed in what looked like some sort of school PE uniform, perhaps to emphasise her youthfulness, but there was no way of knowing her actual age as a person, but the story here was one of a "Lolita" – the young girl seduces the older man. Maybe she was older, I found myself thinking, but why was I trying to justify Rob's potential underage porn? I set it aside in the pile for the police.

The disgusting pig in the video was a man aged around his late 50s. He was wearing a dirty white vest that hadn't been washed for at least a month. The two of them go on to have rough sex. As with all the videos, I fast-forwarded until the end and was relieved when I could turn it off.

There were around forty videos in total. Although I was glad that I had gotten through them all, I continued to feel apprehensive of what I would find next.

Next in my pile to review were images of a personal nature, and the first one I discovered was of him receiving oral sex from a blonde girl orwoman I couldn't identify. There were files full of photographs of Charlotte, some normal, and some were of her completely naked. Did she know that he had these grubby photos stored away in his Mum's spare room? There was even a file of pictures of Charlotte and her younger sister. There was nothing sinister about them other than one taken in a toilet cubicle of them both, but it felt sinister that he simply had these photos at all.

It was evident by the number of pictures he had of the younger sister and the fact he kept them that he must have had an obsession with this girl. Not knowing her age, I decided to put the disc to one side and try to find out at some point.

The following photos were disturbing, to say the least, but I couldn't be sure if he had downloaded them from some kind of voyeur website or if he had taken them. One was taken from a hidden camera of a woman in the shower; another was of a teenager/woman standing naked in a bedroom, slightly bending to put underwear on. It was clear that this unflattering photo had been taken without her knowledge, and my skin began to crawl as I asked myself if Rob had personally taken it. Had he taken any of me? I quickly pushed aside this disturbing idea because I couldn't bear the thought of that sort of betrayal.

I decided that these photos needed to go on the pile of stuff that I would give to the police. I didn't know when I would get to do this, as there were still so many boxes and bags to get through.

The more I thought about Rob's twisted behaviour, the more I started to think about my daughter moving out into the flat with Josh. I already had suspicions about Carla at the time, and the fact that Rob had tried to pre-empt what Carla might eventually tell me brought them all back. I was very sad that Lucie had been very distant since she moved out and pretty much had remained that way until the funeral. I had buried my suspicions about him and Carla as I did not – and could not believe that Rob was capable of sleeping with the daughter of his family friends whom he had known for over 20 years. With what I had witnessed tonight, I believe he was capable of anything.

This suspicion would have to wait for now as I was sure there was still a lot more of this story to be discovered. I found the letters   next.

CHAPTER38
Love Letters

My Gorgeous Charlotte,

When I first met you, you mesmerised me. When I got to know you more I fell head over heals in love with you, from that day on you have been my life, even though the past couple of years I could have shown it a lot more. We have had some great times together rand supported each other, with hardly any arguments, well compared to most people anyway, but I somewhere along the line got lost. I don't know why exactly but I did and regret it so much, the girl who used to adore me is no more, you have hardened up to thinking I didn't care about you and didn't need or want yu, but you could not be further from the truth. I have always wanted you and needed you and always will, I just took our relationship for granted, and should have done the opposite.

I roughly have about forty years left to live and cant imagine living any of them years without you, it's just inconceivable. I am so angry with myself at what I have done to us but more what iv done to you, I will never forgive myself ever, and will never get over you, this I know but that's the sentence I have brought on myself. I do still think that what we have , and what we had , and what your heart really wants, can get us through this, it just needs a different more calmer way of going about it, you say that you can adapt to any situation if needed if we break up, but you don't have to you have a person in your life that adores the ground you walk on and is proud of the way you have grown in the years gone by, a person who loves to see you whenever they can, someone who would gladly give up their life for yours, and someone who wants to be there to take all hit's the world throws at you, a person who will never look at anyone else, a person who wants you for a life time, and who's love for you is endless. That person is me just this time I will never let you forget it or have to guess at it. You are special to me you really are, words are cheap I know that , but all the above is my solemn oath to you, you are my soul mate without a doubt and I believe I'm yours, there is only one soul mate in the world for each person. I came into your world at a particular time, in your own words you might not be here if it was not for us meeting, and I too was in limbo before I met you and was in a particular sad world of my own, we changed each others life. I don't believe in coincidences and I don't think our meeting was, I know it's a bit corny, but I do believe it was meant to be because we both found our place in life, anyway iv droned on enough, just remember no one can love or understand you as much as I do and it's the same the other way round too.

ALL MY LOVE FORVER
ROB XXX

The letter was typed in pink writing and saved as a word document on the disc. Uncanny was the resemblance to a lot of the "love letters" he had sent me. All that bull shit about soul mates! Again, I thanked God that I had my numbness for protection.

The second letter on the disc seemed to be a final letter after the break up:

Hi Charlotte,

This letter is not an angry one, its not to ask you back and its not an abusive one either, its just something I need to say, as this will probably be our last communication.

Iv heard all the stories not just from Stacey but from others as well, it just seems that these past two years or so I was living with someone else i didn't know on reflection, if its all true. But I keep telling myself these people have no reason to lie, Mark, Dave, Leon and i know you still say it didn't happen but you would not talk to me and still wont so i only have there account, so you can understand where I am coming from, i know that if all this went on of course you don't want me to know but we have gone past that point now, i just need to understand why, what the hell went wrong with us that you felt you had to do all this and the lies that you have told about me, i certainly aint no hero but in your own words i helped you immensely and if i had not come along when i did and gave you my support you might not have been here, and im so glad you got throught it, i would of thought that alone would have saved me from the stuff im hearing, never mind the 8 years that followed, I haven't been perfect i know but not many people are, i always say you do what you see fit at the time, and maybe thats what you did, but it doesn't mean its right, was this the real

Charlotte or did you turn into this, am i too blame to some degree? I don't know.

I know I should have left you alone when you was at Staceys, but you go back a couple of years and then imagine me doing that to you, it was damn hard seeing you slipping away.

I always said I could not be friends with someone I broke up with but with u it was different, we went through so much together, the conversations we had, the hard times we had and the good times we had, i thought we had a bond that could not be broke whether we were together or not, im sure at some point in our relationship you felt the same, i know we were not not perfect near the end and for the past year or so, but did i really deserve all this, this is the point where i could get my own back and say ye well i slept with such a body and did this, but i never did no matter where i was or who i was with or what was going on with us i never did, you was always the one no matter what... More fool me? I don't know.

I just feel that we built our relationship up through thick and thin over the 8 yrs and then you have completely destroyed it with all that happened, and not just our relationship, if that needed to end fair enough, but did you have to taint our memories with the lies that you told about me, and all the other stuff that has gone on, its that that makes me sad more than anything that 8yrs had just been wiped within two months,, I wish so much that u had not gone down the road you did with us, i though these memories ment more to you, we always said we would be honest with each other and you was not. If all this is true why didn't you end it two years ago?

I just feel it's a waste don't you? You can lie to everyone else but not to yourself, i know what your like once you have lied or covered something up you will stick to that like hell, if ever you feel like telling me the truth, I would appreciate it, I would really like to know what the hell went wrong, no come backs just the truth between two people who used to be madly in love with each other, don't i deserve it. If you felt that you had no other way to go about things and i know I neglected you through a certain period and maybe all what apparently went on was born through this I don't know. A lot has been said over the past couple of months, and we should have never ended it like this I never wanted it like this, I really didn't. But after all that's gone on I still care about you and yes I still love you, you was the biggest part of my life for a long, long time and iv said it before and I willl say it again you may never need me but if you find yourself on your own, out in the cold or just need help, get in touch, find me, il always be

there for you unconditionally, not out of charity but out of love and care, you can do what you want but you wont break that.
Take care
Rob xx

p.sI've done you a cd with photos and memories and that from 8 years, if there is a bit of the old Charlotte left thought you might appreciate it, it's in one of the boxes clearly marked.

The awful grammar didn't sound like the supposedly educated trainer I thought was Rob. I found the spelling mistakes and general unravelling to be so strange, but I looked at these letters exactly as they were written, the mistakes, the rambling, and all.

After reading these, I felt angry - angry about what he said about lying. It was like he was describing himself perfectly. He would lie and never back down, sometimes even when the proof was right in front of him. He had never spoken much aboutCharlotte, other than they had been together for eight years and that she cheated on him.

He had been so calm when he mentioned the cheating that I must admit I found it a bit strange at the time. He wrote her off by saying that once she had cheated, that was it for them, no going back and that he just left her.

Stranger still was whenever the subject of loyalty and cheating came up with us; he would always tell me he knew he had nothing to worry about with me. I was too honest, if anything, and he knew I was devoted to him. However, he had said on more than one occasion what he would do if he ever found me cheating:"simple if I ever walked in on you and another bloke, I would just stab you both to death."

I know that sounds alarming. If someone told me their partner had said that to them, I would be highly concerned. Most likely, I would tell them to leave that person.

It is difficult to explain, but Rob never said this to me in a threatening way (which sounds like a frightening contradiction, as I think about it now). It was always said in a light-hearted, joking manner. Again, how can those words sound light-hearted? All I can say is that my husband had a way of saying outrageous things sometimes without them sounding outrageous. I would find myself giggling when he said it and reply that it would never come to that and that if I caught him cheating, maybe I would kill him too. Even I find it difficult to comprehend how I did not feel concerned about him saying these words at the time.

Knowing what I know now, I should be grateful that I was so devoted to him and never cheated, or I believe I would not be here in this present moment to tell the tale.

After reading the letters and finding the other things concerning Charlotte, I started to hope that maybe I could somehow contact her, see if she would agree to give me her side of the story or see if she would tell me how Rob acted toward her. I was intrigued to know the details of her relationship with him; after all, she stuck with him the longest from what I can gather.

CHAPTER 39
The Manual

Something I never thought that I would find in a million years was what I can only describe as a Manual, put together by a psychopath. It is extremely difficult to describe to anyone, but I will do my best to convey an accurate insight into what I discovered.

It was a file filled with plastic wallets with magazine articles in each one. I don't know what magazine they came from and I haven't been able to find out where they originated. I know that it is truly troubling to imagine a world where a publication such as this exists. From what I can gather, these articles were selected and collected over a long period of time. It was a time that was unknown to me, so I cannot say whether they were collected over months or years or at what age the monster was when this bizarre hobby began.

Many of the articles started with the sentence "How to," followed by information on how to do a particular thing.

Psych Out Anyone was the title of one article, and it began like this: "Want to know what someone's thinking? Want to know the secrets people's appearance betray? Or what's the best way to hide your feelings? Find out in our complete guide to body language and beyond."

There is then a paragraph about what your body language says about you, followed by images of different men in body language poses: superior, secretive, suspicious, stressed, and uncooperative. Then on the following page, there is the heading:*What are they looking for? A guide to what professional interrogators are looking for when they size you up.*It then gives an account from a Police Officer, Customs Officer, and Job Interviewer.

A similar article I discovered was *Psych Out Life on the Couch: How they see through you -from the very first moment you walk through the door, your psychiatrist is working you out. And then you open your mouth...*Interestingly, a section in this article about how you speak can be as much of a giveaway as the clothes you wear and your general appearance. It does mention that you can train yourself to sound different, but that is no easy feat.

Is this how my husband was able to fool everyone, including me? Had he studied to control his body language? Admittedly he had done an amazing job as he always looked so calm and relaxed, and some had actually used the nickname "Mr Cool" as he never stressed about anything.

Another article was titled: *Scared to Death. Fear has powerful physiological effects, but are they potent enough to kill? According to the evidence, yes.*
Then there were a few articles about how fear can kill people.

How to be a Millionaire was another article in the file, but this was predictable as my husband loved money and worked hard to make as much as he possibly could.

The next article gave information on the following:
- *Obtain a Verdict from a Bent Jury*
- *Have a Bank Account Hacked*
- *Buy a Black-Market Human Kidney*
- *Get a Question Asked in Parliament,* and
- *Can You Train Yourself to Get by on Less Sleep?*

The mind boggles, how many twisted individuals like my husband were these articles targeted at?

A more light-hearted article was titled: *Live Well Survive Anything.* It then stated eight rules to live by and 11 emergency measures to take,ranging from an asthma attack to a smashed thumb.
Another was an article about gadgets and how to become a real-life super hero. You are probably asking, was this directed at children? But no, this was for adults. What kind of adults? I imagine rather strange ones.

A double spread article with Q &A was titled *Weaponry: From Bombs to Handguns, Killing People is Still a Hi-Tech Business...*
It provides answers to the following questions:

- What nations have the atomic bomb?
- What is the most expensive weapon?
- How much land does the Ministry of Defence own?
- Could you survive film-style multiple gunshot wounds?
- Is the .44Magnum still the most powerful handgun in the world? How far can rifle bullets travel?

I get it that some people may have a healthy interest in weapons, but would most normal people keep the article in a file so that they could refer back to it?

How to hotwire a car. Stop! Read this only if you've lost your key and need help, not if you're thinking of stealing a car!
Is this how they got around producing such twisted articles?

How to make money when your parents die. When the Grim Reaper takes your folks, don't let the taxman take their loot.

How to look cool on your own at a party.
This one was laughable, but it is difficult to know if this is the information he was saving or whether it was the small article underneath:
How to get in when you're locked out which is essentially a burglar's guide to breaking and entering.

Considering Rob had never really been interested in exercising and keeping fit, I found a large clump of articles uniquely interesting about how to get the perfect abs, featuring an extensive exercise routine. He certainly did not have the perfect body at anytime we were together, but I loved him the way he was. A bit of a belly wouldn't put me off, and Rob seemed perfectly comfortable in his own skin. The key word here being *seemed*, as I was quickly learning that everything I knew about him was actually the opposite to the truth.

Rob had collected some articles regarding schizophrenia which had eight questions to "test your sanity:"

Q1: Have you felt very low or on edge for more than two weeks?

Q2:   Are you sleeping badly-unable to drop off, waking early, or finding it hard to get up?

Q3:   Are you slower than usual in speech or movement?

Q4:   Have you lost interest in sex, social activities or hobbies?

Q5:   Do you feel worthless or guilty?

Q6:   Have you lost your appetite lately or experienced an unplanned gain or loss of weight?

Q7:   Are you finding it hard to concentrate or make decisions?

Q8:   Are you thinking or even planning to end your own life?

Part of me believes that these articles were to gain knowledge for his nursing career that he had invented, but part of me also believes that he was reading them to get a self-diagnosis. Mentally ill had to be a factor in the evil and twisted life of my husband.

More articles that went towards teaching people to control their body language were:

Don't be Frightened. Now for the Good News: You don't have to feel really afraid ever again. Here's how...

It then gives a list of Do and Don't on how to look calm in the face of fear.

Another was *The Architects of Fear*. This was information about how horror film makers used certain things to frighten their audiences.

There are too many articles to list all of them. I could probably fill a complete book, so I have tried to stick to the most disturbing ones:

The A-Z of seriously badass chemicals,

Treat a toothache in the wilderness, horribly true stories which included a paragraph about the police finding 600 human heads in a warehouse,

What does it cost to:

    Acquire the services of a contract killer

    Purchase a machine gun,

    Set yourself up with a fake ID

    Buy a child- legally or otherwise

"Say Ahhhhh!" So your girlfriend fantasises about George Clooney, but you failed your Biology 'O' level.

Never fear, all you need to pass yourself off as an extra from ER is a lab coat, steady hands and our nine-step guide.

It goes on to give tips on how to examine different parts of the anatomy.

Professional Killers

How to Shut Your Noisy Neighbours Up

The Final Judgement (an article about Capital Punishment)

How to Buy Tanks, Guns and Other Lethal Toys

Find Out How You Got on a Credit Blacklist (and get off)

How to Catch a Burglar in Your Back Garden

How to Perform an Emergency Tracheotomy

How to do a Spock-Style Death Squeeze (about squeezing the carotid artery)

How to Deliver a Baby

How to Wake up Next to a One Night Stand

How to Case a Joint

How to Unhook a Bra with One Hand (something Rob could do with ease)

What's Your Poison? Snakes, Spiders, Scorpions... Which Would You Rather be Attacked by?

How to Dump a Friend, which gave different methods to end a friendship,

How to Win an Argument with a Woman which gave four tips, one that I recognised

Create Confusion if you are Struggling

How to Know She's Cheating on You

How to Hypnotise Away a Woman's Inhibitions and there was even an article about how to have sex

How to Spot if You're Going Mad

How to Tell if that Diamond You Bought Her is Real

Dirty Rotten Scoundrels was a two-page article revealing the tricks of con men.

I came across a few articles about poker. I guessed that this could have been useful for more than one reason. Rob could learn to win money and also how to control his body language. Obviously, some articles were more disturbing than others but added together because they were ripped out of magazines, put into plastic wallets, and kept together in a file made this extremely creepy. Some of the articles convinced me that Rob was definitely a psychopath.

Even normal everyday things like having sex or ending friendships were kept for reference, proving to me that he did not have genuine human emotions and needed some kind of bible to guide him through life. Learning to control his body language and react to situations appropriately empowered him to walk amongst us, the sick and twisted psychopath hiding in plain sight.

The final box revealed some holiday keepsakes and a book that he had once mentioned to me: *The Poor Man's James Bond*. I recall him telling me years earlier that he used to have this book and that it was illegal to own due to the dangerous content. Apparently, there was information about creating poisons, homemade bombs, and other weapons. When he told me about this book, it didn't really feel strange to me. Many people are interested in things that they are not supposed to have, plus he didn't have it any more, or so I thought until I saw it now—something else for the police pile.

There was a small lock knife and a dagger inside the box. When I added these to the other two I knew about;it meant there were a total of four plus his supposedly ornamental Samurai sword. I now questioned if that was the truth. Were any of these purely ornamental, given his joking threat about what he would do if he caught me cheating? Once all these findings were added together, I could, and I felt anyone could, begin to paint a picture of an extremely sick and deranged person.

CHAPTER40
The Best Friend

When I had sent Rob's friend Vinnie a text, inviting him over for a coffee and to give him some of Rob's belongings (things I thought he might like), I never intended for one second to tell him about any of my findings. However, the result was frightening, to say the least.

We sat awkwardly with our coffees at first and just made small talk. We had never met until today, and sitting with him now, larger than life, in my living room was surreal.

Vinnie had expected to see my brother at the funeral and had been surprised that he didn't attend. I explained briefly about the falling out with Carla, who had stayed with Gary and Louise for a while, and how his taking sides had resulted in a text argument and that we hadn't spoken since.

I told Vinnie that I had assumed he was already aware of all this, but I realised it was not the case by the look of utter confusion on his face. Shockingly, he didn't even know that I had a daughter even though Rob and I had been together for five years. Strange that he would not have mentioned that my daughter also lived with us when he moved in with me.

Vinnie commented on it being common that everybody fell out with their family when Rob was about and how it seemed to be quite a pattern in his life. So it went from there, back and forth with us filling each other in on missing information. Vinnie told me that he had been asking to meet me for years, but Rob would always make an excuse, saying that we were working away or busy doing something.

Rob always told me that Vinnie couldn't leave the house because he was a carer for his children who had autism and that he was pretty much housebound after reaching a weight of almost 30 stone. Vinnie laughed out loud at this and told me he has always done bodybuilding and had never been more than 18 stone in his life.

This had been Rob's reason Vinnie hadn't attended our wedding as best man because he could not find a suit to fit. He was flabbergasted when I asked if he previously had a cancer scare, as Rob had told me. Nothing worse than a cold in his life was what he answered.

It was clear he was disgusted that Rob would lie about something like this; it seems health concerns had been an excuse when Rob was constantly texting someone. Rob would say it was Vinnie who he was texting and that he was worried sick about him.

It turns out that Vinnie had a theory as to why we had never met; Rob must have told me some lies at the beginning of the relationship to impress me, and Rob didn't want Vinnie revealing his pile of lies. This made sense, definitely, about the mental health nurse lie, which Vinnie found hilarious.

Vinnie said that this behaviour was the same thing Rob had done when he met Charlotte as he had told her he and Vinnie were both doormen. To make the lie the truth, he talked Vinnie into going to a nightclub with him and asking to speak to the Manager. Neither had SIA badges, but Vinnie said that he was impressed with Rob's powers of persuasion since they both left the club with a doorman job.

I listened intently to every word from Vinnie as I attempted to learn who Rob Carter really was. I discovered more in one afternoon than I did within five years. Here is a list of what I found out:

- Vinnie met Rob when he was about 21 and Vinnie was about 18 –they met at work in Birmingham.

- Rob's Mum's neighbour Margaret had a dog that bit Barbara, and Rob charged round, burst through all the doors, with a knife (with a huge blade) in the back of his jeans, saying to give him the dog because he was going to kill it. He also threatened to stab them. Vinnie dragged him out whilst Margaret was on the phone to the police. As far as he knows, they didn't make friends after that. Rob told Vinnie that Rob beat up her son Steve for trying to protect his Mum. He moved in with Vinnie for a short while after.

Not long after, he moved in with Maxine. Rob was 27, and he had told everyone that Maxine was 17. Vinnie said that after it ended, he found out she was actually only 15. So, more evidence that he was a dirty paedophile.

- He told me that Rob had police ID cards years ago and used to flash a badge at cars and ask them to pull over. Rob laughed when Vinnie told him to stop and made out that it was just a joke.

- Rob had a vile temper when drunk and would constantly cause fights and have to be dragged off people. Was this why he always stayed sober around me? In case his mask slipped?

- Rob was always talking about a special school for mental health for children from age 4-21 years of age and said it was called the Harborne Loonies. He would often talk about a boy named Johnny Barker, who he had hung around with and used to do really crazy stuff. Rob had mentioned him and his brother to me before. Rob was also obsessed with nurses.

So, is this why it seems that Rob never existed until age 21? Barbara didn't own one photograph of Rob as a boy, a child, teenager, or an adult other than the wedding photo we gave her. Strange a Mother having no evidence in her house of her one and only child. The fact that Barbara had been unsure about the school details, and others, indicated she was trying to cover for him and that she always knew he was ill. There is a strong possibility he was a pupil at the special school he so often talked about with Vinnie.

- Rob had bought a car off Vinnie and still hadn't paid him the £3,000 for it after three years, so he finally asked him for it. Rob roped him into doing an inside job, robbing the Aldi he worked at and then paid Vinnie with the money they had stolen. Rob said that when the police came out, he spun them a tale, and they believed it hook line and sinker. Vinnie admitted that when Rob had talked him into the plan, he was so manipulative that he had not even realised he was being played until afterwards.

- Rob told Vinnie that he had borrowed £20,000 from Gemma's kids to start his business and pay for his training. I had found court paperwork showing that the training company had to take him to court as he had not paid them.

- Vinnie didn't speak to him for six months after he hit his girlfriend in the face, knocking her into a chair. Vinnie said that Rob had flown into a rage when Vinnie's girlfriend arrived at their flat unannounced. Apparently, he thought that she was getting in the way of their friendship, and he was angry she was coming between them. When she turned up unannounced and they had plans, he flipped. Rob managed to talk his way back into his life six months later. Vinnie found it hard to explain why he could forgive him for something so terrible, but I knew better than anyone that there was no end to Rob's powers of persuasion. Many said he could sell snow to the Eskimos.

- Vinnie told me about the times they had put false plates on their cars when they were younger to steal petrol and drive away. Rob had told me about this, but he hadn't told me that he used to wear a women's blonde wig whilst he did it. This took me back to a memory of when we were re-watching the *Bad Girls* box set and the scene when Jim Fenner stole Karen's car and dressed up as her, wearing a blonde wig. I remember how much Rob had laughed at that scene, but now I wonder if he was laughing at something closer to home too.

- Vinnie never met Gemma, even though Rob was with her for six years. He also told me that the only contact he had with Rob during our time together was on the phone. There was one time they met to look at a car, but that was all. According to Rob, he was frequently meeting Vinnie in pubs for pints and burgers. Obviously, he was meeting another woman on all of those occasions.

- After asking how Rob and Charlotte's relationship was, I was sad to hear that Charlotte was terrified of him. Vinnie thought that Rob had done something terrible to her, and that's why she left. She also told him she had been stalked and threatened by him after.

- Vinnie thought there was something between Stacey and Rob; he said she was constantly rubbing herself all over him, even when Dave was there. He said it was really weird. It couldn't be a coincidence that he told me this as I had gotten a bad feeling about her when we met that one time.

The fact that she practically stalked me when she found out he was dead was strange too. She found my phone number on the internet and called and texted me repeatedly until I had replied. I was heartbroken about my husband, and then I had her contacting me out of the blue, calling and texting me 48 hours later. She was one disrespectful bitch and needed putting in her place.

I was told that she had put a post on Facebook saying that she would let everyone know when the funeral would be. This was two days after Rob had passed away. I was livid when I called her back and told her to take the post down and that she was not welcome at the funeral, and didn't she think it strange that she wasn't invited to our wedding if they were such good friends?

My biggest fear had been that Lucie or even Carla would hear about Rob's funeral from Stacey.

Stacey ended up telling me that both she and her son Jack (his Godson) had been in contact with Rob during the last six months of his life. So, it looked like another lie had been unleashed. I agreed that she could bring her son to the funeral but warned her in no uncertain terms that if she brought a load of strangers to the funeral, I would "fuck her up" and unleash unholy hell on her. Strong words, but they were appropriate for the circumstance and in a language, she would understand.

She did as she was told at the funeral and stayed right away from me. I had noticed her at the back of the crematorium but had promised myself that I wouldn't cause a scene if she stayed out of my face. I bit my tongue when most people exited the crematorium, and I was saying my goodbyes at the coffin with Barbara. I turned around, and there she was, waiting. As soon as I walked away, she ran to the coffin as though she was the grieving widow.

- Apparently, Rob was obsessed with power when he was younger and had wanted to be in the police. The doormen job was power and image-related too.

- A disturbing revelation was that he was obsessed with knives, often talking about wanting to stab people, but Vinnie just thought Rob was trying to sound like a hard man and had watched too many films. He didn't take him seriously.

I had known that Rob had an interest in different types of knives and had collected a couple, but I wouldn't have known that he was obsessed with knives and certainly not with the idea of stabbing anyone.

- Vinnie was unaware that Rob had got a sofa on credit in his name years ago. I had discovered this when I found an invoice in Vinnie's name but for one of Rob's addresses. I sent Vinnie the invoice, and he was shocked and angry. The company that he had got the sofa from had a bad reputation when it came to collecting debts.

- Vinnie knew that Rob had to retake his driving test because he had been banned. He knew nothing of the benefit fraud he had been convicted of.

- Vinnie believed that Rob had been cheating on Charlotte with Alice, who lived a few doors away from his Mum. This shocked me as I checked with him if he meant the same Alice, who was 30 stone. He confirmed it was. Again, another revelation as Rob would always comment that he did not find overweight women attractive and that this was one of the reasons he did not want to stay with Gemma after she piled on the pounds. Vinnie went on to tell me that this was just one of many, as Rob had a fetish for larger women. Unbelievable, but just another lie for the collection that was growing by the minute. Vinnie said he heard Rob was still in contact with Alice when we were together, and I shudder to think what he was doing with her behind my back.

- One of the more surprising revelations was that Rob was always in and out of work. He had even been signed off with depression for over six months at one time and was actively taking anti-depressants. So much for the "strong mind" and "I never get depressed" claims Rob made.

As our long and overdue conversation came to an end, Vinnie admitted that, although he knew about some of the bad stuff Rob had done, he had no idea as to how dark he was.

After hearing about the things, I had discovered, Vinnie and I agreed that Rob was an absolute psychopath. Vinnie even now believed that Rob had probably killed people. Especially after seeing the folder with the crazy ramblings, codes, random words and numbers, written in two different colours. Teaching himself to memorise and link information, practising foreign languages, studying the different parts of the skull, and so on.

When Vinnie had left, I was shaking. It was getting more and more terrifying by the day to realise what a lucky escape I had when Rob died. The thought he could be a murderer, amongst other things, made my blood run cold.

At that very moment, it crossed my mind that, had I continued to question him about my suspicions, maybe I would have been next. That reality would take a long time to sink in and come to terms with. I don't know if that will ever happen.

CHAPTER 41
The Mother

In the weeks that passed after Rob's death, I regularly went shopping for Barbara and had many conversations with her about her son. Much of what she said from one day to the next was conflicting, and I believed it would be difficult to get the whole truth. She was hellbent on protecting Rob's memory, and although I understood that to some degree, I couldn't help but feel that she had been instrumental in making Rob into the monster that he became. I believe she had assisted him in keeping his dark secrets over the years and that she at least owed me some answers.

I had made Barbara aware of most things that I had so far discovered and hoped this would encourage her to expand on what I knew, fill in some gaps, and give me some well-deserved answers.

The most troubling thing Barbara said to me was when I had told her that I had found out something really terrible about Rob.

"Oh God, he wasn't messing with kids, was he?" She immediately replied.

Stunned at her response, I studied her face and can honestly say there was no evidence of shock what so ever. For a Mother to jump to the conclusion that her son was a paedophile, something so vile and unthinkable, led me to believe that she already knew or, at the very least, she suspected.

What she said next was even more shocking. "Oh, why do men have to do things like that, Julia? I don't understand it."

My anger was overwhelming. I couldn't believe what I was hearing. She was talking like this was an everyday normality, just a bad habit all men had. I told her in no uncertain terms that men don't do things like that, paedophiles do, and her precious son was a paedophile.

She looked genuinely upset, but it was unsettling that there was no shock or surprise at this revelation. Maybe she was just upset I had discovered the truth; she would no longer be able to protect his memory and good name.

Barbara admitted that Rob had always been secretive but that she had no idea he was capable of any of the things I had revealed. According to her, Rob had a terrible temper, and if he was "boxed into a corner," he would turn nasty. She didn't elaborate but told me that there had been many nasty arguments over the years,which had resulted in them not speaking to one another, sometimes for months at a time.

When Barbara talked about Rob marrying me, she said he must have loved me as he was not the marrying type. She was shocked when he had announced that we were getting married.

Good, she had finally slipped up. How could that be the truth when Rob was engaged to Charlotte years earlier. I told her about the booking form for Rob and Charlotte's wedding that I had found. She looked confused by this and went on to say to me that there was no way that Rob would have arranged a wedding abroad and not tell his own Mother. According to her, it would all have been in Charlotte's head. It was apparent by the way she spoke about Charlotte that she was not her biggest fan.

Barbara then proceeded to tell me a bizarre story of the time she had visited the two of them and randomly, Charlotte just appeared in the lounge wearing a wedding dress, asking for Barbara's opinion. When she left the room, Barbara had questioned Rob about it and asked if they were getting married; he had laughed it off and said that it was all in Charlotte's head. Apparently, she had wanted to get married, but he didn't, and she had borrowed a wedding dress from a friend to make a point.

Unimaginably, Barbara says that she believed his explanation. It was a bizarre story that made no sense, but her acceptance of the story was far stranger. Barbara was supposed to be intelligent and sharp-minded, so this did not sit well with me at all. Besides, there were the engagement party photos to confront her with too. Calmly she admitted that she was well aware of the engagement, and she had attended the party.

Barbara's weak argument about the wedding was she knew they had gotten engaged, but she never believed they would get married. Pretty much speechless at her responses, I asked her what she remembered about their relationship and why it ended. I wanted to know if there had been a violent altercation at the end. I explained that I'd been told about Charlotte being scared of Rob and possibly, something violent had happened at the end.

Barbara's account of their relationship was that Rob was the perfect partner and that everything he did was to keep Charlotte happy. She told me that Charlotte had worked in a nursery even though she didn't like children but wanted to be a childminder, although that never happened.

Apparently, Rob was always working hard to earn money to take care of Charlotte. Barbara had a low opinion of Stacey, saying that she was constantly dumping her baby on Charlotte because the baby's father wasn't interested in him. According to Barbara, Rob couldn't stand Stacey and looked genuinely surprised when I told her that Rob had remained friends with her and was even Godfather to her child Jack. She couldn't understand how that could be because Rob never had a good word to say about her.

The day Charlotte left Rob, Barbara had received a call asking her to visit him and bring some food supplies. As he didn't drive at the time, she took the bus down with some shopping and said that he looked so "broken" when she arrived. Charlotte had walked out on him, and he didn't know why, but it was definitely over. Charlotte was never mentioned again. Considering she had been in his life for the last eight years, this was odd, to say the least.

When I asked about the 15-year-old girl Rob had been with when he was 27 years old, Barbara became furious to the point that she was shouting at me. Her face twisted in disgust as she tried to explain the accusation away. According to her, the girl had been 16 years of age, and she had told Rob that she disagreed with it. Apparently, she even went to the girl's house and spoke to her Mother and told her she was not happy about it. Concluding that it was the Mother's fault for allowing Rob to move in with them wasn't one that I agreed with.

None of it would have happened if Rob behaved like a normal human being as far as I was concerned. Barbara didn't comment further on that after I challenged her. She just sat quietly, her expression portraying how unhappy she was at being caught out.

This proved she had known her son had an unhealthy interest in young girls for many years. If she was 16, not that I believed that, this was still wrong in my eyes.

Rob had no problem telling me that he considered my daughter's father to be nothing more than a paedophile for entering into a relationship with me when I was just 16, and he had been 26. He had given a long speech about how 16-year-olds didn't have their own minds, were not adults, and why would a grown man find it acceptable to be in a relationship with someone who wasn't old enough to buy alcohol. Everything that outraged Rob appeared to be things that he had been guilty of.

Barbara's account of what had happened with her neighbour and the dog bite turned out to be quite different to Vinnie's account. However, he had no reason to lie and to be honest, his version sounded the more realistic. According to Barbara, Rob had been angry when the dog bit her. Although Rob had been angry, there was no knife, and she dragged him out of the house as Vinnie stood by the garden gate. She even went as far as to say that she remembered the colour of the T-shirt he was wearing that day. Difficult to believe from a woman who struggled to remember where her only child was born.

Barbara was such a tiny lady, both in height and weight, so the thought of her being able to drag her angry six-foot, two, heavy built son out of a house didn't ring true to me and yet his friend who was a weight trainer stood outside doing nothing.

The fact that the neighbours still had polite words for Rob when they saw him could have been down to fear. This is what I believe anyway.

Angry about what Vinnie had said about Rob, Barbara had a rant, saying that Vinnie was supposed to be a friend and why was he saying such horrible things about Rob now that he was dead? I shut her down quickly and snapped back that Vinnie had only just realised some of the bad things himself, and he was providing me with some much-needed truth.

It was evident that she would never fully come clean about what she knew, like the fact that she hadn't even noticed post arriving for Gemma's husband at her house. Why would she just put the letters with the rest of Rob's mail and not question who the man was? Normal people would have written "unknown at this address" and put them in the post box, not put them with her son's post.

I concluded that Barbara was more than likely as evil as her son, and I wasn't sure how much longer I could have her in my life. It was draining listening to her saying that she wished he would just walk back in the door, and despite all of the bad things he had done, she still loved him and that he was a "good son to her." She would often ask me not to turn on him as she knew that he loved me. Seriously, how could I not turn on him after what I had learned?

CHAPTER 42
The Police

The experience of calling the police to report my suspicions about my dead husband was surreal. I was sobbing as I explained to the operator about all the strange things I had found, including proof of the fraud against Gemma's husband. They arrived around 8am on Easter Sunday, and I gave them the discs, a letter regarding the loans that he had taken out in Gemma's husband's name, the weapons including the Samurai sword, the fake police IDs, and the James Bond book. They advised me that the only criminal activity they had on record for him was regarding the benefit fraud. As clever as he was, I suspect he got away with far worse.

After about half an hour, the two officers left my house carrying a bag of weapons. I was glad to get them out of the house and to have told the police about my suspicions. It felt like a slight weight lifted from my shoulders.

I think that the Police thought he was a bit of a fantasist and that he hadn't been that dangerous. It was strange when I told them about the documents he had saved regarding making mail bombs, a home lab, and learning Arabic that they weren't all that concerned. They said if there had been a change or obsession in religion, they might have been concerned about terrorist activity, but they weren't concerned as it stood.

I asked them to take his phone and iPad away to check for any other criminal activity. Still, they refused and said, even though I had given them permission, this wasn't something they could do because of privacy laws even though he was deceased. They said I was free to look through the devices, which I knew, but I didn't have the same resources and skills as the police. Although I knew I would try, I wasn't confident that it would be easy for me to find the things that Rob didn't want me to find.

CHAPTER 43
Charlotte'sStory

Charlotte had been on my mind since my conversation with Vinnie and my finding all the photos and letters. Vinnie had kindly agreed to pass my number to Charlotte and ask her to call me; I just hoped she would. After all these years, it must be strange to be asked to call the widow of her ex-boyfriend. Thankfully, she called me.

A mobile number that I did not recognise flashed up on my phone, and I knew that it would be her. My hand was shaking as I pressed to answer and I was relieved to hear a kind voice on the other end.

Introducing herself, I immediately sensed that she was a kind person. My voice was breaking as I thanked her for calling and began to explain as quickly as I could some of the shock revelations I had found since Rob had died. I told her about the discs with photos and admitted that some had been given to the police. Charlotte wasn't shocked about some of the nasty things that I had found as she believed he was an "evil bastard."

I listened intently as Charlotte described the life she and Rob had shared. It was far from the fairytale life I had appeared to have been living with him. She explained that Rob had controlled every aspect of her life, including money. She hadn't been allowed access to bank accounts or cash cards and would have to ask for money if she needed anything. An explanation was required for anything and everything that she spent money on, including sanitary towels. He would become angry if he believed that she had spent more than he thought was necessary.

Although this was different to my experience with Rob, it was clear that there were some similarities. I had lived a good life and always had money for whatever I needed or wanted;I could buy what I wanted when I wanted. However, it was true that Rob controlled the money; although, it didn't feel that way at the time.

He would transfer money as and when I needed it,but I would never see a single bank statement. Even when he was ill and I was working, all the money went to him, and he would transfer as and when needed. I would have to tell him what bills needed paying, and he would transfer the amounts to me as everything was in my name.

When we discussed fraud, Charlotte told me about when she had left Rob and had tried to apply for credit. She soon realised that her credit was ruined due to loans and credit cards that Rob had taken out in her name, unknowingly to her. When asked why she didn't report him to the police, she answered that she had been too afraid of him and was just thankful that she had escaped him.

Charlotte explained the relationship with Stacey and Dave. Charlotte had become a childminder (something that Barbara had denied) and was minding their baby whilst Stacey was at work. According to her, Rob never liked them, including the baby, but that he was so two-faced with them.

Often Charlotte would be the one working, and Rob would be in and out of employment. She spoke of how she would often call Rob when she finished work, and he would tell her he was out having lunch with Stacey and the baby. Basically, he was spending her money as she was earning it and spending time with a woman he claimed to seriously dislike. Charlotte always suspected that Rob was sleeping with Stacey and said that she would often sit awkwardly with Dave as Rob and Stacey openly flirted with each other.

My mind was whirring as I listened to how jealous Rob was and that he would constantly be checking her phone, something that I had never witnessed in my relationship with him. She told me about when she went somewhere and how he would just appear out of nowhere, and she had no explanation as to how he always found her. She believed that he must have been stalking and following her the whole time.

Even when she arranged a surprise birthday party for him, he turned up just as she was about to go inside the pub to make her final arrangements. He was in a rage and grabbed her arm, screaming at her to tell him who he was, who was it she was fucking? He went as far as to drag her into the pub whilst she desperately tried to explain herself. Luckily for her, he realised that she was telling him the truth and had, in fact, arranged a surprise party for him. He was able to just switch when he discovered this, immediately appearing calm and happy. He told her that they could still treat it as a surprise and that he would just walk in and pretend to be surprised on the night of the party.

I asked if she was aware of the benefit fraud that I had discovered. She said she wasn't, but she did tell me about a strange occurrence with the police. She said that the police had called the house one day to tell her Rob had been arrested. The first thing the police officer told her was not to worry and that he hadn't killed anyone. They said to her he had been pulled over in his car, and he had been found in possession of CS Gas.

Unaware of what fully happened regarding the arrest, she said she'd been shocked a few days later when he transferred the ownership of his car into her name, telling her it was an early gift for when she passed her test. This made sense regarding the driving ban that I had discovered; although, it was now clear Charlotte knew nothing about it.

A provisional driving licence had arrived in the post for Rob at one point, and when she questioned him, he told her they had sent the wrong one out, and he'd already spoken to them to rectify the mistake.

Not a believable story, but I could see how Charlotte would have taken the explanation from him at the time. I was never afraid of Rob; however, he managed to convince me of pretty much anything. It was like lying convincingly was his superpower.

Charlotte was completely confused when I explained I had found some letters with her name on them that were addressed to Barbara's house, and she was shocked when I told her that I had found a copy of a bank statement on a disc. The statement was for a joint account that she had no clue about, and she was even more surprised when I told her the balance in the account was £21,500. We spoke about the possibility of this coming from a loan that he had fraudulently taken out and put in her name or indeed in someone else's name.

It seemed that Charlotte also had her mental health attacked at every opportunity. He had told her to take time off work on four or five occasions, telling her he had booked holidays. After taking time off, she would be told a few days before that they could no longer afford the holiday, and it had been cancelled.

When Rob had been working as the doorman, Charlotte and Stacey had gone to the club for a night out. As they had been standing talking to him, a woman they didn't know ran over and began to scream and shout at them to stay away from Rob. She told them he was the boyfriend of her best friend Alice (that name again). Stacey appeared more upset than Charlotte, and she ended up fighting with the screaming woman. Again, Rob talked his way out of it by saying his friend "Fat Alice" - as he chose to call her then, was obsessed with him, and it was all in her head about her being his girlfriend.

However, this didn't appear to be the truth as Charlotte found a message in the middle of the night on Rob's phone. He was asleep and had not heard the alert continuing to go off, so Charlotte had gone to switch it off. The message Charlotte said was very clear: *I love you so much, when will I see you again? Xxxxx.* When confronted about this message, Rob stuck to his original story about her being obsessed with him and to take no notice.

Charlotte also believed that Rob had committed a robbery at Dave and Stacey's house. She said that they had a loan of a few thousand pounds intended for their upcoming wedding and put it in a safe in their house. Unbeknownst to them, Rob had been furious that they had more money than him and had kept moaning about it. He was aware that the money had been stored in a safeand one night when Dave was working, Stacey came to the house to visit. Rob told Charlotte and Stacey he was going out but didn't say where he was going. It was a strange thing to do as it was late at night.

That night, Stacey and Dave were burgled; nothing was disturbed or taken except for the safe containing the money. Dave and Stacey never suspected Rob for a second. After all, he had become such good friends with them and often worked with Dave on the doors. In the weeks after this, Charlotte noticed that Rob appeared to have unexplained money, giving her every reason to suspect him; although, theft was not something she would have dared accuse him of.

Although Rob hadn't been physically abusive to her, Charlotte described how he would emotionally abuse her on a day-to-day basis, making her feel unattractive, unwanted, and most of all, stupid. She felt that she couldn't do anything right, and he would constantly call her "thick."

This was like night and day as I was used to being constantly called a strong, beautiful, intelligent woman. Countless times of the day, I would be called beautiful and gorgeous either verbally or by text.

Charlotte seemed to understand the codes I had found as she said when he called her thick, he would use methods with her to get her to remember things. They consisted of words and numbers, so there was definitely a link there. She explained that he was OCD about certain things and insisted that the bed had to be made in a certain way so he could balance a fifty-pence piece on the corners. She asked him where he had learnt that and asked if he had been in the military. She said he had laughed and told her she would never know where he'd been or what he'd done. He would then follow this up by telling her that he was only joking, that his Mum had taught him as she had very high standards. Having had Barbara live in my home and after seeing inside her house when Rob died, I knew this was certainly not the case.

When I asked Charlotte what she knew about Barbara and whether she knew Rob's birth name was different from the name we knew him by, there were more revelations.

Charlotte recalled a time when she had found three birth certificates for him: one as Rob Dixon (his birth name), another as Rob Carter (his known name) and a third for Rob Freeman. When Charlotte asked Rob why he had them, he became angry, snatched them off her and told her to mind her own business. It was never mentioned again, and that was the first and last time she saw them.

Regarding Barbara, Charlotte also found her to be odd but couldn't put her finger on why. Charlotte had never once been inside Barbara's house, even though she was with Rob for eight years. However, Barbara had stayed with them when recovering from an operation and would at times come over for a meal. Charlotte told me about the rude way Barbara had treated her, like when she handed a plate to Barbara; she would push it back at her and tell her to go and cook it properly. Charlotte was unable to stand up to her as she was afraid to antagonise Rob. He would often shout at her to put a smile on her face when his Mother was visiting.

Threats of violence were a regular occurrence in their relationship, but thankfully he didn't carry out his threats.

Charlotte tried to leave Rob on at least eight occasions, but whenever she attempted to go, he would emotionally blackmail her and threaten to tell people personal things she didn't want anyone to know. When she tried to leave him, Rob managed to convince Stacey and Dave that she was mentally unstable and he was afraid she was going to attempt suicide. Bizarrely, not only did they believe him, but they also assisted him in keeping Charlotte confined. Stacey and Dave locked Charlotte in their house for three days and refused to let her leave or have access to a phone. Again, this went unreported due to the immense fear of Rob's reaction that Charlotte felt.

The obsession with knives and stabbing people was reinforced by Charlotte's memories. She, too, stated that Rob would talk about wanting to stab people but was more frightening when he threatened her. If she spoke of leaving him, he would threaten to stab her and all of her family to death.

Rob took her on holiday at one point and, when they arrived, told her he had brought her there to kill her, telling her he would cut her up into little pieces. She was so terrified that he would one day follow through with his threats that she wrote a letter to her uncle to say that if anything ever happened to her or she went missing, he needed to call the police and tell them that Rob was involved.

This brought back memories of my daughter's dad when I, too, would give notes to a friend to keep for the police just in case he ever killed me. It was difficult to hear that Rob was just as bad if not worse, and yet I had never suspected a thing.

Charlotte told me the most concerning thing during our telephone conversation was she believed Rob had committed murder. She recalled when he came home with blood all over his trainers, and when she asked what happened, he told her it was just from a nose bleed. Not wanting to question him further, she accepted the explanation but was worried about what the truth could be.

A few days later, when she was sitting in the car with him, he took a fast corner, and she felt something fall from under the passenger seat. Reaching down and picking it up, she was horrified to discover that it was a large machete covered in dried blood. Distraught, she asked Rob what he had done. Shockingly, he burst out laughing and told her that she didn't need to worry about what he had done but instead should worry about keeping her mouth shut as she was now involved. The knife would now have her fingerprints on it. The fear that she must have felt is hard to imagine, but I believe the fear must have been immense to stay quiet and stay with him after that day.

Charlotte had resigned herself to a life with Rob, and when asked about the booking form for the wedding, she confirmed that they were going to get married. Rob controlled every aspect of the wedding, including choosing and buying both the bridesmaids dresses and booking the venue abroad. A couple of weeks before the wedding, Rob told her that he had cancelled it as they could not afford it.

This was the last straw for Charlotte, who took all the dresses and burned them in the back garden. She laughed when I told her Barbara's explanation of the wedding dress, and she confirmed that Barbara was fully aware of the wedding.

Unable to take much more of the emotional rollercoaster, she knew this was the beginning of the end. She took to sleeping in the spare room until she could find somewhere to go. She had become good friends with a man at work and confided in him about her struggle. This was the man that she began a relationship with and is still with today.

Sickeningly, the last night that Charlotte spent under the same roof as Rob was the night he raped her. She was fast asleep in a separate bedroom when he barged through the door and proceeded to rape her. We didn't discuss the horrifying details; Charlotte did go on to explain that the following day she sent her now-boyfriend a message asking him to come and collect her as soon as possible. Desperate to escape, she left with the clothes on her back and nothing else.

A couple of days later, she arranged to go with a friend to collect her belongings. Rob had different ideas, though, and when she arrived, she found a few items of clothing that had been thrown out of the bedroom window on to the lawn. She collected these and left with no intention of ever going back. It was sad how she lost everything precious to her, sentimental items that she had since a child, her history all gone, thanks to this monster!

It was clear that Rob would not give up so easily and resorted to stalking and making threats. Charlotte received a text describing the front of the house she was staying in and that Rob was watching her. He made threats to kill her and her family, stating that when he got hold of her, he would take his time killing her, slowly cutting her into pieces so she suffered until her last breath. Threats were also made against her new boyfriend.

Rob managed to find out that he had a daughter and threatened to blow his house up with his daughter inside.

Eventually, Charlotte contacted the police regarding the threats and was astonished that they didn't even bother to go and see him. Instead, the police spoke to him on the phone and warned him to stop the threats and leave Charlotte and her family in peace. I believe the only reason he stopped stalking Charlotte was that he was too busy manipulating his new victim. By all accounts, only a couple of weeks had passed after he and Charlotte split up before he began dating Gemma.

Charlotte's account of Rob was so vile and fit perfectly with all of the horrendous things I had found out since his death. The pieces went together like parts of a jigsaw puzzle, but the thing that didn't fit was his relationship with me.

I believe he knew from the start that, after my history with men, he wouldn't last five minutes with me if he treated me the way he had treated Charlotte. Creepily, this led him to mould himself into the man I had waited for all my life, his dark side well and truly hidden.

So much was revealed during that call that I was pretty much left speechless. Managing to gather my thoughts the best I could, I thanked Charlotte for being so honest and agreeing to talk to me. We agreed to meet in person and that I would bring with me any discs I had concerning her, including photos, letters, and bank statements.

Meeting with Charlotte was so surreal because it wouldn't have been something I could have ever imagined happening. She brought her boyfriend with her, and it was clear when we all spoke that Charlotte had been very damaged by her relationship with Rob. Just as she had on the phone, Charlotte came across as a kind, gentle and genuine lady.

It must have been strange for her hearing about how wonderful Rob had treated me as it was for me learning about how vile he had treated her. It was like discussing two completely different people.

During the conversation, I told her she could take comfort in knowing he suffered until his last breath-which was quite fitting considering that he had threatened to torture her so that she suffered until her last breath.

After an hour or so, we hugged and wished each other the best for the future. I was more grateful to her for her honesty than she will ever know. She had provided me with so much insight into my husband than I ever saw for myself during five years of being together.

When I spoke to Barbara about what I had learnt from Charlotte, she dismissed it all and reiterated that she had never liked her. I was learning fast that Barbara would try to defend the monster at any cost. The impression she gave was that she was ashamed of what she knew he had done but wanted her precious son to be remembered as the good man most people thought he was.

CHAPTER 44
Tracked

Over the next few weeks, I tried to avoid Barbara as much as possible, other than dropping food shopping around to her. I could not bear her selfishness in addition to her talking to me about Rob and how she wished he was still with us. She had been told multiple times not to discuss him with me as I was unable to speak about him nicely; therefore, it would not be beneficial to either of us.

I had agreed to collect his ashes and bring them to her because, obviously, I was not willing to have the evil bastard back in my house. I told her one morning when I dropped off her shopping that I would go and collect his ashes shortly and bring them back. She said she was feeling a little tired that day and told me to leave it until tomorrow. Angrily, I explained how tired I was due to me running around every day with things to do and that I was not prepared to come out again the next day. I told her that tomorrow I was going to have a day of rest at home so that it had to be today.

She then said to me I should collect them then but just bring them to her whenever. Furious, I struggled to get my words out without shouting as I explained that I was not happy about even having the bastard in my car for twenty minutes, let alone keeping him in my house for a few days. She looked disgusted when I told her that I would be happy to throw him in the bin if I had my way so that if she wanted them, it was today or never. She agreed with me then that I would collect them and bring them to her today, so I set off to the Funeral directors.

The girl in the Funeral directors must have been shocked by my behaviour when I arrived, but I told myself she was unaware of my circumstances, and well, I would never see her again, so why would I care what she thought. I rang the bell, and when I was invited in, I followed her, and with no emotion, I told her that I had come to collect some ashes. Thinking back now, it was quite a funny thing to have come out with. I didn't state whose ashes I had come for; it was as if I was just asking for a generic item. I must admit she did well to conceal her shock as she asked me for the name.

I gave his name, and I told her that they were my husband's without emotion in my voice. She told me that she would get them and made her way up the stairs before shortly returning carrying a navy-coloured box made of cardboard. As she handed them to me, my first thought was of how heavy the box was. I don't know what I was expecting, but I was surprised by this little box's weight. I thanked her and turned to leave, but she started to tell me about a form she had put on top if I wanted to put them in a crematorium or scatter them. I stared blankly at her, unable to disguise my disinterest in the matter before I thanked her again and left.

It was lashing down with rain at this point, and I was cursing Rob in my head. Why was I carrying him about? I was getting drenched as I walked to the other end of the street to my car. Suddenly I had an overwhelming urge just to let go of the box; I imagined his ashes vanishing into the rain and saving me the job of carrying him. A smile appeared on my face as I laughed to myself about actually doing it. The temptation was strong, and I applied great restraint by tightly holding the box and continuing to my car. Putting him in the passenger side foot-well, I felt angry that he was being driven by me, something I never imagined I would be doing again. Focusing on getting him away from me as soon as possible, I put my foot down and proceeded to Barbara's house.

When I arrived in Barbara's living room, I found her asleep, so I put her monster of a son on the nearest sideboard and turned to leave.

As I did, Barbara called my name, so, unfortunately, I had to stop and speak to her. She asked if the box was Rob - well, of course, it was, it was hardly a box of bloody chocolates, was it? I told her that I would leave the box there and that I was going home, but she started to ask questions about what she should keep him in or take him somewhere to scatter him.

Replying, I told her in no uncertain terms that he was not my concern, I didn't care or want to know what she did with him, and that I wanted to hear nothing about it again. She should just be grateful that I even bothered collecting him at all.

With that, I left her, pretty much gobsmacked, but I had no time to take into account the feelings of an evil old witch like her. I had   enough   to   deal   with   right   now.

CHAPTER 45

Being Stalked

Charlotte had divulged about Rob stalking her and always knowing where she was and how it was something that she could not explain. This made me wonder had Rob also been keeping tabs on me? If Rob was the jealous, obsessive person I now knew he was, then surely, I could not have had all the freedom that I did without him keeping an eye on me.

The first form of tracking that I found was when I was looking through his iPad and discovered that he had it set to "Find my iPhone." This was strange, as Rob never had an iPhone. It turned out to be just as I thought- it was linked to my iPhone. I immediately disconnected it and then thought that I better check my phone just in case he had done anything else. I was shocked to the core when I found something in my settings that said:"send my location." It was set to Rob's phone. Anywhere I went would alert Rob on his phone so that he would indeed be aware of my every move. It was chilling that all this time, I thought he trusted me and wasn't jealous, but he was watching my every move. All the things that he had done with my phone without my knowledge were frightening, to say the least. What if I was planning a surprise for him and lied about my whereabouts? What would he have done to me? Would I have seen the evil side that Charlotte had been so familiar with?

Since the police didn't have the power to search Rob's phone and iPad, it was left to me to investigate further. Through using passwords that he had left behind for me, I managed to hack into old email accounts, some that I knew he used to have and some that I had no idea existed.

One of the things that stood out was an email from a company called Mouse Price. Rob was being sent updates when certain houses went on the market and sold. He was getting alerts for the houses he had rented whilst he and Charlotte had been together. Chilled to my core, my mind started running and trying to think of reasons why he would want these. There was only one reason I could think of, had he left something behind in one of those houses that he did not want a new owner to dig up. A dead body, maybe? Dramatic as that sounded, knowing what I now know, I certainly believe he was capable of it.

This drew my mind back to a conversation about his SAS survival kit. He had a rucksack that he kept in the boot of his car filled with survival gear. He had collected pretty much anything you would need to survive in the great outdoors. His explanation for having this was that he could never be too prepared, and if we had to leave our home in an emergency and camp out, he made sure we would be all set. This was strange in itself, and I recall laughing at him when he told me. However, at the time, I just put it down to boys and their toys.

Now I was beginning to think this was a lot more sinister. What if he was preparing for the day he got discovered for committing a terrible crime, and he was ready to run at the drop of a hat. It didn't bear thinking about, but surely anything was possible with everything he had been doing in his secret life.

CHAPTER46
Police Outcome

When I called the police for an update, all they could tell me was that they had tried to contact Gemma's ex-husband with regards to the fraudulent loans that Rob had taken in his name. They were not going to tell Gemma about the suspicions of what Rob may have done to her daughter. The reason they gave was that they didn't have enough proof, and they couldn't go stirring up such potential, terrible trauma without evidence. They admitted that what Rob had done, taking photos of a 12-year-old girl's cleavage, was undoubtedly inappropriate and, had he been alive, they would have spoken with him about it, but it was not actually a crime.

I believed that there was more to it than this because of the text messages but, again, not enough evidence. The fact that Rob was dead meant that, although he could have potentially committed several crimes, there was nothing that could be done about any of it. All they offered me was their sympathy for everything I was going through.

When I mentioned the Mouse Price email, the detective couldn't hide his shock and asked me why he would be getting those. I linked that to a contract that he had downloaded on his phone in the Janury when he was practically on his death bed. The contract was for a contract cleaning company, what the hell did he need cleaning? He did find that extremely suspicious, but again, with Rob being dead, that was the end of it. I even joked that maybe we would talk again if any bodies showed up, to which I received an awkward giggle.

To this day, I still have my dead husband's toothbrush in a bag in my safe, for access to his DNA, just in case one day my worst fears   are   proven.

CHAPTER 47
You Tube

Although I had already established that my husband had an unhealthy interest in young girls, I struggled to process it fully.

One thing that I still hadn't checked was his browsing history on his phone and iPad. Knowing that he always deleted every message and call from his phone history, I expected the same with his browser. However, this was something that he hadn't bothered to do, possibly because I had never used his devices to access the internet.

Tears welled up in my eyes as I looked through the YouTube videos in his history. There were *Britain's Got Talent* auditions of young girls dancing in gym knickers - not something a grown man should be watching.

There were videos of cheerleader mishaps where their costumes would let them down, and people would see more than they should.

Videos about young girls who had been kidnapped and raped and showed images of the girls bound and gagged; another video was about the most beautiful children in the world.

The video was innocent, but there was no innocent reason for my husband to be interested in the little girls who were featured. Their ages ranged from approximately five to ten years old, but the most disturbing video was of a little girl aged between two and three years old in a bikini. Throughout the video, she is walking around the stables, saying hello to horses. The language was foreign, so I have no idea what was being said but literally the whole video (about four minutes long) was just of her walking around in her bikini. Sickened, I discovered that my husband had watched the entire video. There was no entertainment value to it, and my only conclusion was that he was leering at this tiny girl who was little more than a baby. I had been sharing my bed and my most intimate moments with a disgusting paedophile.

Memories of things he had said to me that seemed innocent at the time now took on a whole new meaning for me. He would often comment on how little and cute my hands were. He would often mention my little mouth and say he thought smaller mouths were much nicer to look at. The worst was when we talked about underwear as I had just bought some sexy lace knickers. He commented that he wasn't really into stuff like that and said he found nothing sexier than basic white cotton panties. Combined, these comments indicated to me that what he found attractive were things that looked childlike. There was no end to my dead husband's   deceit   and   depravity.

CHAPTER 48
Bank Statements

It emerged that when my husband passed away, not only did he have almost £40,000 in personal debts and £64,000 debt with the Inland Revenue for unpaid taxes, but he had managed to spend close to £100,000 within three years without me even knowing.

I have found where some of it went, but I will never know the true extent of what he was spending the money on. Here are some of the things I found:

- Paying car tax payments for a '54 plate car for years (probably Gemma's car)

- Over £2,500 of mortgage payments for Gemma after 2015, which is when he officially left her. He was making payments until at least 2017 when we got married and possibly longer.

- He had paid his friend £37,000 over a two-year period from his savings account. Considering the said friend did just a handful of courses for him, this proved to me that Rob must have been pretending to go to work but was, instead,sending his friend. God only knows where he had been going; I can only assume to be with another woman or women.

- There were regular payments of £200 a month that were transferred to an account named *"Kid's Money."*So, was it true that he had borrowed money from Gemma's kids to start his business?

- There were other payments to an account that just said
  "*Work*" and these were also mostly £200 a month.

A feeling of stupidity consumed me when I recalled all the
times that we had argued about money. I would always be asking
where all the money had gone as we could earn as much as £9,000
some months and, OK, we had expenses like hotels and travel, but
there was still no way we could have spent it all in a month. He
would tell me that we hardly had anything left and we needed to
stop spending so much.Then he would get angry when I would ask
him to go through the outgoings with me. He would snap at me to
grab a pen and paper and would sit reeling off figures to me and
telling me what they were for. He was apparently on his banking
app going through his statements at the time; now, I think he was
probably reading the news or on social media. He would ask me to
add it up as we went along, and he would have been making the
figures fit.

All of our income went into his account and did until the day he
died. I would be earning money, but instead of being paid, I would
have to ask for money to pay the bills or if I wanted to buy
anything. He would then transfer it to me, which would be
annoying at times, but the way it was done, I had never considered
it to be controlling. Now and then, he would transfer a large
amount to me and tell me to just use it as I needed, but then, every
day, he would ask what the balance was, and I would find myself
explaining what I had spent. After a few days, he would ask me to
transfer back whatever I had so that he could keep all the money
together and keep a check on what we had to make sure everything
was covered.

Looking back, I can't believe I went along with it for so many
years. I had always been independent and to become so dependent
on someoneelse was not the norm for me. Yet unquestioningly, I
accepted it. The level of trust I had for that man is one I never had
for any other man, and yet he was the most untrustworthy person
that has ever entered my life

Rob would control all of the finances, and he would just tell me
what money had come in and what he had paid out. He would
often tell me that people had paid late, and when I wanted to chase
them up, he would get angry and tell me that you do not behave
like that in business and that you gave good customers a long time

before doing so. I have since discovered that the late payers were never late, so my husband must have constantly been juggling figures to balance with what I expected us to have coming in. He even went as far as to tell me that one customer's husband had gone into a hospice and that was why we hadn't received payment and obviously, under the circumstances, we couldn't chase payment. This, too, was revealed to be a lie. This particular client had never paid late; in fact, she always paid the day after a course had been delivered. Furthermore, this particular client was someone who I needed to speak with as she was Gemma's boss, and I wanted to know how Rob had first become her trainer. This was how he got his reputation to obtain some very good clients with   large   contracts.

CHAPTER 49
Reputation Building

Calling Teresa was not an easy thing for me to do as I had only met her when Rob was ill and I was delivering a course at her agency. Due to Gemma's history, Teresa had spoken to Rob and asked that, if she made sure Gemma was out of the way, would I agree to go and deliver a course there? I agreed, and after the course, Teresa and I had a bit of a heart to heart about Rob and his illness.

When Rob had passed away, I had contacted her and let her know about the funeral arrangements. I was now going to call her and tell her that the man she had known for many years was, in fact, a fraud and a monster, and I was going to ask her what she knew when she took him on.

I can't recall how I started the conversation, but I was soon asking her if Rob had told her he had been a mental health nurse, and she confirmed that he was. However, she said that he had started out working for her as an agency worker because Gemma worked there. She said although he was a nurse, he had only worked for her as a support worker. She was shocked when I told her that he had never been a nurse, and she asked me if I was sure as she had always believed he was.

I asked her about his DBS check, as the one I found had criminal convictions on it. Teresa explained that his DBS had been clear but that it was strange because she had never seen a DBS like his before or ever again since. This led me to believe that he had supplied a fake one somehow and that maybe Gemma had assisted by saying that it had been received through the post.

I had to ask Teresa why had she taken on Gemma, who had been to prison for fraud, and then her partner, who now was proven to be a fraud. Teresa paused in shock before asking me about Gemma going to prison. Teresa said she knew that Gemma had a few problems and had discussed some of them with her but hadn't been told she had gone to prison and didn't know any important details. It was difficult to believe as you only have to google Gemma's name and you get the whole sordid story. However, Teresa did appear to be genuinely out of the loop.

When I mentioned the testimonial that her company had done for Rob, which resulted in him securing contracts with other clients, she appeared not to know anything about it. Was this something Gemma had done without the knowledge of her boss?

Teresa explained how nice and charming Rob had been and that she used to nickname him *Mr Cool*. She had never met anyone so calm, someone who never appeared to stress about anything.

However, she said that Gemma told her he had left her in a lot of debt, but that was none of her business, and she didn't get involved.

I ended the call, leaving Teresa understandably speechless and asked that she pass my number to Gemma as I wanted to speak to her about things that involved her children.

I also sent Gemma a Facebook message, but to this day, she has never contacted me. Is this because she wants to leave Rob in the past nowt hat she has moved on, or could it be that she knew more than me? Could she have been assisting him with the fraud against her ex-husband? I don't think I will ever get an answer to that one.

CHAPTER50
A real mental health nurse

Thankfully in life, I believe that sometimes Angels come into your life disguised as humans at precisely the right time and for exactly the right reason, and that is what happened with my friend Jaxon.

I was delivering a course a few weeks after my husband had been diagnosed with terminal cancer. The class should have had eight people attending, but only one person had shown up on this particular day. This was the first time it had ever happened, and I just sat making conversation with the one lady who had attended when there was a knock at the door. One of the consultants asked if they could put a nurse called Jaxon onto the course. Of course, I invited him in, and now the three of us were laughing at how small the class was.

Jaxon and I instantly connected. He had a genuine sorrow for what I was going through and offered to stay in touch with me and send me any helpful information he could find regarding helping my husband beat the unbeatable.

At that stage, I remained optimistic that we could save him; looking back, it was probably denial, but it was all I could do to keep myself going.

Over the months, we exchanged many messages regarding my husband's health, and then I let Jaxon know when Rob had passed away. After discovering all the horrors relating to my husband, I contacted Jaxon and asked him if he would come over for a chat.

I told him absolutely everything that I had found out, showed him the weird manuals and codes, showed him photos of the weapons and the police IDs. I went deeper into it by telling him about things that I had found suspicious in the past and about me going to CBT due to my "paranoia." Even things Rob had said in passing that did not seem peculiar at the time maybe had some significance now.

Rob and I used to watch *Breaking Bad*, and he would defend Walter White's actions for lying to his wife, saying she was an "ungrateful bitch" and that he had done it all to make money for her. We used to watch a program called *Evil Lives Here*, and at the beginning of the program, it would say, "there were signs." My husband would repeat it in a mock creepy voice and laugh. He had also said that he did not understand how people could live with someone for so many years and not know they were a psychopath, and surely their mask would slip. He even went as far as to say that I was safe in the knowledge that he wasn't a psycho as I would have known by now. The only relationships he ever experienced had been long term, and none of them ever said a bad word against him. After all, they did live locally, so I'd think that something would have gotten back to me by now.

Saying that after he died, I had reactivated my Facebook page, and when I looked in my blocked lists, there were so many names of people that I had never heard of, which made me think he was concerned about people he was involved with contacting me.

My Facebook was just another part of my technology that Rob had managed to hack and control. Something else that I had never batted an eye at was when we were watching *Dexter* about the serial killer; my husband commented that he liked his dress sense. As he had lost so much weight, we did have to keep ordering new clothes for him. He managed to find a shirt just like the one Dexter wore and some beige chinos and he stated he already had similar trainers so that he would have the full look. He never even tried them on when they arrived, as he barely left the bed and lived in his pyjamas unless we had a trip to the QE hospital.

Scenarios like these as isolated incidents are not suspicious, especially when you think that you have the most wonderful husband, but put into context of who he was, these become troubling, to say the least.

After what was actually hours of going through all the information with my friend Jaxon, he asked me why I thought my husband behaved in the manner he did. Something I had done a lot over the last few weeks was research about personality disorders, something both of my GPs had mentioned when I discussed some of my findings with them. Answering my friend, I told him I was unsure whether Rob had been a psychopath or a sociopath, and he nodded, saying that I was almost right. In fact, he believes that my husband had a cluster personality disorder and was a psychopath, sociopath, and narcissist rolled into one. Jaxon had worked at Ashworth with severely mentally ill criminals and explained that he had worked with a few people with this disorder and that they are the most dangerous people you could ever meet, with 99% of them having committed murder.

Hairs stood up on the back of my neck as cold chills ran down my spine whilst I listened to Jaxon explain that he believed I was lucky to be alive and had I kept prodding Rob about things had he not been diagnosed as terminal, I would probably now be dead. His words were, "Julia, you've been living in a shark tank for five years without knowing when he could strike."

The gravity of the situation was beginning to sink in. Having no emotion about my husband's death was apparently good as I had detached to protect myself. Jaxon explained that what I should be feeling is gratitude, and I should be grateful to have escaped such evil clutches. Hence, I was no longer the grieving widow but instead the grateful widow.

Jaxon made sense of many of my husband's behaviours, which helped me feel less stupid. In the hands of a master manipulator, you cannot feel bad that you got tricked or caught out. It is like a full-time profession to them; after all, my husband had gone as far as to accumulate information and collate it into his very own manual. Psychopaths have no real feelings; therefore, they often mirror the other person's emotions.

CHAPTER 51
Coming to Terms

In the months since Rob died, I was consumed with investigating the man I knew as my husband but never really knew him at all. To try to deal with the grief that has been so tarnished with evil is nigh on impossible.

Acceptance that I will never know the full extent of my husband's secret life is something that I hope will come. Fortunately for me, the numbness acts as some protection emotionally, but, unfortunately, that is a double-edged sword. I genuinely feel emotionless in my day-to-day life, and when bad things happen, I automatically detach as I know that it could be the end for me if I try to deal with anymore heartache.

I feel nothing most of the time, making me feel like I am no longer human. That maybe he has turned me into a psychopath with no real emotions. It has been over a year since he died, and the numbness and emotionless sensations are showing no signs of leaving me, so I live a robotic life. I work to pay the bills, wear a smile all day which exhausts me, and then head back to the safety of my lonely life.

The only time I feel relaxed and moderately happy is when I am home with my dog. I am not interested in doing anything else with my life and wish that I could stay home all day, every day with my dog. Real-life is something that I don't want to deal with, as the energy it takes is more than I can handle.

My family and friends joke with me about how antisocial I have become, but the reality is that this is how I want to be. I have not and cannot deal with anything that has happened, and I just want to stay home and forget that the rest of the world exists. He died on the 10th April 2019, and by July 2019, I had to get a job and start working to pay my bills because I had been left with nothing when he died. He had spent everything that I had worked so hard to build up.

The business had to be closed due to his gigantic tax bill, and I was forced back into the rat race to earn a living.

Although some friends and family knew what the real truth was, many others did not and to hear how sorry they all were and how sad it was that my husband died made me want to scream.

The thought of the people who didn't know the truth judging me was also tough as it was always in the back of my mind that they were wondering if I should look sadder, look at me going on holiday and her husband just died. It was sad enough becoming a widow at 38 but to add all of this to the mix was enough to send someone over the edge.

Friends who know the truth have often told me how strong they think I am and that if this had happened to them, they would have had a full-on breakdown. I still worry that mine is to come if this numbness ever wears off; when I spoke to the GP, he was at a loss what to suggest as the situation was just so unique.

Bereavement counselling wouldn't be any good as why would I want to grieve for this monster? I am looking into possibly getting trauma counselling; if this hasn't been traumatic, I don't know what is.

People say that writing the book will help as it is cathartic, but I just find it incredibly draining, and it doesn't make me feel any less numb.

My friend Jaxon, the mental health nurse, explainedthat I was showing signs of human hibernation. You feel OK in the safety of your home, but you feel anxiety if you have to leave the house for any reason. Once you're back in the safety of your own home, you begin to relax again. This was definitely how I felt and still feel over a year later. I am happy living in my reality but having to engage in real life makes me anxious.

Apparently, we have two parts to our brain, the human aspect and the monkey aspect. My friend drew me diagrams and explained the difference between the monkey making decisions and the human. The monkey does not care about what is good for you in a logical way but instead only cares about the natural instincts of keeping you safe and well-fed. The human side of things is about what is best for your future.

We have a computer in our mind which is full of files made up of useful information and memories. It is good to access information that we need for day-to-day life. Unfortunately, our brain's monkey side is not rational, and if it finds a bad memory, it will catastrophise and encourage us not to do something.

Going through such unspeakable trauma for me meant that the monkey took over, and I allowed it to so because all I wanted to do was stay home in the safety of my bubble and protect myself.

Difficult as it is, I am trying to overcome the monkey's urge to give up on life and stay home. However, if I could afford to pay my bills, with the way I feel, I would stay home, close the door on the world, and never venture out again.

I am much like a functioning alcoholic but instead a functioning severely depressed person. Not that I wasn't almost an alcoholic after drinking every night from the day Rob was diagnosed with cancer until around May 2020. I would never get drunk but would have to have at least two drinks a night. I felt like I deserved them, and if I could get myself through a whole day, then I deserved them. I would say, "Well done,Julia; you made it through another day; you're still alive."

Something that did consume me was that Rob hadn't been the first bad man in my life, as I have already explained. He was one of many in a long line; he was even worse than my daughter's father, yet he seemed like the total opposite. The creepy thing was my husband knew my history with men, and he knew that I had learnt from some of my mistakes; therefore, Icould and would be able to see the signs and not be accepting of the same behaviour again.

This made his job easy; he could morph into my dream man, concealing any of those tell-tale signs I had seen in the past. Warning signs which should have been clear were just not there. My friend Jaxon was the first person ever to help me understand my relationship history with toxic men. According to Jaxon, most people have sensors and alerts that should go off when they encounter dangerous people, such as psychopaths. Something doesn't feel right and they don't feel safe in their company or comfortable with their behaviour or what they may be saying.

In my case, I was immune to these feelings of concern, not because I am stupid and don't notice anything, because I did question many things throughout our relationship. It was because I had been comfortable in the company of psychopaths since being a baby that I was immune to their odd behaviour.

I believe that my father, who I won't go into detail about as that's a whole other book, is also a psychopath and pathological liar. From birth to the age of four, I lived with this man, and then I saw him every weekend until I was around 15 years of age. The first few years of a child's life are so important, as this is where they absorb so many things which mould them for life.

In my situation, I was raised around a psychopath and was witness to many odd behaviours that, over the years, became normalised behaviours to me. Shocking behaviour was not shocking to me. Normal to a young child is what they see and hear in their environment as it is the only thing they know at that time.

Relief was certainly something I experienced when discussing this with my friend Jaxon because, finally, after all these years, there was a reason for why I was attracted to men like this and why they were able to attach themselves to my life so easily.

It was a shame that it took such an extreme situation before I found these answers. Nevertheless, it was empowering to know why I was caught in a cycle of meeting and forming relationships with such evil men.

I will need to engage in a lot of personal work before I believe that I can trust my judgement ever again. My friend will spend time teaching me how to install those warning signals that most people have instilled from being a young child.

Although it is important to do that, it is not at the top of my priority list. Staying alive and keeping a roof over my head are basics necessities that currently drain my energy to the point that it is all I am capable of.

Besides, the thought of ever being with another person does not even enter my head. People say that this will change in time, yet I don't want it to,to be honest.

My experience has proven to me that I do not need someone else in my life to be happy. I am almost 41 years old now, and all I had ever wanted was a husband and family. Now that I have had that, albeit not a normal one, I know it isn't the be-all and end-all to life.

If I can continue to be strong and maybe do some good in this world by helping others escape abuse, I will be happy. Some people maybe like me, not realising that they are in an abusive relationship. Abuse comes in all shapes and sizes, and each aspect is wrapped in different paper.

Controlling and coercive behaviour and gaslighting were things that I was subjected to daily whilst thinking that I was living the life of a princess. Only now do I look back and realise that I had no finances of my own and had to ask for every penny (from money that I had earned). I was not paranoid and damaged by asking legitimate questions.

Anything that I had felt suspicious about was proven to be correct. How could someone make me believe otherwise if I am so intelligent? Easy, I am a normal human being, and I was playing a game against a master manipulator, who was highly intelligent, with no emotions, no guilt. I was no match for someone like that. Who would be? Yes, there had been signs that some things were not right, but his skills, added to me being comfortable in the company of psychopaths, enabled him to reel me into his twisted life.

The scariest part is that if I had done one thing differently, the day that I met my husband, then there is a strong possibility I would not be in a position to write this story. Jaxon, the mental health nurse, believes that if the day I met my husband, I had shown an interest in him, then I would never have heard from him again. It really could have been that simple.

Jaxon asked me if I had even fancied my husband when I first met him, and I had never really thought about it before, but the answer was no. I actually didn't think much of him at all. I was asked how my husband looked at me that day, and I answered that he had looked at me as though he had fallen in love with me at first sight. This was a standing joke I had before we even got together as I always knew that we would be together from the way he had looked at me that first day.

According to Jaxon, this would have been a look of obsession. It would have been a challenge for him as I had paid him no attention. This obsession led him to do what is called "love bombing", where someone is over the top to gain your affection. Certainly true with my husband, the number of calls and texts were ridiculous, but I saw it as romantic at the time. The fact existed that there could be twenty or so kisses at the end of every message. The early morning surprises, turning up at my door at 7am before I went to work, just to make me coffee and to share a few precious minutes with me. These were ulterior motives to check if I had another man in my house, yet that never crossed my mind.

Before I knew it, I was head over heels in love; everything about him was perfect, including his looks that I had never noticed before. I had never felt this way in my life, and it was a glorious feeling, like walking on sunshine. Jaxon explained to me how love bombing works, and it definitely fit the profile of my husband.

The person goes all out, showering you with affection, but after a while, they start to lose interest and often become cruel. When the victim begins to pull away from the person, they apologise, make excuses for being distant and step up the love-bombing once again. It's rather like a cat and mouse game, and we know that there is only one winner in that game.

For all the pain I have endured and am still trying to deal with even now, I have learnt a lesson first hand that not many people live to learn.

I have seen evil up close and have come out with invaluable knowledge that I hope to use to enrich others. I believe that there is a reason I met my husband, that he died, and that I survived. Fate put me on this path because, although I have often doubted my strength, I believe that I am strong enough to keep fighting, tell my story, and help others, maybe even save lives.

I imagine some single people could read this book and then possibly go onto meet a psychopath. Hopefully, my warnings will go off like an alert and pull them away from that person.

Maybe someone reading is feeling self-realisation of the situation they are in and will find the strength to free themselves, or some may be feeling recognition and solidarity if they too have been through similar trauma.

Everything for a reason and a reason for everything.

CHAPTER 52
Still Around?

I mentioned earlier that I have always believed in the afterlife, and call me crazy if you like, but the things I am going to tell you happened; some have witnesses, some are without.

A few days after Rob passed away, I was lying in bed when I heard a thud. Not sure where it came from, I froze for a few seconds then said out loud, "Rob, if that's you, do something else."

Almost instantly, the TV turned itself off. I loved and missed my husband so much that this was such a comfort to me; I liked to think that he was close by and still with me, watching over and taking care of me. However, this was no longer the case when I started to discover who he really had been.

When Rob had been ill, he had an illness smell to him. So difficult to describe, but I call it the cancer smell, just a smell of being unwell. This smell started to reappear when I was up in the middle of the night looking into more things. It would appear and follow me from room to room, or sometimes when I would be texting his friend saying negative things about him, I would feel that someone was looking over my shoulder and then the smell would appear.

Some nights, the dog would jump up, ears perked with a look of fear on his face, eyes wide looking behind me or up at the ceiling. His eyes would follow something (invisible to me) around the ceiling, just like Rob's eyes had done on the day he passed away.

THE ~~GRIEVING~~ GRATEFUL WIDOW

One day, I left the house to pick up my Mum as she was coming to stay with me as support. My front door was playing up, so I was using the back door, which is closest to my bedroom. I had Alfie on the lead, and just as we were about to leave, I realised that I had left the TV on in my bedroom. Letting go of Alfie, I went back to my bedroom, switched it off, and away we went.

Upon returning with my Mum, I opened the back door to enter the house, and we could hear music blaring from my bedroom. Shocked, I ran in to find my TV, not only on but changed to the music channel. My Mum thought maybe I had just left it on, but I explained that I had purposefully stopped in my tracks to go in and turn it off. Her face dropped.

That night my Mum got an experience of her own. I had left her in the living room, which is only next door to my bedroom and gone to bed. Less than five minutes later, I heard a large bang and then my Mum shouting my name

I leapt out of bed in fright, dashed into the living room to see what all the commotion was about. My Mum was sitting on the sofa, white as a ghost. She explained how one of the photo frames on the wall behind her had just fallen off the wall. It hadn't even fallen forward as you would have expected; it dropped straight down behind the sofa. When I picked it up, I found the frame was damaged and that all of the photos had become dislodged.

The next day when I had walked into the living room, the lights on the TV stand lit up. This can't happen without using the TV remote and turning the TV on.

When I got home from work that evening, my Mum told me that she had heard an alarm going off during the day and found it was the timer on the cooker. The timer hadn't been used for months, and to set it, you have to go through pressing lots of buttons. I didn't know how to explain it.

There were other times when Alfie was stood at the gate, tail wagging at something or someone who, again, we couldn't see.

One night I was in the bath when suddenly I heard the television come on, but it was making that hissing noise like it wasn't tuned into a channel. It was so loud that I couldn't ignore it.

At first, I thought that the dog must have sat on the remote, but Alfie was asleep on the sofa and the remote was on the fireplace when I checked the living room.

As I checked my bedroom, the noise stopped. I walked in, and again there was no television on in there either.

Another night, I sat in bed watching TV when I heard a tap running loudly, so I got up, checked the bathroom and kitchen to find nothing, and then the sound stopped. This happened another five or six times before I got annoyed and said, "if this is you, you can stop it. I'm not playing along with you, so fuck off!" It happened once more, I ignored it and then it stopped altogether.

In June, I had planned a short getaway to Spain with my cousin and was ironing my last few things for my case when I suddenly got a fright. For some unknown reason, my phone started playing a song from my library from across the room. The song it was playing was called *Not Too Late* and was the theme tune of a programme Rob and I used to watch together.

The last creepy thing to happen in the house was when I talked to my friend on the phone. She lives in Leicester, and I was in Birmingham. I was reading our angel cards on the phone and *had* asked them out loud, "Is Rob still haunting me?" As soon as I finished the question, two things happened, my lamp started going dim and then bright, dim then bright whilst my friend was shouting about her lamp doing the same. Although nothing much freaks me out, that did as we both called it at the same time.

It happened another two times during the call, and on both occasions, we were shouting at the same time.

A few weeks after my visit to the clairvoyant, my husband finally seemed to get the message that he would not be forgiven this time.

CHAPTER 53
The Clairvoyant

I have been to the clairvoyant several times over a twenty-year period, but this was the most anticipated meeting of my life.

I had read up about how long you should wait before seeing a psychic when someone had passed away and the general consensus appeared to be three months. I patiently waited before making my appointment, and I managed to get an appointment for 29th July 2019 for my friend and me.

Some people don't believe in psychics and their abilities, but it is one of those things where seeing is believing. Just to note that I was not on Facebook at the time, and other than people connected closely with me, not many people even knew that my husband had passed away.

My friend decided that I should go first, so I followed Amelia into the kitchen whilst my friend waited in the lounge. Once we had settled down in our chairs, I had held the crystal ball for a few minutes (something you are asked to do when you arrive).

Leaving my friend in the waiting area, Amelia then took me through to a small room and placed the crystal ball on the table. There were lots of candles burning, filling the air with fragrance. The room was small and dimly lit, but it felt comfortable. Amelia indicated I should take a seat, and we sat down opposite each other with the crystal ball on its stand in between us.

I waited as Amelia made herself comfortable and found her connection with the other side. Her bracelets chinked as she moved her hands, placing them on either side of the crystal ball. She closed her eyes.

Amelia began to talk as I listened intently.

"The first thing is that you have a man standing at the side of you, and I feel like he has been on edge for a few months. Who has passed away in the last year?" she asked.

"My husband passed away this year," I replied, watching the

flame flicker on the candle.

Amelia looked thoughtful. "OK," she said. "He's on edge with you because you've been stressing too much. OK? Now was this a quick passing?"

"Not really." I placed my hands under the table so she couldn't see I was nervous.

"Was he ill?" she asked.

"Yeah, for a short time.," was my reply.

"I'm still getting that he had passed away last year..." Amelia sounded puzzled.

"He started being ill last year."

"I think that he'd got it sorted in his head," she looked at me. "He knew the outcome and was under no illusion that he was going to survive, and he'd come to terms with a lot of stuff. Did he leave you letters to find?" Again, the sudden subject change.

"He was supposed to have, but I've not found any."

"He has left you some letters, and they will be in the stupidest of places – right under your nose." Again, she stared into the distance. "But I don't think he wanted you to find them straight away. He wanted to have time pass so that you had time to grieve. Did he pass in March?"

"April."

"And whose birthday was it in March or April? A child maybe?"

I frowned as I tried to remember. "I don't know," I finally admitted.

"Never mind," she answered. "So, who is the one who had the problem with their head? I sense crippling headaches, with flashing lights."

"That would be me," I wondered how she knew. "I have migraines."

"Do you see him when you have them? In the flashing lights?"

"I don't want to see him."

"Why not?" Now she sounded surprised.

"I've found out a lot of bad things about him."

"Can you give him the benefit of the doubt, he's not here to defend himself now is he?"

"I've got proof," I answered. "I don't need his answers."

"I don't want to darken his image, when he is coming through as a good man who has made mistakes along the way."

I thought that was a strange thing to say.

"…I like him."

"He's a psychopath, which is why everyone likes him." I didn't feel that he deserved to be liked.

"Is that what it is as he is coming across really charming.He did love you."Again, she looked thoughtful. "He's sorry for a lot of things but the letters – there are three - will explain."

"Do you have something to do with your daughter?"

"Not really."

"He's saying he's sorry." Amelia continued. "You need to find the letters."

"I found an envelope with my name on it, but it was empty," I told her.

"He has definitely written them."

"Have you checked the car?"

"Could your daughter have found one of the letters?"

I frowned. "I don't know how she'd find one."

"He's got himself into a real pickle, a real state."

"He had his own business didn't he?" Her face thoughtful now. "One where he was able to make his own choices?"

"Yes."

"What happened to it?"

"I had to close it."

"Why? It was a nice little money earner, wasn't it?"

"It was, but he didn't put things in place, and I had to redo all my qualifications."

"Did you leave ashes at the funeral parlour?"

"They're with his mum," I smiled, thinking that I was getting used to these sudden subject changes.

Amelia nodded. "She didn't know anything about this, did she?"

"She knows a lot more than she's telling." I still didn't like the woman. "She knows a lot of terrible things about him, but she's really a nasty woman."

"He's mega sorry," Amelia repeated. "Now I've got a Louise around you."

"Could be my sister-in-law."

Amelia nodded. "Has she stood by your daughter and her friend?"

"Yes."

"That's good. Have you taken a sideways step with work?"

"I'm doing what I did before but for someone else."

Amelia smiled. "It will get your confidence back, and you can change later. It's good that the people also seem really nice."

At least that part was true.

Amelia's eyes looked dark as she explained that she was now seeing visions of my husband before asking me if he was involved with a girl called Carla. I gulped as she proceded to tell me that she knew that Carla had a baby boy, however the next question stunned me.

"Is he the father of that baby?"

I explained that my husband was unable to father children but that when I had seen Carla and her partner for a moment with the baby during a trip to Tesco, it was plain as day that the child belonged to Carla's partner, he was like a carbon copy of him. Feeling relieved that I had seen that for myself, I sat expectantly awaiting the next revelation.

"If I knew he was around small children, I would notify the authorites, he couldn't be trusted" Her face saddened now.

"Why do I feel that my throat is being …" she paused, frowning and to my horror started moving her hand across her throat in a cutting motion. "Why am I feeling this?" She looked concerned. "And what's going on with the head and neck?"

"After he died, I found that he had been watching videos of people being beheaded. I have had nightmatres about them ever since." I replied, attempting to speak clearly without shaking.

"Is that what you're trying to do with me. You can piss off! Get out of here and do not come back, you are not welcome!" She was shouting now as I sat quietly trying to process what was happening.

I continued. "Rob had a thing about strangling people and stabbing people, and he put a knife to my throat."

"OMG, did he?" She was horrified.

"Terrifying," Amelia actually shivered.

"I'm not frightened of him."

"He keeps saying he's sorry."

Oddly enough, I didn't care.

"I feel cross and angry with him," Amelia told me, "mostly for pretending to be nice."

"Yes, because when I last saw you, you thought he was all lovely and nice, and you were saying he was like out of the movies, like an actor, but he's fooled everyone."

"He is like an actor," she put her hands on the table. "A man who is playing lots of different roles."

I didn't say anything.

"Has he got a younger sister?"

"I don't think so."

"There is someone around him."

"He's been messing with everyone, including his ex's daughter..."

"Have you been in touch with her?"

"I've messaged her, but she's not been in touch."

"She will when she's ready."

It was up to her, and I had already made the first move.

"You need to write everything down," Amelia said suddenly. "You need to get your story out there."

"That's what I'm doing."

"Who is helping you with that? Who is encouraging you, pushing you to do it?"

"I've got a couple of friends who are helping."

"When you've written it all down. And you get someone to proofread it and publish it. You'll find a weight lifted off your shoulders."

I believed that.

"So, how close are you to doing that?"

"Probably by the end of the year," I told Amelia. "I've made a start, but it's such a big story; it's going to take some time."

She nodded. "Were you with Rob for nearly ten years?"

"I knew him for ten, but we were together for five."

"Oh, right, so why am I getting ten?" A frown crossed Amelia's face.

"Possibly because I knew him for ten years, but I think he had been stalking me before we got together."

"I would say so because he knew a lot about you. He was a dangerous man."

"Someone was watching over you," She looked me in the eye. "He wasn't going to get away with it."

I nodded again.

"But I do know that you need to find those notes."

"I have cleared tons of stuff out but haven't found them."

"Have you still got stuff of his?"

"Not much. I've got rid of most of his things."

"Check everything. Find these notes. You need to know what's in them. You definitely still have them"

Again, a tilt of the head. "He knew he was dying, so why was he so calm about it?"

"I think he knew his time was up because all the stuff was coming to catch him up."

"I hope you weren't with him when he died," Amelia remarked.

"I was."

"He didn't deserve that. How come you were there?"

"He came home to die. That's what his wish was. He was in the hospital. I had nursed him all through his illness, and when he was dying, he wanted to come home. He didn't know he was dying at that point as he was so out of it."

"Did he die at home then?"

"In my bed."

"Get rid of the bed!"

"It's too expensive to buy a new mattress." I had thought of it, but I just didn't have the money.

"I don't want you to have it. Get rid of it and any photographs. He doesn't deserve anyone's sympathy."

"I took it all to the tip, even the wedding photos."

"I bet you had a lovely wedding."

"Hmm."

"And you looked beautiful." There was another pause. "It's time for you to have someone nice around, you know. Time to have some fun."

"It's hard," I told Amelia. "Literally everything he has ever told me has been a lie. There's no truth in any of it."

"How awful for you."

I continued, "He had even convinced everyone that he was a mental health nurse."

"And that was a lie?"

I nodded.

"There is a film in this!" Amelia looked over her shoulder.

"I've been told that," I replied, thinking of the people who had said similar things to me. It was hard to believe that my story was interesting enough to be a film.

Amelia turned the crystal ball. "Did you get some money when he died?"

I shook my head. "He left nothing but debt - £100,000 worth of debt."

"He really was a nasty man, wasn't he?"

"Can I ask you a question?" This was something that I wanted to know, something that kept me awake at night.

Amelia nodded.

"Who came for him? Who came for Rob when he died?"

"Well, I don't really believe in heaven or hell," she ran her fingers over the crystal ball, "but…"

"He could see someone on the ceiling," I explained. "And my dog kept looking around the room, but there wasn't anyone there. And when the nurse came round, Rob told her there was a man under the stool where she was sitting."

"I need to ask you if he had a drug dealer friend?"

I pulled a face. "I don't know."

"This man is a dealer; it isn't nice stuff. It's bad stuff." She closed her eyes. "It's not necessarily drugs. I am seeing trafficking, maybe even children, It could be something else. I feel as though he owed someone personally money…"

"I don't know I repeated."

"I can tell you he didn't want to go with this man, whoever it was."

Oddly, I felt pleased.

"Rob said to one of his friends, the day before he died, who was that? Do you know that man? The one who walked out of the room."

"He never said anything to me."

"It was someone he didn't want to go with. Someone who was waiting for him."

"He wouldn't go for ages. He was terrified and making all these horrible noises…" I remembered.

"Tough luck," Amelia said. "It was someone like the Grim Reaper or someone he owed something to."

"Good." I knew I sounded nasty, but I didn't care.

"And get rid of the bed. Please." Amelia circled back to the bed. "Everything of his has to go. Get rid of his essence. Wipe him out and try not to think of him. I know that's going to be difficult as you're doing a book, but he doesn't deserve you thinking about him."

Amelia was right. He didn't deserve that.

THE ~~GRIEVING~~ GRATEFUL WIDOW

CHAPTER 54
The Final Chapter

After months of being numb and putting on an act for the world, I had reached a breaking point. I had to accept that there was no way all of these things can happen to one person, and I just had to numb it out and continue with life.

The numbing was the easy part as I didn't even have to try. My brain realised that what had happened could easily kill me, so it did its job well and protected me by blocking out any emotion associated with these events.

Since April 2019, I had felt like Rob had never existed on this earth. I never knew him, he did not live in this house, and I was never married. I became detached from the entire series of events and felt like I have been told a crazy story about a man called Rob. I am just writing what I'd been told.

Everyone who knows the truth tells me that I am so strong and to keep going, but the truth is, strength wouldn't get me through. Numbness and an ability to act is why I was still here. The only way to explain my life right then is that I feel like I died in April 2019.

Julia is no longer here; however, her body existed, and someone else stepped into her body and kept it alive. They look like Julia, they sound like Julia and even make the same jokes as Julia, but it isn't really Julia.

Had my husband turned me into a psychopath? I walked around all day on autopilot with no real feelings and pretending to be happy and coping with life, but I felt nothing except exhaustion. Every day, Pretending took every bit of energy that I had to a point where there was nothing left after a day at work.

It is shocking for someone who was such a social animal to see that I have turned into a complete recluse—not even wanting to see friends or family because even with them, a switch flicks in my brain, and the act is on again.

Receiving a text message frustrates me. *"Hi, Julia how are you? How is your week going?"* I feel like screaming. I can lie and say *all is ok* or tell the truth, but do I want to text people every week telling them how bad I feel? No! Who would?

I have fallen into a dark depression where even wanting to get better is tiring. My only salvation, the only way to keep myself safe, is being in my bubble. Just me and my dog, locking out the world.

I don't want to bother the world, and I don't want it to bother me. People who advised me to get out more, go to work and be around people all thought they were helping, but until you have been to such depths of despair and have lost everything, including your mind, they simply cannot understand. Forcing myself to put on an act and be around people and go to work was physically and mentally killing me.

After almost 18 months of doing it, I was ready to kill myself. I could see no point in an artificial life that I indulged myself in to pay the bills. If I were dead, then there would be no bills, no people, no numbness, no nothing. The only comfort in life is being with my dog, who is a real angel without wings. Sitting with him, losing myself in mindless television, is the only time I didn't have to pretend. I can just be.

Can this go on forever? Of course not, but it was the one thing keeping me alive right now and to be forced out of it would be like stopping someone's life-saving medication.

THE ~~GRIEVING~~ GRATEFUL WIDOW

Lockdown was a blessing for me as it gave me three and a half months to stay home with my dog and relax. I enjoyed being alone and not seeing anyone; it was what I needed at the time. Going back to work after the lockdown was the beginning of my unravelling as I had to put on the pretence again and this time, I just wasn't capable of keeping it going.

About three weeks ago, I had a meltdown at work, and I don't know what caused it other than a build-up of the pretence. I began to cry (not something I have done much of this past 18 months) and couldn't stop. I wanted to die, and that was that.

After listening to a work friend, I went home, rang the GP, who directed me to my local mental health crisis Team and told them how I felt. I struggled but continued to work whilst I waited the two weeks for my initial assessment.

That day was such a turning point for me. At first, when the nurse read the notes for the call I had made two weeks earlier, she had wondered if I was psychotic and that my mind had fabricated what I had been saying. However, after reading my medical notes and seeing me face to face and speaking with me, she realised that it was all real and was astonished by what had happened to me. She listened to how I felt, and when she agreed, I needed to be in my safety bubble with my dog to keep me safe for now. It was such a relief.

Finally, someone understood that surrounding myself with people was, in fact, the worst thing for me; it was killing me. I felt vindicated, and finally, I was going to get the real help that I needed.

I have just started taking anti-depressants and a tablet to help me sleep, which is already helping me get a night of restful sleep and help with my mood as I'm not constantly exhausted.

THE ~~GRIEVING~~ GRATEFUL WIDOW

When I look back at all the things I have done in 18 months and what I have "achieved" it feels unreal. There were red flags with my behaviour, and now that I've accepted what the doctors and nurses have told me, I am "very unwell"; I can now recognise them.

Somehow, I had started a full-time job three months after my husband's death, undertook and passed three new qualifications by studying after work. How my brain got through all that when it was not firing on all cylinders still surprises me even now.

In October 2019, I decided that I would go away to Turkey by myself, which concerned my family and friends. When asked if it was a safe thing to do, my answer had been, *"probably not, but what's the worst that can happen? I might get murdered, but so what? If I get murdered, I won't be here to complain about it."* I had and at the moment still don't have any real sense of consequences and am told that this makes me vulnerable, but when you have no value for your life, you really don't care.

Returning from Turkey, I got a taxi to collect my car from my cousin's house and making my way along the M56 at around 3:30am. I was in the fast lane doing 70mph when a black, small, SUV type car swerved into my lane in front of me. I sounded the horn in disbelief at what they had done, and they thankfully got back in the middle lane.

I decided there and then that there was something wrong with this person and the best thing was just over to take them and get away from them. As I was by the side of them getting ready to overtake, the car started coming towards me into my lane alongside me.

Everything happened so fast; I don't know if they clipped me or I moved to avoid being hit. Still, the next thing my car scraped the central reservation, turning the wheel to the left backfired, and the car started to spin in the lane before heading at high speed towards the central reservation. I don't know if I shouted out loud or just said it in my head. "You're dead!"

The next thing I knew, the airbags were up, and smoke was entering the front of my vehicle, beginning to choke me. My first thought was that I would need a cigarette, so I grabbed my handbag and sort of stumbled out of the car to find myself at 3:30am standing in the middle of the fast lane of the M56. It was 4°, and I was wearing a little summer dress covering my lovely new tan.

An ambulance had its lights on and was slowing down in front of me as I just stood there, confused. I looked for the other car, but the bastard that had caused the crash had continued on his way without a care in the world.

The driver got out of the ambulance and explained that he was a private ambulance and that he would leave it there with its lights on to avoid another crash. He took my arm and crossed me over the three lanes of traffic to the hard shoulder.

Scrambling over the barrier with my jelly-like legs, I fell and scraped my leg. The shock kept the pain away, and I stood shivering as the ambulance driver called the police and an emergency ambulance. He was such a kind man and even went back across the motorway to get me a blanket out of my car to wrap around me. I had bought it at the airport to keep my legs warm on the plane and was so glad I had it now.

The ambulance drivers remarked that a guardian angel must have been looking after me, and once I had been checked over at the hospital, it was confirmed that I had a couple of cracked ribs and whiplash. Not bad for a 70-mph bust-up with a steel reservation. The doctor who saw me told me that I should be thankful to God as he had given me another life that morning. He told me that at 50mph, you would expect traumatic injuries, but at 70mph, well, I should not have been sitting up on the end of the bed chatting with him. The thing was, I wasn't grateful. In some ways, I was angry as to why it hadn't finished me off. The odds were that it should have, so why save me when I didn't even want to save myself?

I left the hospital with a bag of pain killers, and like everything traumatic in my life, I blocked it out. After six weeks of resting the physical injuries, I went back to work, and the pretence commenced once more.

A lot has certainly happened in the past 18 months, and even though I'm awaiting treatment, I am doing OK in my bubble. I have people behind me wanting to see this book finished, and I sometimes think, is that why the car crash didn't kill me, was I meant to stay and finish this book?

More people know the truth about my husband now, which helps a little as I would sometimes worry about how others perceived me. Did they think I was a cold-hearted bitch who didn't care that her husband had died? Who could blame them if they did think that? After all, I was giving such a good impression of someone coping very well and getting on with life. Some of those people now have taken the sympathy they had for my husband and redirected it to me.

I hope that my writing this book serves as a warning to many people so that if they were to meet someone new and are "swept off their feet," maybe they would think twice before jumping in feet first. Perhaps someone will recognise some of the initial signs and change their mind about that second date. Perhaps someone is already in this type of relationship, but like I was, you are too far in and too isolated to check if your suspicions are founded; maybe this book can help you.

I already knew before I met my husband that there are many evil men in the world, and after many terrible experiences, I thought I knew all the signs and that it was not possible to reel me in. This book shows that even I, someone who should have seen it as clear as day, missed the signs and was carried away with a sense of love.

I was love-bombed to the extreme, something an abuser does to hook you at the beginning. They shower you with more love than you ever could have imagined, and it makes you feel on top of the world. If they lose interest and you start to back away from them, they kick start it all again, and before you know it, you are dependent on them to make you feel happy.

I can't feel too stupid for falling for my husband's lies as I was up against a far more intelligent person than myself. The evidence suggests that he could train himself for many years to create his charismatic, charming persona. A man who had a mind that could use complex memory codes to retain any information useful to him to create gains for himself, no matter what the cost to others. My husband often used the saying "retain what is useful and reject what is useless." Something he'd have done every day in order to collect information about his victims or information he wanted to con and impress people with. It takes an extremely clever individual to take away relationships from you that you have had your whole life without you recognising the part they played.

I believe that I won't ever let another man into my life again and who could blame me. If you can even call him this (I prefer the word monster), this man invaded every part of my mind, thoughts, and life and demolished everything I had that was good.

If this book can help just save one person from losing everything to a psychopath, sociopath, narcissist or worse still, a combination of all three, then it will have been worth it.

THE ~~GRIEVING~~ GRATEFUL WIDOW

As for me, I will continue with my medication in the hope that the Trauma Therapy can make some kind of life for me, whilst keeping my dead husband's toothbrush wrapped in a bag inside my safe (for DNA purposes) just in   case   a   body   shows   up...

EPILOGUE

After being put on the mental health crisis team's books, I would have daily phone calls and the odd visit from nurses. My first visit from a senior nurse who had come to give me a second assessment was scary, to say the least. The words "you are acutely unwell at the moment" bothered me so much. I was on the verge of a nervous breakdown, one step away from being admitted to a mental health unit. I would rather be dead than have that happen. Did the professionals think I was crazy? Was I now a psychopath with no real feelings?

The nurses assured me that no one thought I was crazy, and even the strongest of minds wouldn't have been able to cope with everything I had in such a short space of time. A terminal diagnosis for my husband of only a year, two weeks later, in a car crash (car is written off), keeping a business going whilst taking care of my dying husband, the death itself, the funeral, then the revelations that were to come, then forced back to work due to debt, then a 70-mph car crash into the central reservation of the M56, and losing my dear friend during the lockdown—quite a list for an 18-month period.

In January 2021, and I was still going, not better, not back working, but much stronger. Therapy began, it started as CBT, and and then moved on to full trauma therapy. I was hoping it would make me face things and that I would feel something so that my memories could be processed and dealt with so that I can move on.

Alongside my therapy, I had become a spiritualist. This has helped me so much as I no longer feel alone with my issues. I put all of my problems in the hands of my angels and allow them to guide me, and just knowing that someone else will find a solution and take the daunting responsibility away from me is just mind-blowing.

I pray every night and thank my angels for all of the things that I am grateful for, and I pray for myself and my loved ones. I have joined a spiritual church, and it is amazing, something I should have done a long time ago. With the spirituality and my therapy, I believe that I'm going to come out the other side as a stronger, kinder, and better version of myself. I'll be able to make changes so that I will not follow the same paths that have led me to bad men, and I have faith that, with my new judgement skills, I will one day be able to find my way to a life where I am truly happy.

May 2021

People say things have to get worse before they can get better. That is so very true. Barbara passed away just 6 months after her precious son so I believe they are now reunited in Hell. Carla's son is now four and a half and other than the quick glimpse at the supermarket, I have never set eyes on him again. Sadly Lucie for some unknown reason sided with Carla, although I still to this day do not know what I did wrong to either of them. I have never spoken with my brother, sister in law, half sister again. I did reach out to them at one point but they made it clear in no uncertain terms that they were unwilling to speak to me. I am so relieved now that they made that decision as I firmly believe that things happen for a reason and none of those people made a positive impact in my life.

Leanne and Mark had already stopped speaking to me in 2018 and it was only in March 2020 that I found out what had happened there. Rob had convinced me that Mark was a control freak and that is why Leanne stopped answering my messages for months at a time. However we had both been surprised after months of ignorance to receive a beautiful card and gift for our first wedding anniversary. I did send Leanne a text to than her but to ask what was going on with her but again I never received a reply.

It was only when I made a call to her out of the blue in March 2020 to advise her of what had happened and that Rob was dead did I finally get an answer. She told me that she thought it was I who had stopped communicating with them and that for months and up until she sent the anniversary gift that we had been communicating back and forth regularly by text. My blood ran cold, Rob had been impersonating me for months and telling me that Leanne and Mark were the ones behaving oddly. I am not sure how he did it, whether he mirrored my phone or contacted her to say I had a new number and did it that way. It does not matter how or why, it happened and it destroyed another relationship. Leanne was lovely on the phone and told me she would call me the next day. I am still waiting now over a year and have accepted that the past is best left in the past.

I am grateful for each and every person that turned their back on me and walked away as it sent me on a whole new path. A journey with amazing new people that have become closer to me within a few short months than some of my longest friends and family members.

Some say life begins at 40 and for me, this is absolutely the caseand I have never been happier My spiritual journey is on course and as I pack my last case to head off to a sunnier climate, I am indeed The Grateful Widow.

ABOUT THE AUTHOR

Maria Morrissey (pseudonym) was born in 1980 in Billinge, Wigan. Although she has moved around a lot during her life, she spent most of her years in Sale in Cheshire before returning to her home town of Wigan. She has had an eventful life, to say the least, and has always thought that she would put it into words one day. However, life was always busy, and it was only after the unbelievable events of the past six years that she knew she had to start writing. Whilst suffering from PTSD and reactive depression, Maria has struggled but succeeded in producing this fictional psychological thriller based on true events in the hope of changing the lives of others.

Printed in Great Britain
by Amazon